She

A Cautionary Tale

Carla Howatt

She
A Cautionary Tale

By the Book Publishing
3 Donnely Terrace Sherwood Park, AB T8H 282 Canada

Printed in the United States of America
First Printing 2019
First Edition 2019
ISBN: 978-1-7751605-3-3

10 9 8 7 6 5 4 3 2 1

Dedicated to my husband, whose endless patience and faith keep me going.

Chapter One

Olivia

Olivia sat staring at the slender man sitting across from her, wondering how she could make a graceful exit. There seemed to be a thin line between engaging in such a way to not encourage someone to keep talking and not being outright rude. After years of online dating, she was beginning to get the hang of it. The trick was to smile slightly in the right spots while not asking any questions. And not laughing. Whatever happened, she must not laugh.

The problem was, she'd known as soon as he'd started talking that there was not going to be a second coffee date. It had begun with his long drawn out explanation of how he was not responsible for being late, assuring her that the blame rested squarely with his ex-wife. Her tardiness had always been an issue and was ultimately the reason why they divorced. That and the fact that after his brain injury, caused by a motorcycle accident - he had decided he wanted to live in an RV. Not because he couldn't afford it otherwise, he was quick to assert, but because he had longed for the simple life. His ex-wife was hung up on material possessions and had an unhealthy attachment to shallow, material things… like savings plans and investments.

Bringing her coffee cup to her lips, she blew lightly on the hot drink and wondered how long they had been sitting there. Taking a sip, she set the coffee down and glanced casually at her watch. Crap. It had only been fifteen minutes. Another fifteen to go and she could make a graceful exit. She often wished she could be mean-spirited and get up and walk out, but she couldn't help but reason that while these failed attempts at dating meant they weren't a match for her, it didn't mean they were less deserving of some basic respect.

While he continued to talk, she pushed her sunny blond hair behind her ear and leaned her head on the palm of her hand. Her eyes were a soft blue, and they looked kindly on the man in front of her.

"I'm telling you, the big companies want us to be tied down by debt," he was saying. "If everyone did what I'm doing, they would have a hard time sucking us dry the way they do."

"Uh-huh," Olivia said, nodding imperceptibly while looking over his shoulder and avoiding eye contact.

"I have my RV and I can go anywhere I want - nothing holds me down," he continued. "If I decide I want to see the mountains, I go. If I need some money, I work, and if I don't, I don't."

"Mmmm," with a lift of her chin, Olivia expressed neither agreement or disagreement, just an acknowledgment he had spoken.

Exactly fourteen minutes later, Olivia gently broke into his conversation, saying she was sorry, but she had to get going. She had mentioned when they set up the meeting that she had another commitment and couldn't stay longer than half an hour.

"Oh yeah, sure! No problem at all," he said. "So, I guess we'll be in touch then?"

"Sure, we can do that," Olivia responded with a smile as she quickly reached out her hand to shake his. She had learned this trick after being caught in an unexpected hug after another awkward coffee date. she was already composing in her head the let-down email that would say "Thanks, you are a lovely person, but I don't think we are a good fit." As she headed for the door,

The fresh air outside was welcome after the stuffy coffee shop, and she slipped into her car with a relieved sigh. As she waited for her phone to connect to her Bluetooth, she looked in the mirror to tie back her hair and check her makeup.

She couldn't wait to tell Terri about this one! One of Olivia's go-to friends when she wanted to debrief about the latest online dating bomb, Terry was a fellow single woman who understood how frustrating and discouraging dating could be in your thirties. Petite in stature but large in personality, Terri could always be counted on to have time to chat. Olivia could imagine Terri throwing back her head, light blonde hair cascading down her back as she laughed at Olivia's latest dating foibles.

As if her thoughts were a summons, the phone rang and Terri's number showed on the call display.

"Hi, Terri! I was just thinking about you!"

"So, how did it go?" her friend asked, effectively skipping any welcoming niceties.

"Wellllll, you know how I was pleased that he just asked to meet and didn't want to spend days and weeks chatting online first?"

"Yeah?"

"There was a reason why he wanted to meet right away. He was using a free computer in the local library to access his account because he lives in an RV," she explained.

"Oh no!" Terri exclaimed, trying to suppress her laughter.

"Oh yes, he is 'off the grid' most of the time and didn't want to fool around chatting online," Olivia said.

"You certainly haven't had the best of luck, have you?" Terri said.

"Nope. I thought the guy who wanted to sell me his book was a bad match, but this fella was even worse," Olivia said with a smile in her voice. "Can you imagine me deciding to live the simple life in an RV, going on and off the grid, depending on how paranoid I was feeling that day?"

"Oh no, not paranoid too?" Terri asked.

"Oh yes, not only are 'they' all out to get us, but all these power lines and the radiation from WiFi may have caused complications while healing from his brain surgery,"

"His WHAT?" Terri sputtered as she broke down, howling with laughter. "Where do you find these guys?"

Olivia asked herself precisely that as she drove home, making a mental list of dating disasters as she changed lanes. So far, she had met a man who wanted a mother for his six children, a young man who wanted a mother figure, another who worked an entry-level job and lived in his aging parent's basement and, of course, the guy who sold her his book at their first meeting.

She was 37 years old. Way too old for this she thought as she turned into her suburban subdivision. Having married young, she had her children and was divorced by her early thirties. Now, she lamented ever being able to find someone to spend the rest of her life with.

That night, after sending off a thanks-but-no-thanks message to her RV-loving coffee date, she slipped between the crisp, cool sheets of her bed. As she lay there looking up at the ceiling, she felt a deep sense of longing. It frustrated her because she had a great life. She worked at a job she loved and that gave her a sense of fulfillment, her kids were great, and she had some fantastic friends. Why was it that no matter how hard she tried, nothing filled the empty spot deep inside her that became so noticeable in the dark of the night? She tried to focus on the freedom her life gave her. She had the freedom to travel, to spend weekends in the mountains, she could watch any channel she wanted on the TV and fighting for the bed covers was never an issue.

Flopping onto her side, she punched the pillow next to her as though trying to force the negative emotions away.

~ ~ ~

"Hurry Up!" Olivia yelled down the stairs. "I'm not driving you if you miss your bus!"

The sounds of trudging teenagers coming up the stairs were the only answer she received. A moment later, grabbing their lunches and stuffing them into their backpacks, her boys filed out the front door with a mumbled goodbye flung in her direction.

Olivia looked at the clock and decided she had just enough time to check her messages online before she would need to be on the road. Sliding in behind her computer, she wiggled her mouse to activate her screen. Clicking on the browser icon, she quickly loaded up her Facebook profile. Seeing no messages needing a response, she moved on to the dating site she had found. There was a message from her coffee date from last night, insisting that she had not given him a chance. He assured her that he was going to be in town for another day or so if she changed her mind, and would check his emails from the library before he left.

With a roll of her eyes, she clicked delete and moved on to the next message in her inbox. She deleted that one almost as quickly. Why did so many men think that pictures of their penis were a sure-fire way to interest a woman? Worse yet, were there women that responded? Some women must, Olivia mused, or they wouldn't keep doing it.

With a deep sigh, she closed down her browser and stood up to collect her briefcase, lunch, and purse. Slipping her feet into her heels, Olivia adjusted her black pencil skirt over her slim but curvy hips and faced her day.

Chapter Two
She

Driving home from work, she tried to silence the voices in her head and calm her upset stomach. Her fingers were wrapped around the steering wheel, her white knuckles betraying her anxiety. She wasn't sure what she was going to face when she arrived home, but she tried to tell herself it didn't matter. She was not responsible for other people's actions. There was nothing she could do about things. Her husband may or may not be home but either way, she was okay.

She caught a glimpse of herself in the rearview mirror as she cast a quick look and did a shoulder check before switching lanes. Her brown hair hung straight to her shoulders and the sun caught her highlights, but her face looked tired. She had recently lost weight, and instead of making her feel svelte and sexy, she felt gaunt and worn.

She took a moment to ponder how things had gotten this far; where all the hopes and dreams had gone. It didn't seem so long ago that her spirit was light, and the possibilities were endless. Now, she felt diminished, shrunken down to this perpetual sense of uncertainty.

She would never have considered herself insecure before, but now it seemed to define her existence.

Weaving in and out of the thick rush hour traffic, she tried to stop her mind from visiting last night's scene in her head; - the yelling, the tears, and the accusations. Home was supposed to be the place one went to withdraw from the world and find peace and comfort. But her home had become a tense, anxious place where she rarely felt truly at home. She was spending more and more time at work, immersed in the day-to-day reliability, the ebb and flow of deadlines and emails. She was never uncertain at work. That was her domain and the place where she shone. Lately, work had become her escape from home.

The drive home seemed to take forever, and several times she glanced impatiently at the clock in her car's dash. It was like this most days now, the desire to be home and battling the urge to stay away. She wanted so badly to be able to go home and relax, knowing her husband would be there, waiting for her expectantly. She wanted to feel the love and unconditional acceptance she felt in the beginning before it all went wrong. Every day she wondered if this would be the day. The day she finally figured out what had happened and was able to make it all right again. The day the husband she thought she knew magically re-appeared.

She banged the palm of her hand impatiently on the steering wheel. Why couldn't she turn off this treadmill in her brain? She continually went over the same thing, looking at it from every angle, trying to make some sense of it. She kept trying to make sense of that which was unfathomable. She asked herself questions that she didn't have the answer for, driving herself crazy.

Crazy was just how she felt these days. The last year or so seemed like a split existence, divided between the then and the now; when he loved and when he didn't. No matter how hard she tried, she couldn't figure out where the line was between the two was located. When did the change happen and why?

Breaking loose from the worst of the traffic, she coasted down the highway, feeling a sense of both relief and dread. She pulled up to her home, parked, and grabbed her purse. Entering the house, she tapped the button on her key fob and heard her car lock. As she stood just inside the front door, she felt the emptiness first and then heard the quiet. He wasn't home. It didn't surprise her that he wasn't there, and she felt a bit of disgust with herself for still being a bit disappointed.

Slipping out of her heels, she walked to the fridge and pulled out a frozen dinner to pop in the microwave. The coolness of the hardwood felt good against her bare feet, and she rolled her shoulders to help release some of the tension. She walked to their bedroom and gratefully changed out of her work clothes into a pair of jeans and an old sweatshirt. Washing up in the bathroom, she splashed warm water on her face. As she wiped dry with a towel, she couldn't help looking at herself in the mirror. When had those lines appeared under her eyes? Was it from a lack of sleep or was her age starting to show? At 39 she had hoped she would have a few more years before worrying about such things. Peering closer, she couldn't help but notice the weariness in her face. Maybe it wasn't time that was causing the lines, but life itself?

Later that evening, she curled up on the couch with her book, the TV playing in the background. She preferred a bit of noise in the house when she was here by herself, as it made the house seem a little less empty. Around midnight she jerked her head up as a loud sound from the TV startled her awake. Great, she thought, now I'm going to have a crick in my neck and not be able to get back to sleep.

Stabbing at the remote to turn off the tv, she gathered up her book and glass and began flipping off the lights as she headed for the bedroom. As the house went dark, she wondered again when her husband would make it home. Or if he would come home at all this time.

She slipped into her bed, pulling the sheets up to her neck and willing her mind off the path of imagining where he might be at this very moment.

It seemed like only an instant later that she felt his presence as he sat at the edge of the bed and pulled off his socks when in reality two hours had gone by. Standing up, he undid his belt and pulled down his pants, pulled his t-shirt over his head before crawling into bed beside her.

She lay on her side with her back to him, trying to keep her breathing regular as she listened to him in. Two in the morning was not the time to confront him or to ask questions.

He spooned up against her back as he nestled in, and when he breathed on her neck, she caught a whiff of alcohol. She could feel his hard-on pressing up against the small of her back as he moved his hand down and slipped it between her legs. Inserting one finger into her, he moaned slightly in her ear. Damn it, she thought, don't do this, not tonight.

Pulling her hip towards him, so that her weight shifted her over onto her back, he pushed himself up using one arm while at the same time shoving her nightgown out of the way and moving his knees in between her legs. Spreading her legs apart, he entered her immediately. He began moving in and out, and his breathing grew more rapid. She lay there wondering if she should say something to him - if she should try to kiss him or offer any encouragement. Not that he appeared to need it. He was oblivious to her as he moved faster and faster until, with a shuddering climax, he made a loud grunting noise and fell on top of her.

After catching his breath, he rolled over to his side of the bed and was soon fast asleep. She turned back onto her side and stared at the bedroom wall, quiet tears dripping down her face.

Chapter Three

Olivia

That isn't going to work," Olivia said patiently into her phone. "The deadline is at 4 pm, not tomorrow."

A colleague walked by her desk and gave her a pitying look as he slid new copy into her inbox. The entire office knew that the day the final text was due at the designer's was an especially stressful time for the department. Inevitably, someone wasn't prepared or threw up one roadblock or another.

"But if you're late handing it in, I'll be late editing it and so on and so forth," Olivia explained, a note of frustration in her voice. "It isn't just your copy that I have to have ready, Derek!"

Hanging up the phone a bit harder than usual, she leaned back in her chair and was rubbing her tired eyes just as someone knocked on her door before popping their head into her office.

"I'm doing a coffee run. Do you want anything?" Wanda, her supervisor, asked.

"Nothing for me, thanks," Olivia responded with a sigh.

"How is the schedule going this month?" Wanda inquired, leaning against the door frame.

"The usual," Olivia responded with a smirk. "Everyone has a legitimate reason why they should be given extensions, and those reasons are always completely outside their control."

"Ah yes, the deadline that changes every month, and sneaks up and surprises the poor unsuspecting staff," Wanda laughed. "You really ought to be more clear about the deadline being the 12th of every single month Olivia!"

"Oh, go and fetch some coffee!" Olivia said, laughing. "You're not helping me one bit!"

Wanda headed down the hall a few feet before swiveling back to Olivia's office.

"Are you still planning on going to the awards show the chamber is putting on this weekend?" she asked.

"Wouldn't miss it for the world," Olivia answered. "'I'll be there 'with bells on', as they say!"

Turning towards her computer, Olivia clicked on many files before finding the one she needed. It was several hours later when she lifted her head, realizing the office had grown very quiet. It must be lunchtime already, she thought. Rubbing the tightness out of her neck, she arched her back and looked out her office window. Deadline day was always intense, but she thrived on the pressure.

Four hours later, her phone interrupted her concentration.

"Olivia here," she answered distractedly. It was her 16- year-old, Jonathon letting her know that her ex-husband would be picking them up in half an hour.

"Okay, don't forget your homework this time," she said. "No excuses!"

Being a single parent wasn't always easy. As the kids grew older, the issues didn't become fewer, but the types of problems she had to deal with were different. She now had the freedom to work late, knowing the boys would get themselves ready for their weekend with their father. No more rushing home to make sure they were packed and waiting in time for pickup, but she still needed to harp on them about some of the everyday things. She looked at the time and gave herself another hour to work before she headed home. Olivia hated working too late on the Friday night of what she called Her Weekend; the weekend her husband took the kids provided her with some much-needed alone time, away from work and the day to day rigors of raising two rambunctious teenagers.

After wrapping up final editing on the articles she was working on, she turned off her computer and straightened up her desk. As she locked her office door, she couldn't help noticing that she was one of the last people to leave.

"Night Earl!" she called to the janitor, "Have a great weekend!"

"You too," he responded with a nod of his head and a smile, "you stay out of trouble, you hear?"

Laughing and shaking her head, Olivia headed to her car in the parking lot. She slid behind the wheel and reached down to take off her heels. Throwing them in the back seat, she wiggled her toes and sighed wearily. Another week down, another edition put to bed, and now the whole weekend to herself.

She dodged traffic as she made her way home, careful to avoid the more congested parts of town. The last thing she wanted was to get caught up in a traffic jam when there was a bottle of wine with her name on it, just waiting at home. Sitting at a red light, she decided that she was going to indulge and forget making dinner. A baguette at the deli and a wedge of cheese would be just what she needed. With no kids to prepare a meal for, she didn't have to worry about balancing the nutritional intake of her dinner.

After a quick stop at the store, she made her way home and into her garage. Hitting the remote attached to her vehicle's visor, Olivia entered her house. Whenever she came home, she felt the worries of the day ease. It was the first home she had bought after her divorce and it symbolized independence and liberation. The tall ceiling in the entryway with its large skylight, beckoned her to come in and relax.

Later that night, she sat on the bar stools at her kitchen counter, opened up her laptop, and signed into her online dating profile. Balancing a glass of red wine in one hand and her computer mouse in the other, she noted that her inbox had an alert.

Olivia opened the inbox and opened the new message that waited for her.

"Hi, my name is Luke, and I noticed your profile because you have a great smile and we share a love of hiking. Check out my profile and drop me a line if you are interested in chatting."

She clicked on the small square profile picture next to his screen name "Luke39" and his profile loaded. Luke39 was two years older than her, liked hiking and running as well as quiet evenings. He had an undergraduate degree in business and had gone to the local college to obtain a journeyman electrician certificate. Her eyebrow raised just a bit as she scrolled through his pictures and she carefully set her wine glass on the counter. Grabbing her phone, she hit the memory one button, and the phone began to dial.

"Hi Olivia," Terri answered cheerfully, "what's up?"

"I'm online, and someone just contacted me that looks interesting. Thought you might take a peek for me and tell me what you think," Olivia said. "his handle is Luke39." Terri also had an account on the same site and would be able to access the Luke39 account easily.

"Nice!" Terri exclaimed. "He's a fine specimen! How did you respond?"

"I haven't yet," Olivia explained. "I wanted to see what you think first."

"Why? He's adorable, and from his profile, he sounds literate and potentially even sane. What have you got to lose?"

"I don't know. I guess I'm just a bit leery. He is a bit too good looking, don't you think?" Olivia asked tentatively.

"Too good looking? He's quite handsome, but so what?" Terri scoffed...

"Well, I'm just wondering why he's contacting me," Olivia said.

"What is wrong with you woman? You're a catch. You're good looking, and you're smart and funny, why wouldn't he want to contact you?" Terri encouraged. "I wish you could see yourself the way others see you."

"If you say so," Olivia hedged, "I guess I'm just a bit skeptical after some of the people I've met on here. Good looking, sane and smart? That seems like too big of an ask these days, so there must be a catch."

Although Olivia was usually a confident, strong, capable woman who was looked to by her friends for reasoned and well-thought-out advice on their lives, deep down she harbored a belief that she wasn't worthy. That in some basic way that truly mattered, she wasn't enough and would be found lacking. This was something only those closest to her realized and they often wondered what had triggered such deep-seated insecurity. It always surprised Terri when Olivia revealed her true feelings about herself.

"Just respond to him and see where it goes," Terri advised. "If it's too good to be true you'll figure it out pretty quickly."

"You're right," Olivia agreed. "I'll respond and see what happens. For all I know he's a robot, and I won't hear back from him."

Hanging up the phone, Olivia took one more swallow from her wine glass before turning to the keyboard and typing out a response to Luke39.

"Hi Luke, thanks for contacting me. Your profile looks very interesting, and I would love to chat further. Perhaps we could exchange a couple of messages on here and then, if you are comfortable sharing a phone number, we could talk "in real-time"?"

She hit send and then closed her laptop. Oh well, she thought. What will be will be.

Chapter Four

She

She pushed the button on the toaster down after inserting the bread and reached for the coffee pot.

"Hey, did you make my lunch?" her husband asked as he entered the kitchen. "I'm running behind, and I can't be late again this week."

"Yes, it's in the fridge." She answered. "So where were you last night?"

"Nowhere," he responded in a distracted tone while adding milk to his coffee-to-go mug.

"Nowhere?" she asked quietly.

"Just met up with a friend," he said. "I have to go now; not sure what time I'll be home."

"That's okay. I have a hair appointment tonight anyway," she said, forcing lightness into her tone. "Time to get my color touched up again."

Her voice tapered off as she realized he was already walking out the door. Staring at it as it closed behind him, she ran her fingers impatiently through her hair. What an idiot I am! She thought. I should confront him and tell him he either gets his act together or we need to take a serious look at where this relationship is going. Even as she thought it, she knew she wasn't ready to go down that road. How could she, when she had experienced an intensity of emotions with him that she had never felt in any other relationship? The passion, the excitement, the sheer joy that came from feeling so incredibly loved and adored! If she walked away from him now, she would lose any chance of ever experiencing that kind of emotion again. As long as she kept trying there was a chance, no matter how small, that he would go back to the loving, passionate, and attentive man she had fallen head over heels in love with a short two years ago.

She finished getting ready for work and headed out the front door, no closer to resolving the turmoil that raged continually inside her.

That afternoon, as she ate her lunch in the cafeteria at work, her cell phone began to ring.

"Hi Mom," She answered with a grin, "Aren't you supposed to be deep in a crossword at Aunt Sherry's?"

The good humor drained from her face and her eyes widened with surprise and fear as she listened to her mother speak.

"Okay, which hospital are you at?" She demanded. "I'll be there as soon as I can!"

Her boss looked at her with concern as her voice carried across the room, and she stood up abruptly.

"Everything okay?" Wanda asked. "That didn't sound very good!"

"I don't know," She responded. "They think my Dad had a heart attack. I have to go now."

"Do you need anyone to drive you?" Wanda reassured her. "Do you need us to call anyone?"

"No, I'm okay," She replied distractedly, as she discarded her half-eaten lunch.

Hurrying towards the lunchroom door, her heart in her throat, she walked briskly to her office, pausing only long enough to grab her coat and purse from the hook on the back of the door, and left the building. As soon as the Bluetooth in her car hooked up to her cell phone, she punched in her husband's number. His phone rang and rang, finally going to voicemail.

"Where the hell is he?" she mumbled as she left him a message. "Hi, can you call me as soon as possible, please? I'm driving to the hospital. They think my Dad had a heart attack."

Although traffic was light, it felt like it took forever to get to the hospital and find a parking spot. By the time she was standing in front of the information desk, she was a bundle of nerves, and her hands were shaking. She gave the woman at the desk her father's name and waited while his name was searched on the computer.

"He's on 4D4 ma'am," the information clerk informed her.

Without waiting for directions, she flew down the hallway towards the elevators. She arrived at the unit a few minutes later. She saw her mother in the waiting room and immediately went up to her and wrapped her arms around her tightly. They stood there for a few minutes, offering each other much-needed strength and support.

To the casual observer, it would not have been immediately apparent that the two women were related. Where her mother had grey, wispy hair that seemed to have a mind of its own, her own carefully manicured brunette style was shot through with burnished highlights that grabbed the light whenever she moved her head. The older woman had a strong, patrician face that gave nod to her British background, while her daughter had delicate features, a tiny nose, and eyes that tended to avoid contact with others.

She pulled away slightly and took her mother by the arm, leading her to a row of chairs to sit down.

"What did the doctor say?" She asked. "Do they know if it was a heart attack for sure?"

"They're running some tests, but they believe it was," her mother replied. "However, they think it may have been small enough to serve as a warning."

"That's good news, isn't it?" She asked.

"I think so, but right now they aren't saying anything for certain," her mother sighed, "They're just talking about 'maybe' and 'likely' and 'hopefully' right now."

"When will they be able to tell us more?"

"I don't know. They took him to run some more tests and said the doctor would come to see us when they get some results."

"Do you want me to go and get you some coffee or something?" She asked her mother.

"No, I'm okay, I'm just so glad you're here," her mother answered, leaning her head against the waiting room wall and tiredly closing her eyes.

She reached for her purse and pulled out her phone. No phone calls and no messages from her husband. Where the hell was he? She could use some support right now.

She picked up a magazine and flipped idly through it before throwing it back down on the low table. Standing up, she paced the length of the waiting room, before sitting down and picking up the same magazine again. After a few minutes, she realized she was not going to be able to concentrate on anything, and she resigned herself to staring at the industrial-looking clock on the wall.

She felt her mother's hand as it reached out and touched hers. Sitting together, each caught up in their thoughts and fears, they waited.

Chapter Five

Olivia

Her first impression was just how his voice was so much deeper than she had imagined. It was robust and manly, seeming to come from the very center of his being.

"Thanks for agreeing to chat with me Olivia," he greeted her. "It's so much more personal than email."

"I agree, exchanging email always leaves me wondering if I'm chatting with a 13-year-old boy in his mother's basement," Olivia laughed, "You can just never be 100% sure."

"Well, I'm no 13-year-old boy," he responded with a chuckle.

"No, you certainly don't sound like it," Olivia reassured him, "and can I assume your name is Luke?"

"Yes, it is Luke. Luke Bowden," he reassured her. "When we meet I can even show you my ID."

"Perfect!" she said, laughing, "One can never be too careful!"

"You have a nice laugh," he lowered his voice slightly.

"Thank you," responded Olivia.

"So how does this work? We have all the stats about each other already, so I can't ask you the usual questions," he teased. "I feel like all my openings are useless."

"Well, I could start by asking you how you landed on a dating site," she offered.

"That's easy. I was in a long-term relationship until about four months ago," he began, "I didn't know where to go to meet some nice, down to earth women who weren't just out there prowling and looking for a sugar daddy. Going online allows me to weed through some of those types right off the bat."

"My reasons are similar. As I said in my profile, I'm looking for a long-term, serious relationship, and that isn't something easy to find at our age," she explained. "Going to the bar isn't my thing, but online allows me to meet different people on my terms."

"How long have you been online?" he asked.

"A couple of years, give or take," she responded.

"Wow! Are you sure you don't have two heads or something? Your picture is gorgeous so it can't be that," he teased. "Or maybe men are just not all that smart?"

"I think it's specifying a serious, long-term relationship that does it," she smiled. "That tends to scare off all but the hardiest."

"Fools, all of them," he said with a deep-throated chuckle. "So, would you be interested in meeting in person?"

Olivia felt something like a teenager who had just been invited to prom as she answered, "Yes. Yes, I would."

"Great! I'm out of town right now, but I will be back in two days," he said. "Can I call you then and set something up?"

"I'll wait to hear from you then," she said.

Hanging up, she felt a surge of excitement and quickly phoned her friend April. Next to Terri, April was Olivia's closest friend, and she knew she could count on her to join in her excitement.

"Hi April," she said. "How are things?"

"They're good. You sound happy!" April responded with a chuckle. "How are things with you?"

"Pretty good! I just got off the phone with someone from the site, and he sounds mighty nice!" Olivia said. "And by nice, I mean normal. And manly. And did I mention normal?"

"Ha! Isn't it a sad state that we're at the point where normal is something to state twice?" April laughed.

"I know, and it's been so long since I've been excited about anyone. We've chatted a bit online and today was our first phone call. He's out of town, but he'll call when he gets back so we can meet in person!" the excitement in Olivia's voice was hard to ignore.

"I'm happy for you! It's so nice to be interested in someone, isn't it?" her friend asked. "Did I tell you what happened with John and me?"

After an hour or so of good conversation, punctuated with laughs and groans, the two women hung up, with a promise to get together in the next couple of days for a girl's night out, just April, Olivia, and

Terri. Olivia spent the rest of the day with a slight smile on her face as she cleaned up the house in preparation for the upcoming week.

One visit to her son's school for parent-teacher interviews and a week of work later, Olivia found herself sitting at a table at a Starbucks coffee shop. Blowing on her hot chai tea latte, she looked nervously at the door again. Darn it, she thought, he's going to be a no-show. The past week they had chatted more online, and as the days went by, she became more and more interested in meeting him. She was afraid she had put too much of her hope into this guy; she certainly should know better. How many times had she gotten her hopes up only to have them dashed? She supposed it would be better to find out now after just a week or two, as opposed to the two or three months she had spent chatting with that guy who lived a few hours north. What a disaster it had been when they finally met. She learned the hard way that no matter how great things appear online, or even on the phone, it's only when people meet in person that they find out if there is a connection. Or, in the case of the two-monther, when there was no connection and, in fact, there was more than just a little bit of repulsion. After that experience, she swore that she would fast track the amount of time spent chatting with any one man online and get straight to meeting face to face.

The door opened, and she quickly looked up, dismayed to see that it was two young mothers, toddlers in tow. Watching them with their long hair pulled up in fashionable ponytails, wearing skintight yoga pants, Olivia felt insecurity wash over her. What on earth would a man who looked like him want with someone like her anyway? She was 37 years old, had two teenagers, and baggage from a broken, unhappy marriage. She had to work hard to keep the pounds off, and she had never been a real head-turner. She was so engrossed in her thoughts, she didn't hear the door open again or see the man approach her until he was standing right beside her table.

"Olivia?" he asked, nervously.

"Oh!" she started. "Yes. Yes, hi."

"Hi, I'm Luke," he introduced himself as he held out his hand. She took his hand and felt it engulf hers. She looked into his blue eyes and immediately felt her breath catch in her throat.

"Hi Luke," she managed to say, "So nice to meet you."

"You too," He responded with a smile, "You were easy to find; you look just like your pictures."

As he sat took off his coat and sat down, she had a moment to look at him before he turned his attention back to her. He was the perfect height- about six inches taller than her- and built solidly. His broad chest and thick arms were a perfect match for his deep husky voice. She was surprised to find her body reacting to him already, and they had barely exchanged a dozen words.

"I thought we were never going to get a chance to meet," he said. "my schedule has just been crazy lately."

"That's life these days isn't it?" she responded.

"It sure is," he said as he looked her straight in the eyes.

"So, what exactly do you do?" she asked, a bit thrown off balance by the obvious appreciation he showed on his face.

"I'm an electrician, and I work for a local plant," he answered. "It means I have to make some road trips once in a while, but not very often."

"An electrician with a business degree?" Olivia asked with a smile.

"I know, it isn't your usual combination, but the degree was for my mother," Luke said. "The second career was all for me."

"Well, they do say everyone will have several careers in their lifetime," Olivia noted.

"Yes, but I intend for this one to be my last. I enjoy my work and am quite content," he said.

Olivia went down the must-have list in her head and made a mental checkmark next to the one called 'stable and settled'. She also couldn't help but notice that good taste in clothes was another one of his attributes. He was wearing a simple t-shirt with a casual shirt over top, but the t-shirt was the perfect shade of blue for his eyes, and the shirt strained attractively across his shoulders.

Wow, she thought, stable, normal, attractive, and able to dress himself. What more could I ask for?

Chapter Six

She

The doctor finished relaying the results from the testing done on her father and laid down his clipboard.

"In a nutshell, he's going to need to change a few things and take better care of himself, but we have every reason to believe he's going to be just fine," the doctor assured them. "He will need a change in diet, some more exercise, and a little less stress."

"Oh, he's going to do all those things, or I'll kill him!" her mother exclaimed.

Laughing with relief, she reached out and hugged her mother. It had been a long afternoon and evening spent in the waiting room. With small breaks to go for a walk or do a coffee run, they had spent hours pacing the waiting room. Her sister, Rebecca, had shown up and taken turns distracting their mother with talk and pictures of her grandchildren.

Whenever her mother and sister weren't looking, she would check her phone to see if her husband had called. There was nothing until around 8 pm when she received a text saying:

"Sorry to hear that. Keep me posted."

"Keep you posted? Honey, I need you here."

"I'm at a friend's, and there is nothing I can do at the hospital."

"You can give me support – be there for me!"

After half an hour when he hadn't responded, she sent him another text.

"Are you coming?"

"I told you, I'm at a friend's, there's nothing I can do. I'll see you later."

She sat in the waiting room chair, stunned. She was facing one of the hardest days of her life and her husband, the man who was supposed to support her, to encourage her, hold her hand and be her rock, couldn't bother to show up because he was at a friend's? She knew things were bad, but he wasn't that callous, was he? Surely, he cared about her more than this?

Her worry for her father, coupled with the stunning realization that her husband had no intention of being there for her, brought her to tears. She struggled to keep them from falling so she could support her mother. She didn't want her to see her fall apart. She didn't want to have to explain to her mother that her husband was a complete ass.

"This sucks," her sister said, as she plopped herself into the chair next to her.

"You have no idea," She said; a bitter twist in her voice.

"Thank you for being here for Mom," Rebecca continued. "I would have been here sooner, but I had to wait for Jake to get home to watch the girls."

Rebecca and her brother-in-law Jake had two adorable one-year-old twin girls. The four of them made for a picture-perfect family, and she tried hard not to hold that against her sister. It was hard though, because every time she was around them, it seemed to highlight how much her own marriage was lacking. Where Jake and her Rebecca were obviously in love and worked together like a well-oiled machine, she and her husband were lucky to even be on the same page these days.

"Well, at least we know he's going to be okay," her sister continued. "How about we set up an alternating schedule to check in on them when he gets released."

"Check in on us?" their mother interjected, "What is this I'm hearing? Have we suddenly become old, and frail, and unable to take care of ourselves? Your father had a heart attack, that doesn't mean there's anything wrong with me!"

Seeing her mother and sister together, sharing good-natured ribbing back and forth, made her smile. They were so much alike, but neither of them wanted to admit it. Physically they were similar, as her sister shared their mother's aristocratic appearance and her ability to command a situation. While her sister's hair was a rich honey gold, it also appeared to be out of control most of the time.

"No of course not Mom," her sister said, trying to pacify her. "I just meant there may be extra work with his medicine and trying to get him to exercise and all that. We'll be there to help you."

"Oh, okay. I guess if it means I get to see you girls more often, I'm okay with that," their mother said with a small smile of concession. "And those grandbabies of ours! They'll have your father back on his feet in no time, if for no other reason than he's going to want to get back down on the floor and play with them!"

The three of them chuckled as they each imagined the scene. It wasn't unheard of for him to spend hours laying out on the floor, letting the toddlers crawl all over him.

"Well, why don't you two get along home now; you both have husbands waiting for you and Rebecca has kids to get into bed!" their mother insisted, all the while gathering coats and purses and ushering them towards the door.

"Glad to see you've bounced back from the stress Mom," Rebecca laughed. "Back to running things!"

"No point in wallowing," their mother responded with a smile. "Life goes on!"

Exchanging hugs and good-byes, the two sisters left their mother and headed for their cars in the parkade.

"I guess it's pretty clear where we get our resiliency from," Rebecca said with a smile, as they entered the elevator.

"Yup, nothing gets her down for long," She replied.

"Hey, are you okay?" Rebecca asked as she noticed the tears welling up in her sister's eyes. Wrapping her arms around her, Rebecca drew her close as the tears turned into sobs.

She buried her face into her sister's shoulder and let herself release some of the tension and despair of the day.

"I'm sorry, it was just stressful, and now finding out Dad is going to be okay..." She trailed off.

"I know, sometimes it's when the worst part is over that we fall apart. It's okay, let it out," Her sister soothed, patting her back.

The ding from the elevator caused her to straighten up, pull away from Rebecca, and compose herself.

"Thanks for being here today Rebecca," she said.

"Hey, what is family for?" Rebecca said. "If we aren't there for each other, who will be?"

She smiled wanly and walked slowly towards her car, her sisters parting words ringing in her ears. If she couldn't count on family, who could she count on?

Chapter Seven

Olivia

As she drove away from the coffee shop, Olivia chatted excitedly with Terri, sharing with her every detail of her meeting with Luke.

"It sounds positive," Terri asserted. "How did you leave it?"

"After the visit, we just said good-bye and left," Olivia answered. "I'm not sure if he'll call me, or email or if I will even hear from him again. I mean, I think it went well, but who knows?"

Just then, Olivia heard a beeping noise come through on her Bluetooth speakers.

"Oh my god, oh my god, it's him!" she squealed. "It's Luke on the other line!"

"There you go!" Terri said with a laugh. "Now take a deep breath and answer it! Goodbye!"

Clicking through to the other line, Olivia said hello, hoping that her voice didn't sound too eager or breathless.

"Hi, it's Luke," he said. "I forgot to ask you before you left if you would like to go out for lunch sometime this week?"

"Yeah, sure that would be nice," Olivia said, trying to play it cool. "Did you have any particular day in mind?"

"How about Tuesday?" Luke suggested. "I have some commitments tomorrow, but Tuesday is free."

"Sure, Tuesday would work," Olivia replied. "I could meet you. Just let me know where."

"Oh, I can pick you up," Luke said. "How about you send me your work address, and I'll be there on Tuesday just before noon?"

"That sounds good," Olivia responded.

"Okay, until then..." Luke said.

As she disconnected the line, she let out a loud shout of excitement. She could barely believe she had met someone intelligent, sane, stable, and attractive - and to top it all off, he was interested in her! She drove the rest of the way home, unable to wipe the grin off her face.

That night, as she organized her sons for the upcoming week, her mind kept drifting to her coffee date with Luke. She was still amazed at how he made her pulse quicken, and how just thinking about him made her smile. It had been so long since she'd felt this way. Oh heck, who was she kidding? It had been almost forever. Her first marriage was to her high school sweetheart, and she didn't remember there ever being a time when she had felt the kind of attraction for him that she was already experiencing with Luke. While she had been attracted to the father of her children, it was a slow, easy, and comfortable attraction, not the thunderbolt she had felt as soon as she met Luke.

Once the boys were in bed, she sat down at her laptop and logged into her profile page. There was a card from Luke saying how much he had enjoyed meeting her. The message inside the card took her breath away. He explained that he felt like a schoolboy and that he hoped he hadn't made a fool of himself, but it had been a long time since he had felt such a connection to a woman.

Olivia sat back in her chair and took a deep breath. It was one thing to feel this kind of attraction, but to realize it was mutual? That brought things to a whole new level in her mind. What should she say in return? She didn't feel comfortable coming right out and saying she felt the same, but she also didn't want to discourage him. Oh, crap! Why was it so hard to date these days? And for the umpteenth time, she reflected on the fact that she felt way too old to be wrestling with these issues.

In the end, Olivia sent a note back thanking him for the card, reassuring him that he had not made a fool of himself and that she was excited to have lunch with him on Tuesday.

After sending him the message, she closed up her laptop and prepared for bed. Washing her face, brushing her teeth, and laying out clothes for work the next day were all part of her routine, and she walked through it step by step, all the while reveling in the sense of hope and anticipation she felt as she looked forward to Tuesday.

As it turned out, she didn't need to wait until Tuesday to hear from him again - there was another card waiting for her when she woke up the next morning. It was a pretty card wishing her a wonderful Monday and a quick note saying, "One more day!"

That morning, she drove to work with her music turned up just a bit louder than usual, singing along with her favorite musicians. She walked into work with a smile on her face that her colleagues found impossible not to return.

Chapter Eight

She

When she returned home from the hospital, her husband was sitting in his favorite chair in the living room, with a drink in one hand and a remote in the other.

He barely moved his eyes from the TV as he asked, "Hey, how'd things go with your Dad?"

"He's going to be okay. It was a small heart attack," she responded. "He has to watch his diet and get some exercise going forward."

"Good," he said.

She stood in the doorway watching him as he watched the sports channel. He was so engrossed in it that he didn't seem even to notice she was still standing there.

"I could have used you there tonight, for support," she stated.

The only acknowledgment he made was to lift his chin once and nod. He continued to watch TV, making no move to respond or engage with her in any way.

"Did you hear me?" she asked.

"Yes, I heard you," he said, clearly irritated. "I told you, I was visiting a friend. There's nothing I could have done anyway. We've been through this already."

"Do you care about me at all anymore?"

"Oh Christ, not this again!" he said, clearly exasperated. "Just because I won't do everything you want me to do, doesn't mean the sky is falling. You knew what I was like when you married me. Stop bitching!"

The worst part was that he was right. She had known what he was like when she married him. She had married him and hoped that against all the odds he would be who she thought he was. She had hoped all her dreams would come true and that they would be together as she felt they were always meant to be. She couldn't fault him, because in the end he had told her the truth and she had chosen to jump in anyway. She remembered the conversations they'd had when they were first dating. He had told her he was damaged. She'd thought he meant that he had some baggage. We all have baggage. We are all damaged. she had thought then. Now she knew he'd meant what he'd said and she hadn't listened; he really was damaged. She had no one to blame but herself.

With a deep sigh, she turned around and went into the kitchen and poured herself a glass of wine. Cutting some up some cheese, she put it on a plate and added some olives and pickles. All the stress of the day, combined with pre-wrapped hospital food, had left her with little appetite for a big meal. Taking it all to the kitchen island, she nibbled at her food and flipped through the day's mail.

Where was she going to go from here? Could she stand staying in a relationship where she always wondered where she stood and if he was going to be around from one day to the next? Could she stand leaving him and giving up on any chance at love? She wasn't getting any younger, and she couldn't imagine, after everything she had been through, that she would be able to find anyone else. She was too old, she had too many defensive walls up around her, and she wasn't sure it was even possible anymore. So that left her with a bad marriage on one side, and loneliness on the other. Taking another drink from her wine glass, she reassured herself that it wasn't a decision she needed to make tonight.

That evening, she was getting ready for bed when she heard her husband in the other room, and she assumed he was turning in for the night as well. As she walked out of their washroom, she thought she caught a whiff of his cologne. That's odd, she thought, why would he be putting cologne on before bed?

Pulling her pajamas on, she heard him close the bathroom door and walk down the hallway - away from their bedroom. A cold ball formed in the pit of her stomach as she hurried in his direction. When she reached the front entryway, he was pulling on his shoes.

"Where are you going?" she inquired in a surprised voice.

"Going out for a bit," he answered brusquely. "Meeting a friend for a drink."

"What friend?"

"Just a friend from work," he said.

"How many drinks did you have tonight?" she asked. "Do you think you should be driving?"

"I'm fine. I can hold my booze," he responded.

"It's already ten. How long are you going to be?"

"I don't know- a few hours," he said in an irritated voice.

"This doesn't make any sense," she protested, her voice rising. "Why do you have to go out now?"

"I just do,"

"Please, don't go!" she pleaded.

"Don't be like this," he scowled, "I told you I'll only be a few hours!"

"But why don't you stay, and we can stay up for a few hours," she asked, in what she hoped was an enticing voice, as she sidled up next to him, using her hand to caress the front of his jeans.

"Stop it, that isn't going to help!" he said, annoyed. "I'll see you tomorrow."

The door slammed as he walked out of the house, leaving her standing there, her face reddening with humiliation. Was there no limit to how low she was willing to sink? What was it going to take for her to cut the tie that bound her to him? He treated her horribly, disregarded her feelings, and she didn't even want to think about what he was doing when he was out with his nameless friend. She was still willing to beg and plead with him to stay, ready to throw herself at him in the hopes he would choose her.

She sat on the bench at their front door, tears streaming down her face as she once again felt the pain of being rejected by the man who was supposed to love and cherish her.

Chapter Nine

Olivia

Two more online cards, and a phone call later, Tuesday had finally arrived. Olivia couldn't believe how attentive Luke was being; it was certainly not anything she was used to experiencing from men. She was a bit nervous meeting him again, as she was starting to second guess herself and her reaction to their coffee date. Maybe she had been mistaken, and he wasn't as great as she thought? She had begun analyzing his emails and cards, looking for the show that gave away some oddity, some major flaw. So far, nothing.

She certainly hadn't noticed any less attraction on her part when she climbed into his car to go for lunch. The mischievous glimmer in his eyes was still there, his heavenly scent, and strong hands clutching the gearshift were just as she remembered.

Over lunch, he peppered her with questions about her family, her friends, and her life. He talked about his family who he didn't have a chance to see nearly as often as he would like, and his mother who was living on the West coast.

"So, what do you do in your spare time?" she asked.

"Oh, this and that," he answered vaguely. "To be honest, because I'm coming out of a long-term relationship and I just got all that settled, I haven't had an opportunity to do much of anything but work."

Olivia saw what appeared to be a life of dedication and work, with little time for play.

"What about sports?" she probed, hoping to get a clearer picture of his life.

"Nah, not much into them at all," He said, shrugging, "I like to go hiking once in a while, but that's about it."

"Wow! A man who doesn't like sports and isn't glued to Sports Night," Olivia teased. "You are a rare breed!"

They laughed together as the waitress cleared their plates.

"You have an amazing laugh," Luke said, gazing at her appreciatively. "It makes me smile on the inside."

"Gee, thanks," she said, feeling a flush rise in her cheeks.

"Has no one ever told you that?" he asked.

"I don't recall. I don't think so," Olivia said, shifting uncomfortably in her chair.

"Then they're crazy," he said. "Now, let's get you back to work."

Gathering their things, he helped her on with her coat. With his hand on the small of her back, he guided her out of the restaurant. She couldn't help but notice the admiring glances of the waitresses as they watched him leave. She didn't blame them. His square jaw, deep blue eyes, and commanding presence screamed masculinity. She felt a thrill of pleasure as she enjoyed the knowledge that he had chosen to be there with her.

On the drive back to work, she realized she was nervous again. Was he going to kiss her goodbye? This was the second time they had met, and they had talked twice on the phone and exchanged copious emails and cards. It wouldn't be surprising. Did she want him to? Of course, I want him to! Then why was she so nervous? You're not fifteen for Heaven's sake! she chided herself, Get a grip! She was so wrapped up in her thoughts that she hadn't realized he had gone quiet until they were almost back at her office. Then she started to worry about why he was so quiet.

Pulling up into a parking spot at her office, he put the car into park and turned around in his seat to face her.

"Look, I want to tell you something, but I feel kind of awkward about it," he said.

Oh great, she thought, he needs money. I should have known.

"I want to kiss you, but I don't want to do it in front of your office," he said, bluntly. "but I don't want you to go back to work thinking I don't want to."

"Oh." She said, unsure what else to say.

"So, if you don't mind, I would love to be able to give you a hug and save our first kiss for a more appropriate location," he said.

"That sounds fair," she said with a smile.

He reached out and wrapped his arms around her, engulfing her. She took a deep breath and breathed in his masculine scent. God, he smells and feels so damn good, she thought.

He released her and Olivia wasn't sure, but she thought it was reluctantly.

"We'll set up a night for dinner?"

"Sounds good," she answered, as she opened the car door and stepped out.

The rest of the day went by in a blur. She typed at her desk, she answered her phone and chatted with her colleagues, but for the life of her, she couldn't have said what it was all about. A steady hum of excitement coursed through her body as she replayed their lunch date minute by minute. She couldn't wait until their next date! Dinner next time. They were stepping up on the unspoken hierarchy of dating. From coffee to lunch and now dinner. She smiled as she recalled one of her online dates who asked her, after their second dinner date, if they could now go on to just hanging out at home watching TV because he was ready to be done with all the formalities. Dare she hope that Luke didn't see all of this as just necessary formality to get through? Maybe, just maybe, he also saw it as a journey to enjoy and experience together.

At the end of the day, she was getting ready to turn off her computer when she decided to do a quick check on the online dating site. The dot was lit up next to her inbox, indicating she had a new message. She opened it up and found a card with an adorable puppy on the cover that had a sign propped up on him reading "I like you."

Giving a furtive look around her office and seeing no one, Olivia placed both her hands over her face, stamped her feet rapidly and giggled. She was like a woman who had been roaming the dry parched sands of the desert for years and had just received her first sip of water. She could sure get used to this kind of attention!

Chapter Ten

She

Laughing at a co-worker's joke, she took another sip from her glass of wine. Going out tonight had been a good idea. Getting out of the house, and away from all the negative self-talk, was something she should do more often. She was so caught up in her marital unhappiness that she sometimes forgot there was a big world out there.

"Hey, you want another glass of wine?" Justin asked.

"Sure, that would be great," She responded with a smile. It was nice to remind herself that some people didn't mind being around her. In fact, some people actually liked her company.

She was distracted from her thoughts by a loud laugh from the woman on her right.

"I was just telling him that joke about the man with webbed feet," Judy from accounting explained. "Remember, that one I told you the other day?"

"Ah, yes," She smiled and exclaimed "JUST DON'T FORGET THE LEMONADE!" in perfect unison with Judy, causing them both to dissolve into giggles as they clinked their glasses together.

Laughter really was medicine for the soul. There was just nothing like laughing with friends to help lift a person's mood. She wished she had more opportunities to spend time with friends, but she didn't have many that she still stayed in contact with these days. As a newlywed, she had thought it was only natural that she spends most of her time with her husband, working on nurturing their relationship. Now she wondered how she had managed to lose touch with so many people that she had once considered essential in her life. At the time it just seemed easier to turn down the invitations when her husband felt uncomfortable around her friends – most of whom he felt didn't like him or were too high on themselves. It was easier just not to rock the boat. After a while, her friends stopped calling so much and eventually drifted away. Even her family played less of a role in her life now. They were polite and respectful around her and her husband, but it was apparent they picked up on his attitude towards them. Although he never actually said anything, his sullen silences and piercing stares were enough to make them realize that their presence was neither wanted or appreciated.

The isolation had crept in so slowly, she hadn't even been aware it was happening until recently. It was only when he started withdrawing, and she needed support the most that she found had herself alone.

"Here's your wine," Justin chirped as he placed a glass in front of her. "The bartender is swamped so hopefully it's what you wanted."

"I'm sure it's just fine, thank you," She said, raising the glass and taking a large sip. "Yup, perfect!"

"Do you dance?" he asked.

"Badly," She said with a laugh.

"That works for me," he grabbed her by her wrist and pulled her towards the already over-crowded dance floor.

Half an hour later, they returned to their seats, sweaty and breathing hard.

"Yikes! Who knew a line dance could be such a workout?" She laughed.

"I did!" Justin exclaimed. "Whoever said country music is for wimps never did a line dance after two-stepping to a couple of songs!"

She wiped her forehead with her drink napkin and leaned up against Judy.

"Save me, Judy," She grimaced with mock horror. "I'm a hot mess!"

"You're on your own lady!" Judy laughed.

"Then at least pass me that menu so I can fan myself,"

She fanned herself, waiting for the sweat to dry and the redness in her face to subside. She knew she would pay for all the wine and dancing when she woke up the next morning, but right now she was having fun for the first time in a long while.

She reached for her glass and raised it to her lips while she looked out over the dance floor. Her heart skipped a beat as she saw a familiar back sitting at the bar. She set her glass down carefully and stared. Her husband had told her he was watching the game with a friend tonight, but here he was instead. Drink in hand, he laughed at something the bartender said.

"Wanna dance some more?" Justin asked.

"Umm, no I'm okay," She answered.

"Come on," Justin insisted as he grabbed her wrist.

"No," she snapped sharply. "I said I don't want to."

"Okay, okay," Justin responded, raising his hands and backing away in mock surrender.

"I'm sorry," she muttered, gathering up her purse and jacket. "I need to go to the ladies' room."

With her head down, she maneuvered through the crowd and made it to the washroom. Her fingers shaking, she locked herself in a stall. Closing her eyes, she took a deep breath. Why was it she couldn't have even one night for herself? Why did he have to be here? Why had he lied to her? That last thought caused her to sit on the toilet lid and bury her face in her hands.

What was she going to do? Her gut wrenched at the thought of walking away, but she also knew that staying was slowly killing her. He would continue to treat her with little to no regard, and she would keep trying to find the love he had for her in the beginning. She felt so hopeless.

After a few minutes, she stood up, smoothed down her shirt, and opened the stall door. Going to the sink, she rinsed her face with fresh water and patted it dry with paper towels. She didn't have to make any decision tonight, but she knew the time was approaching when she was going to have to face the facts.

She returned to her table, careful to keep her back to where he was sitting. She didn't want the humiliation of him realizing she knew that he had lied to her. It was better to just pretend she didn't know.

"Sorry guys, I gotta get going," She mumbled to her co-workers.

"What? Already?" Judy said. "We're just getting started!"

"That's what I'm afraid of," she joked. "I have to get up early in the morning, and if I stay any longer you guys are bound to get me into trouble!"

She made her way out of the bar and into the chilly night. Taking a deep breath to steady her shaky nerves, she pulled out her phone and opened an app to hail a ride. She would get home and be sound asleep before he was, she reassured herself. She wouldn't have to face him tonight. But she knew she was kidding herself. The reality was that she wouldn't be sleeping much for quite a while; instead, she would lie in bed wondering where her husband was and what he was doing.

Chapter Eleven

Olivia

Preparing for her dinner date, Olivia carefully applied her makeup. Butterflies fluttered in her stomach, and as she drew a line over her eyelid with a black pencil, she had to concentrate on making sure her hand remained steady. For heaven's sake, she admonished herself. You aren't a child anymore! But even as she told herself that it was just dinner, her face grinned back at her in the mirror.

Straight out of the shower, she had chosen a new matching set of underwear. Not that anyone but she would see it, she assured herself. She had made that clear in her online profile that she was not interested in jumping into a physical relationship. She wanted to make smart decisions at this point in her life. Sex just clouded a woman's perspective and made it more difficult to make wise choices. But even if only she saw it, the underwear made her feel sexy and strong. It gave her confidence.

She wasn't sure where they were going for dinner, so she chose black, dressy Capri style pants and a casual jacket over her delicately trimmed white blouse. Matched with a string of long pearls and her gorgeous new red patent leather purse, she couldn't help but think she was ready for just about anything.

Now, if she could just get this breathing under control! She had already brushed her teeth twice, but the adrenaline pumping through her body caused her mouth to dry and feel slightly furry. She rummaged through the drawer in the kitchen that held all the bits and bobs of life and had just found a package of breath mints when the doorbell rang.

Taking a deep breath, she ran her hands along her shirt to make sure everything was in place and went to open the door. He stood on her front step, a bunch of flowers in hand.

"Oh my! These are lovely!" she exclaimed as he passed the flowers to her. "You didn't have to!"

"Maybe not, but I wanted to," he said, with his heart-stopping smile.

"Come in, come in," she invited. As he walked past her, she noted that he seemed to have taken a lot of care with his appearance as well. Freshly shaved, he smelled manly and musky. She inhaled deeply, the smell and the fact that this date was important to him as well helped to calm her nerves.

"Would you like a glass of wine or something before we leave?" she asked him.

"No, I'm good," he reassured her. "I don't drink much. But you go ahead."

"No, that's fine," Olivia reassured him. "So where are we going tonight?"

"I made reservations at the new steak place that just opened," he said, sounding a bit uncertain. "I hope you're okay with that?"

"Absolutely, I've been wanting to try it," Olivia said with a smile.

"Are these your kids?" Luke asked, looking at the pictures on the living room wall.

"Yes, from a few years ago," she responded, "They have grown up quite a bit since those were taken!"

"They are handsome young men," Luke said. "You must be very proud of them."

"Yes, I am," Olivia responded.

"Well, should we get going?" Luke asked.

"Lead the way," Olivia answered as she grabbed her jacket and purse.

As they walked out the front door and down the driveway, Luke rested his hand on her lower back, gently guiding her to his truck's passenger side. Reaching out, he opened the door for her.

When they arrived at the restaurant, Olivia noticed that the waitress gave Luke a second look while she was gathering their menus and taking them to their seats. She felt a bit shallow about the spark of pleasure it gave her to know that other women noticed her date. She couldn't help but feel proud to be there with him as they settled into their booth.

"Would you like some wine to start?" Luke asked her. "Don't let my not drinking stop you."

"Oh no, I don't feel right drinking alone," Olivia said. "I'm good, really. I don't need to have wine."

"Go ahead," he insisted. "I don't want you to abstain on my account."

"Really, it's okay," she said. There was an awkward pause before he continued,

"Okay then," he said, changing topics. "I've heard the steak here is good, and I've been dying to try it."

They chose their meals and ordered, the entire time finding it hard to wipe the smiles off their faces. They talked about their day, and how much they had looked forward to the evening. Enjoying their appetizers, they asked each other questions about their childhoods and backgrounds.

She learned that he had lost his father at a young age in a workplace accident and that his mother raised him and his three siblings by herself. She was pleased to hear the pride and love in his voice as he spoke of his mother. It was apparent that he thought the world of her. He wasn't overly close with his siblings, but he attributed this to living a long way from each other and being unable to spend a lot of time together. He painted a picture of someone who loved his family but was separated by distance.

"Do you miss not having family close by?" Olivia asked.

"Nah, sometimes it's best," Luke replied. "It's easier to miss them the further away they are."

Olivia threw her head back and laughed at the off-handedly astute observation he had made. Her laugh seemed to unsettle him, as though he wasn't quite sure what he had said that was so funny, but he soon joined in the laughter.

By the time the entrees arrived, Olivia's nerves had settled down considerably, and she was enjoying her evening. Luke looked more at ease too, as he cut into his rare steak and popped the first piece in his mouth.

Olivia eyed his steak skeptically and raised an eyebrow, "Are you sure that isn't still mooing?" she asked.

"What? This is the way steaks were meant to be eaten!" he said, grinning.

"Yeah, back in caveman days when there was no fire," she joked.

By the time they were finished eating, the conversation had slowed to a comfortable lull. Leaning back in his seat, Luke patted his stomach and proclaimed the meal perfect.

"There is no way I can finish the rest of mine," Olivia said. "I'm stuffed!"

"What? No room for dessert?" Luke asked, and then, seeing the decidedly horrified look on her face. "What happened to all the talk about loving chocolate and how you can always eat chocolate? Your profile said you were a chocoholic."

"Oh no, not tonight," Olivia said, with a groan. "Not even for chocolate!"

The waitress had approached while they were talking and asked with a smile if they would be interested in some coffee instead.

"Do you have some peppermint tea?" Olivia asked.

"Make that two," Luke said.

They lingered, chatting that way for another hour while sipping their tea contentedly. It seemed like a short time later when they looked around and realized most of the customers had left and the servers were wiping off the tables.

"I guess we better get going," Luke announced as he grabbed the bill.

"How much do I owe?" Olivia asked, pulling her wallet out of her purse.

"Nothing," Luke stated decisively.

"Are you sure?" Olivia asked. "I don't expect you to pay for everything."

"If I can't afford to pay for us both myself, I shouldn't be asking you out," Luke stated. "I don't want you to offer to pay for anything any time we go out."

Olivia couldn't help but notice his assumption that they would be going out again and she felt a small thrill run through her. She reached into her purse and reapplied her lipstick as he settled the bill.

Back at her house, he parked on the driveway, and they walked up the path towards her front door. The conversation slowed, and the same awkwardness that was present at the beginning of the date returned. Unlocking the door, she stepped inside, battling with herself about whether she should invite him in. Would he take it as an invitation to more than she was interested in right now? Luke's next words were the answer she needed.

"I have to get going, I'm expecting an early morning phone call," he said. "But I'm wondering, would it be okay if I kissed you?"

"Umm... ah... yeah, sure," she stammered. She couldn't recall the last time a date had asked her permission for a kiss. As he leaned toward her, she caught his eyes with hers. Piercing and blue, she felt almost swallowed whole by his gaze. Pressing his lips to hers, he gave her a tentative kiss, closed-mouthed at first, but opening as she responded. He slipped his hand along the small of her back and pulled her towards him. She could smell his cologne once again and be was overcome by the sheer manliness of the scent. His tongue slid between her teeth and touched hers carefully, gently exploring. Her knees weakened as he pulled her closer, nestling her hips into his.

Suddenly, she was standing alone. He had pulled away abruptly and was backing out the door.

"Thank you for tonight," he said. "I can't wait to see you again!"

She waved goodbye and then closed the door. Leaning up against it, she closed her eyes and took a deep breath.

"Oh boy, Olivia," she said to the empty room. "You're in a heap of trouble!"

Pulling her shoes off, she flexed her toes and ran her fingers through her hair. It had been a wonderful evening. Great company, terrific food, and a kiss. And what a kiss! She couldn't recall feeling that way about a kiss in a long, long time. A kiss that made her feel so wholly female.

She sat down at her computer and pulled up her email. She wrote out a brief message to Terri and April. As her best friends, she knew they would be wondering how the evening went, and she wanted to let them know she was home safely. After sending the email, she tidied up the kitchen and set out some breakfast for the morning. She went into the washroom and cleaned her face, preparing for bed. Just as she was ready to crawl between the sheets, she noticed a red dot next to the dating app on her phone. Tapping on it, her heart skipped a beat when she saw that she had a message from Luke! She had thought the evening couldn't get any better, but it did as she read his sweet words:

"Thank you for a great evening. I can't believe I have found someone as wonderful as you! I wasn't sure if I was supposed to kiss you or not, so I figured I best just ask, I hope that was okay? I have to say, even if it wasn't, I can't say I regret it. That was an incredibly hot kiss, and it was all I could do not to stay longer. You have the most beautiful eyes, and your lips are amazingly soft; I could have kissed you all night. But enough from me, I hope you sleep well - I know I will."

Olivia threw herself onto her bed with what she was sure was the most ridiculous grin on her face. It had been such a long time since she had felt the heady rush of attraction and romance, and every nerve in her body seemed to tingle with anticipation.

Chapter Twelve

She

She found herself staring out the window instead of dealing with the deadline looming in front of her. Picking at the cuticle on her left thumb, she barely winced when she pulled it back so far that it drew blood. Jumping when someone laughed loudly in the hallway, she realized her nerves were strung more tightly than she had thought. Damn it! She needed to get a handle on her life and her emotions. This wasn't doing her any good, and now it was starting to interfere with her work. It was growing increasingly difficult to worry about things like deadlines when she was faced with so much uncertainty and unhappiness in her marriage.

She turned away from the window and faced her computer. Calling up her browser, she did a quick search for bed and breakfasts in a nearby mountain town, which was an easy drive from her home. She was surprised to see that there were several options available for the weekend, and she felt her burdens ease a little as she began preparations for a get-away.

After spending some time investigating, she settled on a bed and breakfast that offered a private balcony off a rustic styled bedroom. A small breakfast was included in the price along with the promise of some silence and privacy, all sitting nestled in the Rocky Mountains. It was perfect. For the first time in quite a while, she felt in control of something in her life. She may not be able to say how her husband treated her, when he came home or what he said to her, but she was still in control of what she did, where she went and how she spent her time.

Pushing away from her desk with renewed determination, she rose and went into the lunchroom to refresh her coffee. As she added milk to her coffee, she began to think about the deadline ahead and mentally walked through the steps she needed to finish to get the project done on time. She would get this project out of the way today, tie up some loose ends tomorrow and be off for the mountains the day after for two glorious nights of fresh mountain air, some light reading and a brisk hike along scenic trails. For a fleeting moment, it crossed her mind that the trip would be more romantic if only her husband would come with her. She pushed that thought away as she knew that to even bring it up would probably cause another fight. She didn't want to hear him make excuses, and worse yet, she didn't want to listen to herself beg.

Making a determined effort to shrug off the negative thoughts, she sat down at the lunch table and tried to join in the conversation her colleagues were having. She was tired of feeling isolated and alone. She needed to make more of an effort to engage with the people around her. She needed to stop obsessing about herself.

"Any big plans this weekend?" Stacey asked.

"As a matter of fact, I just booked a lovely little B and B in the mountains," She said a big smile on her face.

"Ooooh, that sounds lovely!" Stacey responded. "Is your husband going with you? How romantic!"

"No, this is just a 'me' weekend," she said. "Time for me to recharge my batteries and spend some alone time."

"Oh, I wish I could do that!" she said enviously. "There is no way the hubs would be okay with me going away and leaving him with the gremlins for a whole weekend!"

"I guess that's one of the benefits of having kids young," She smiled. "When I was married to my first husband, and the kids were little, I never had the chance to spend time just on me."

"So, you're saying one day I too will be so lucky?" Stacey asked with a smile.

"Something like that," She laughed.

"Well, I'm envious," her coworker said. "But I better get back to work, these invoices won't pay themselves you know."

"Talk to you later," She waved. "And take care of those kids and that husband!"

She still had a smile on her face as she walked down the hallway towards her office. It felt good to take some positive steps.

For the next several hours, she worked almost non-stop on her project, and as she gathered her things at the end of the day, she realized it would easily be completed before the deadline of noon tomorrow. Walking out to her car, she knew she wasn't ready to go home. She unlocked the door and sat there, just thinking. After a few minutes, she decisively started the vehicle and headed out of the parking lot.

Instead of heading toward home, she turned in the opposite direction and ended up in the parking lot of a group of big box stores. It was time for a new outfit. She couldn't remember the last time she had bought new clothes for herself, and this trip was the perfect excuse. She wasn't sure exactly what she was looking for, but she also knew the hunt would be part of the fun.

A few hours later, she returned to her car, bags in hand. She had found a lovely pair of lounging pajamas that would be perfect for her weekend getaway. Although soft and comfy, they were also stylish so she didn't feel like she was in her mother's clothes. She also picked up a new tote, just large enough to fit her camera, phone, and wallet. It would be ideal for nature walks this weekend. And of course, she picked up a bottle of wine. Not the usual inexpensive kind she often drank, this was one she had wanted to try for a while but hadn't been able to justify the price tag.

Buying for her weekend, made it seem all the more exciting and somehow exotic. She mentally shook her head. How many times in the past had she jumped in her car with a friend and taken off for the mountains at the last minute? It had been no big deal and something that happened regularly. For some reason, this trip felt different. It felt freeing and daring. To take time for herself, to spend money frivolously, was something she missed. She wasn't quite ready to stop. She smiled to herself as she placed her bags in the trunk, slammed the lid shut, and headed off toward the upscale lingerie store. Who said she needed her husband along to feel good about herself? Nothing like some new underwear to help a woman feel ultra-feminine.

She found herself staring out the window instead of dealing with the deadline looming in front of her. Picking at the cuticle on her left thumb, she barely winced when she pulled it back so far that it drew blood. Jumping when someone laughed loudly in the hallway, she realized her nerves were strung more tightly than she had thought. Damn it! She needed to get a handle on her life and her emotions. This wasn't doing her any good, and now it was starting to interfere with her work. It was growing increasingly difficult to worry about things like deadlines when she was faced with so much uncertainty and unhappiness in her marriage.

She turned away from the window and faced her computer. Calling up her browser, she did a quick search for bed and breakfasts in a nearby mountain town, which was an easy drive from her home. She was surprised to see that there were several options available for the weekend, and she felt her burdens ease a little as she began preparations for a get-away.

After spending some time investigating, she settled on a bed and breakfast that offered a private balcony off a rustic styled bedroom. A small breakfast was included in the price along with the promise of some silence and privacy, all sitting nestled in the Rocky Mountains. It was perfect. For the first time in quite a while, she felt in control of something in her life. She may not be able to say how her husband treated her, when he came home or what he said to her, but she was still in control of what she did, where she went and how she spent her time.

Pushing away from her desk with renewed determination, she rose and went into the lunchroom to refresh her coffee. As she added milk to her coffee, she began to think about the deadline ahead and mentally walked through the steps she needed to finish to get the project done on time. She would get this project out of the way today, tie up some loose ends tomorrow and be off for the mountains the day after for two glorious nights of fresh mountain air, some light reading and a brisk hike along scenic trails. For a fleeting moment, it crossed her mind that the trip would be more romantic if only her husband would come with her. She pushed that thought away as she knew that to even bring it up would probably cause another fight. She didn't want to hear him make excuses, and worse yet, she didn't want to listen to herself beg.

Making a determined effort to shrug off the negative thoughts, she sat down at the lunch table and tried to join in the conversation her colleagues were having. She was tired of feeling isolated and alone. She needed to make more of an effort to engage with the people around her. She needed to stop obsessing about herself.

"Any big plans this weekend?" Stacey asked.

"As a matter of fact, I just booked a lovely little B and B in the mountains," She said a big smile on her face.

"Ooooh, that sounds lovely!" Stacey responded. "Is your husband going with you? How romantic!"

"No, this is just a 'me' weekend," she said. "Time for me to recharge my batteries and spend some alone time."

"Oh, I wish I could do that!" she said enviously. "There is no way the hubs would be okay with me going away and leaving him with the gremlins for a whole weekend!"

"I guess that's one of the benefits of having kids young," She smiled. "When I was married to my first husband, and the kids were little, I never had the chance to spend time just on me."

"So, you're saying one day I too will be so lucky?" Stacey asked with a smile.

"Something like that," She laughed.

"Well, I'm envious," her coworker said. "But I better get back to work, these invoices won't pay themselves you know."

"Talk to you later," She waved. "And take care of those kids and that husband!"

She still had a smile on her face as she walked down the hallway towards her office. It felt good to take some positive steps.

For the next several hours, she worked almost non-stop on her project, and as she gathered her things at the end of the day, she realized it would easily be completed before the deadline of noon tomorrow. Walking out to her car, she knew she wasn't ready to go home. She unlocked the door and sat there, just thinking. After a few minutes, she decisively started the vehicle and headed out of the parking lot.

Instead of heading toward home, she turned in the opposite direction and ended up in the parking lot of a group of big box stores. It was time for a new outfit. She couldn't remember the last time she had bought new clothes for herself, and this trip was the perfect excuse.

She wasn't sure exactly what she was looking for, but she also knew the hunt would be part of the fun.

A few hours later, she returned to her car, bags in hand. She had found a lovely pair of lounging pajamas that would be perfect for her weekend getaway. Although soft and comfy, they were also stylish so she didn't feel like she was in her mother's clothes. She also picked up a new tote, just large enough to fit her camera, phone, and wallet. It would be ideal for nature walks this weekend. And of course, she picked up a bottle of wine. Not the usual inexpensive kind she often drank, this was one she had wanted to try for a while but hadn't been able to justify the price tag.

Buying for her weekend, made it seem all the more exciting and somehow exotic. She mentally shook her head. How many times in the past had she jumped in her car with a friend and taken off for the mountains at the last minute? It had been no big deal and something that happened regularly. For some reason, this trip felt different. It felt freeing and daring. To take time for herself, to spend money frivolously, was something she missed. She wasn't quite ready to stop. She smiled to herself as she placed her bags in the trunk, slammed the lid shut, and headed off toward the upscale lingerie store. Who said she needed her husband along to feel good about herself? Nothing like some new underwear to help a woman feel ultra-feminine.

Chapter Thirteen

Olivia

Come on boys!" Olivia yelled from the kitchen. "It's time for supper!" Honestly, she mumbled to herself, what is with these boys?

They ate non-stop until it was time for a meal, and then they couldn't pull themselves away from their games. She swore she wouldn't keep calling them next time. Let them miss out on the meal entirely, and maybe they would learn to take her seriously. If they didn't come up after she had called them three times already, they could eat their meal cold for all she cared. She sat down at the table and cut into her chicken, rationalizing that there was no reason for her to have to eat a cold meal.

A few minutes later, she heard the boys trudging up the stairs, chattering to each other about the latest game they had played. They sat down at the table and dove into dinner, totally oblivious to their mother's frustration.

"Mom, I need a note to miss my chem class tomorrow," her son, Jonathon, said between bites of his chicken.

"Why are you missing chem class?" she asked.

"Because I wasn't there for the last class and now, we have an exam on it," he said, matter-of-factly.

"You want me to write a note so you can miss a class because you haven't prepared?" Olivia asked, her fork stalled midway to her mouth.

"How could I prepare? I told you, I wasn't at the last class!" Jonathon said with more than just a little outrage in his voice.

"Well, I would suggest you contact someone who was there and get their notes," his mother patiently explained to him. "because I'm not writing you a note to get out of chem class."

"Ah, Mom!" he protested.

"Suck it up, buttercup," his brother taunted.

"Adam, knock it off!" Olivia admonished. "There is no reason to torment your brother."

The rest of the dinner was spent eating quietly, one brother picking at his chicken with a sullen look on his face and the other inhaling the meal almost faster than he could chew. As they finished dinner, Olivia began stacking the plates and passed them to Adam. The cups and cutlery went to Jonathon.

"Don't forget to rinse off the pots before they go in the dishwasher," she instructed them as they took the items into the kitchen. As she watched them moving around, she took a moment to appreciate that although they drove her crazy at times, they were, at heart, good kids. They helped out at home, they didn't get into trouble at school, and their grades were decent. What more could a mother ask?

Later that evening, she settled in for her phone call with Luke. For the past week, they had been talking every evening and meeting every second day or so for either lunch or dinner. She usually preferred lunch because of the boys – she didn't want them to meet until she felt more confident in their relationship - but she knew at some point she was going to have to introduce him to them. She couldn't keep juggling spending time with him and taking care of the boys while keeping them apart. She didn't like the idea of introducing her boys to just anyone, but it appeared as though Luke was going to be around for more than a couple of dates. Generally, the boys weren't even aware when she went on one of her coffee dates or even to dinner. She didn't want to be the type of mother who had a revolving number of 'friends' coming in and out of her son's lives.

Luke had picked her up from work at lunch today, and they grabbed a bite at the local sub shop. It was nothing fancy, but she just enjoyed spending time with him and getting to know him better. Tonight, they would talk for at least an hour and the same again tomorrow night. Luke also routinely sent her cute cards through the dating site, and frequent texts, just to let her know that he was thinking of her. She had never received this amount of attention before and she wasn't sure she would ever get tired of it.

She still couldn't believe what was happening. After several years with no romantic interest in sight at all, she was being swept off her feet! There was no other way to describe what was happening. He brought her flowers almost every time they met, paid for every meal, and ended each evening with a kiss. And oh, what kisses! She had thought that maybe the first kiss had just been the result of nerves from a first date, but it turned out it wasn't. He kissed her again the next time they were out, and the next time, and the one after that. Each time, Olivia felt it from the tips of her toes all the way up to her head. And every place in between. She had begun to look forward to their goodnight kiss. If she were honest with herself, she would admit that she had started to crave it.

The phone rang at precisely eight pm, as usual. He was always right on time, as though he had been watching the clock and didn't want to keep her waiting.

"How was your day?" he asked, his deep baritone voice making her smile.

"It was great," she responded. "Work went by quickly, the boys haven't killed each other, and I haven't killed them, so we're all good!"

His laugh of appreciation caressed her ear, and she settled down into the pillows on her bed, ready to spend time with him.

"Glad to hear," he said. "I'm glad we went for lunch today, I miss you on the days we don't see each other."

"I miss you too," Olivia murmured shyly. She was still unused to his ability to express how he was feeling and found herself answering somewhat awkwardly. She did miss seeing him when they weren't together, but she was still coming to terms with the fact he felt the same way!

They talked about their work, her boys, and which movies they were interested in seeing the coming weekend. The boys would be with their dad, and they would have a lot of time they would be able to spend together.

After about an hour, Olivia began to stifle a yawn or two. As much as she tried to hide it from him, he noticed right away.

"Are you ready for bed, Olivia?" he asked.

"I'm afraid so. Sorry for yawning in your ear," she answered.

"It's okay, don't worry about it," he said. "Are you in bed now?"

"Yes, I am, I think that's one of the things that is making me tired," she answered.

"Are you in your pajamas?" he asked, his voice lowering slightly.

"Um, no, not yet," she responded, the tone of his voice caused goosebumps to rise on her arms.

"Why don't you put the phone down, go change, and then crawl into bed," he suggested. "I'll talk you to sleep."

Feeling silly, Olivia nevertheless did precisely that. She slipped her nightgown over her head, quickly splashed some water on her face and crawled in under her covers.

"There, I'm ready," she told him.

"Good, now let me talk," he said. "You don't need to say anything, and I won't ask you any questions. If you feel yourself nodding off, just go with it."

She felt a bit odd, but also strangely giddy at the thought of him doing such an intimate thing. He lowered his voice slightly and began talking about his home town and what it was like growing up there. He spoke of carefree days playing with his brother and his uncles, of growing up the oldest in a single mother family and how he tried so hard to be there for everyone. After a while, he talked about leaving home and moving to a brand-new town. As he spoke, his voice seemed to get deeper and slower. Olivia's eyelids grew heavy, and she smiled sleepily to herself as she realized once again how much she enjoyed his voice.

After a while, his voice trailed off, and she lay caught in a state between slumber and awareness, a twilight area where she was aware of what was happening, but she didn't really care.

"Olivia, click the hang-up button and have a good night's sleep," he commanded quietly. With a murmur of agreement, she tapped the button and fell into a deep slumber.

When she woke in the morning, she felt like she was climbing up a dark well, struggling to gain consciousness. Her eyes were encrusted with sleep, and her throat ached. Oh no, she thought, a cold. No wonder she had been so tired the night before - she had been coming down with a cold.

Dragging herself out of bed, she forced herself to go into the washroom and turn on the shower. The hot water soon had the room filled with steam, and she sat on the bathtub edge, hoping that the warm, moist air would clear her nasal passages. She sat there for a while before getting up and splashing water on her face before peering into the mirror. Yup, she was definitely sick.

Although she hated to do it, she went into her bedroom, picked up her phone and dialed work. She didn't miss many days, but she always felt slightly guilty when she did. She grabbed her housecoat and wrapped it around her as she trudged out to the kitchen.

"Whoa, Mom!" Jonathon exclaimed. "You look grody!"

"Don't be such an idiot Jonathon, you don't say that to a woman!" Adam chimed in.

"Okay, okay, no arguing this morning guys! You're right, I'm not feeling well, and I'm just up long enough to make sure you two get off to school okay," Olivia said in a croaking voice.

"We're okay, Mom, we can handle it," Adam reassured her. "Go back to bed."

"Yeah Mom," Jonathon reassured her. "Best to stay away, we don't want to catch what you have!"

"Subtle dude, real subtle," Adam laughed as he punched his brother on the arm.

Olivia dug through the medicine basket above the fridge to find some type of cold medicine that might help her sleep away the morning. She managed to find some nighttime flu medicine and a few cough drops. That would have to do for now. She went back upstairs and crawled under the covers. She picked up her phone and checked her email for messages. Sure enough, there was one from Luke:

Good morning sleeping beauty! I hope you slept well last night. You sounded so adorable as you nodded off, I couldn't help thinking about what it would be like to be there, holding you. I'm not talking anything sexual (not that I haven't thought of that mind you!!!), but just to hold you as you fall asleep. I hope that one day I will have that opportunity. Talk to you tonight!

She smiled to herself at the thought of falling asleep in his arms. But not with this cold, that's for sure. She almost snorted at the thought of it and quickly succumbed to a spasm of hacking coughs. Oh yeah, she thought, Sexy. Really sexy.

She slept for a few hours and when she woke, she decided to try some soup. She wasn't really hungry, but she hoped that by eating some soup and maybe some toast, that the liquid would help soothe, and the toast would have a scratching effect, on her beleaguered throat. She entered the kitchen, bathrobe wrapped tight around her, her slippers flip-flopping on the floor. While the soup was heating, she went to her computer and checked the dating site. Sure enough, there were a couple of cards from Luke. One had been sent early this morning and had a cute puppy dog on the front and inside it read, "I find you adorable!" The second card had flowers on it, and a short message written by Luke that said, "Thinking of you!". It was nice having someone thinking about her all the time, although she was beginning to wonder where he found the time.

Curled up on the couch, she napped on and off throughout the afternoon, the sound of the TV her only company. As she slept, couples squealed over finding their ideal home, audiences oohed and ah-ed when the war veteran's house was renovated.

The boys came home from school and checked to make sure she didn't need anything. She got up a couple of times to use the washroom and to make sure the office hadn't left her a message on her phone or sent her an important email. She sent off a message to Luke, letting him know she had received his messages but that she was sick.

Her phone rang shortly after she sent the message.

"Hi, are you okay?" Luke asked, concern tinging his voice.

"Oh yeah, it's just a nasty cold," she reassured him. "I stayed home and nursed it today, so hopefully I'll feel better tomorrow."

"I hate to hear you sounding so sick," he said. "But on the upside, your voice is even sexier sounding than usual."

Olivia laughed, which caused another fit of coughing. When she came back on the phone, she apologized for leaving him waiting.

"Seriously though Olivia," Luke said. "You should maybe get that checked out, you don't sound so good."

"Oh, I'll be fine," she brushed off the suggestion. "It's just day one of the cold from hell."

"Okay, if you say so, but I'm keeping an eye on you, young lady!" he joked.

They talked for a while longer, and then they agreed that they should call it a night so Olivia could get to bed earlier than usual. The cold was exhausting her, and she wanted to take care so it would be gone as soon as possible.

"Goodnight Olivia," he said. "I'll see you tomorrow."

"I'm not sure I'll be able to make it for lunch tomorrow as we had planned," Olivia said. "Unless I feel radically different tomorrow, I imagine I'll be home from work for the next couple of days."

"Don't worry, you not being at work won't stop me from seeing you," he stated, decisively.

"Oh, believe me, you don't want to see me and risk catching this cold!" she assured him.

"We'll see," he said. "For now, you just get some rest."

Having felt progressively worse as the evening went on, she didn't need to be told twice. Dosing up on the overnight flu and cold medication, she climbed into bed and was soon sound asleep.

~ ~ ~

She lay in the morning sunlight, wondering what she had ever done to deserve this cold. It had been a long time since she had been knocked on her butt so thoroughly by the common cold. She had vaguely heard the boys get ready for school a couple of hours ago, but she hadn't been able to convince her body to fully awaken. Now she reluctantly slid out of bed and grabbed her housecoat. Heading into the kitchen for some tea, she stopped by her computer to check her messages. As she expected, there was one from Luke:

"Hope you are feeling better today. I can't wait to see you. I'll come by around noon with some lunch."

Oh no, there was no way she wanted to see Luke while she was in this condition, and she certainly didn't want to give him this cold. She looked at the clock and realized she needed to let him know quite soon not to come as it was getting later in the morning.

"I'm sorry Luke, but I'm not fit for human consumption today. I look like hell, and I really don't want you to get this. Let's plan for something in a day or two?"

She hit send and took another sip of her tea. The hot liquid soothed her sore throat and gave her a reprieve from the scratchy pain. She laid her head on the desk and closed her eyes for a moment. The ringing of the phone interrupted her moment, and she reached for her cell.

"Hi, Olivia speaking," she answered, without looking at the call display.

"Hi, it's Luke speaking," he responded.

"Hi Luke, sorry about having to cancel but I really feel awful," she said.

"Oh, we're not canceling, I'm going to bring you over something to eat so you keep your energy up and can get well soon," he informed her.

"No, really Luke. I would rather just crawl back into bed," she insisted.

"But we were supposed to see each other today, and I've been looking forward to it," he cajoled. "I'll only come by for a bit, and then you can get some more rest."

"But I don't want you to catch this," she argued.

"Don't worry about me. I'm not afraid of a cold bug," he said, a touch of irritation in his voice. "And don't worry, you look great no matter what."

"Okay," she said reluctantly.

"I'll be over in about an hour," he said, the decision made.

She hung up the phone feeling out of sorts and annoyed. She didn't want to see anyone today, but she supposed it might do her some good to have a reason to get dressed and cleaned up a bit. She stretched her arms over her head in an attempt to shake off the cobwebs in her mind and her body. She would rather go back to bed, but instead, she headed to the washroom to jump in a hot, steamy shower so she could get dressed and be ready for Luke.

An hour later, almost to the second, the front doorbell rang. Olivia met him at the door and guided him to the table and chair set on her front deck.

"If you insist on being around my bugs, at least we can limit the exposure and eat out here," she said.

"As I said, if I want to see you, I won't be letting some bug stop me," he said decisively.

Setting down a bag from a nearby sandwich shop, he began to pull out containers of soup, salad, and wrapped sandwiches. She slipped back into the house to get the spoons and forks and a jug of juice from the fridge. Soon they were settled in to eat lunch on the front deck, the midday sun playing peekaboo behind low floating clouds.

"Mmmm, this is good," Olivia said, as she tackled the fresh salad. "I didn't think I had an appetite, but this is great."

"See, you needed someone to take care of you and make sure you eat," Luke stated.

"Yes, you were right," Olivia said with a smile. "I couldn't manage without you."

"That's better," Luke said, a twinkle in his eye.

They ate the rest of their lunch in silence, enjoying the treat of a midday meal out in the sun. Afterward, the garbage was collected and put back in the bag. They each stretched out in their chairs; Luke, looking content and at ease, Olivia struggling to keep her hacking cough to a minimum.

"What time do you have to be back at work?" Olivia asked.

"Trying to get rid of me?" Luke joked.

"Of course not," Olivia said with a smile. "Just don't want you to get in trouble."

"Yeah, I should probably get going," he responded reluctantly. "But it was nice to see you today."

"You too," Olivia smiled sincerely. "Hopefully I'll be better company the next time I see you."

"Speaking of that, is there anything, in particular, you want to do this weekend?" he asked.

"Not really. I'll leave that in your capable hands," she answered.

"Sounds good. Now you take care of yourself and make sure you're drinking a lot of water and getting a bunch of sleep," he said.

She walked with him down the front steps to the driveway. Waving as he left, she felt a wave of exhaustion flow over her. Lunch had taken more out of her than she'd realized, and she couldn't wait to get back into bed. The truth was, she was feeling uncomfortable after their visit. It confused her because while she loved spending time with him, his insistence today made her feel like she didn't have a lot of control over the pace of their relationship. She struggled with her emotions for a while before deciding that she was probably being overly-sensitive because she was so sick.

Chapter Fourteen

She

Hands full of bags, she walked into her house and wrestled her way down the hallway. Laying the bags on the dining room table, she threw her purse on the counter and noted that the house had that telltale empty feeling that houses have when no one is home. He wasn't home again tonight. But for once she wasn't going to let it get to her. She'd had a good day, she had plans for this weekend, and she was on schedule to get her latest project completed.

She walked over to the wine rack and chose one of her favorites. If her husband didn't want to spend time with her, then she was just going to have to take things into her own hands and take care of herself. If that meant spending money and going on road trips by herself, then so be it!

She turned on the TV and flipped it from the sports channel that her husband regularly watched to a 24-hour classic rock channel. She began putting together a salad for her dinner while dancing to the music. It amazed her how little it took, how easy it was really, to make her happy these days. Why hadn't she decided to do this sooner? It was time to take her life back into her own hands and gain some control. When had she gotten to the point where she was waiting around for a man to make her happy?

She ate her dinner, drank almost half the bottle of wine, and was wiping things up when she heard the door. Her heart sank a little. It was only then that she realized that she had been hoping that she would be in bed before he came home. She hadn't been waiting for him as she usually did. She was happy making her plans and being in her contented little world.

"Hi, how are you?" She said as he walked into the room. "Did you have a nice day?"

"Yeah, it was okay," he said, walking over to his chair in the living room and flipping the channel back to his sports shows.

"Good. So, what's new?" She asked, putting on a smile and making an effort to engage him in conversation.

"Nothing is new, just the same old," he responded, eyes glued to the TV. She waited for him to ask her questions about her day so she could tell him about her plans for a road trip on the weekend. The questions never came, and the heavy silence continued. Feeling frustrated by his lack of attention, she got up and walked toward their bedroom.

"Okay then, I'm heading to bed," she told him. "I'm going to have a bath, read a bit, and then go to sleep."

"Uh-huh," he said.

Pouring her bath, she sat at the edge and watched the bubbles grow. Her eyes misted over as she reflected once again on her marriage.

It was like living on a roller coaster. One day you're up, and the next day you're down. The difference is that when riding a roller coaster, you can see what's coming.

She had been so excited about her plans, but just a few non-committal responses from him and her heart had sunk, taking her buoyant mood with it. She sipped on her wine, analyzing the beginning of their relationship. She told herself that there was no way she could have seen this coming. He had been so loving, so attentive, and so head-over-heels in love with her back then. What happened? she asked herself for the umpteenth time. What had she done to deserve this? To be ignored, disrespected, and shunned?

She stood and took off her clothes, draping them across the clothes stand, and slipped into the hot water. The water soothed her body, if not her mind, and she felt some of the day's tension begin to melt away with the hot, soapy water. Running her hands up and down her soft, slick and wet body, she closed her eyes and remembered what it had been like on the trip they took just before they were married. Making love in the shower, the warm water cascading over their bodies, the soap causing hands to smoothly glide over the skin. Flesh pressed up against hard, cold tile creating a mixture of sensations. She sank deeper into the tub, and her fingers found their way all over her body, caressing, probing and stroking. Damn, how could she be married and still feel so utterly lonely?

The night was spent tossing and turning, the product of drinking too much wine in a hot bath and a lot of lonely questioning. When she got out of bed in the morning, her husband was in the shower, and so she quickly dressed, went downstairs and had her breakfast. By the time he was dressed, she was heading out the door with a quick goodbye and a rushed comment about needing to work on a deadline today. The truth was she had lots of time today to get her work done, but she just didn't feel up to trying to talk to him or having him bring her mood down any further.

She took the long way to work, driving through the local park and enjoying the early morning sun on her face. She knew she was going to have to let her husband know that she was going away tomorrow, but his behavior had pushed a rebellious button within her. If he didn't want to talk to her, that was fine; she wouldn't speak to him either. She knew that wasn't helpful, but it was how she felt. She would deal with him tonight.

Pulling into the parking lot at work, she saw a co-worker struggling with multiple trays of coffee. She rushed to help her and grabbed one of the trays.

"Thank you!" her colleague exclaimed. "I thought I could manage them all, but I think I overestimated my abilities. Apparently, my waitressing days were longer ago than I recalled!"

They laughed together as they entered the building and set the trays on the lunchroom counter.

"I'm not looking forward to the staff meeting this afternoon, I was hoping to get some stuff done early and then get working on that huge pile of filing I've been avoiding."

"What staff meeting is that?" She asked. "I think I missed something."

"Don't you remember?" Her coworker said. "We're having those consultants come in to talk about efficiency in the office and how we should all be working better together?"

"I seem to have blocked that one out," She mused.

"Lucky you, but you still have to come," her colleague laughed.

"Yeah, yeah," she laughed in return. "I'll be there!"

She entered her office and sat down at her desk, turned on her computer and began to deal with her work for the day. For the first time in weeks, she was able to immerse herself in her work, and the hours sped by. She ate her lunch at her desk while reviewing files, and before she knew it, her project was done and it was time for the staff meeting.

~ ~ ~

At the end of the day, she gathered up her things and headed home, determined to have a real conversation with her husband. She needed to let him know what her plans were for the weekend. She needed to make him understand that it was important for her to start taking better care of herself. He was, of course, welcome to come along, but she knew there was no way he would even consider it.

She sent him a text as she got in her car, asking him if he was going to be home for dinner, and by the time she was pulling out of the lot, he had responded saying he would be back in time for a late meal. She stopped at the grocery store and picked up some good quality steaks, potatoes, and some quinoa salad.

~ ~ ~

Their meal was ready to eat just as he walked in the door. He smiled a rare smile at the smell of the barbecued steaks and walked into the kitchen as she dished up the salad.

"Wow, what did I do to deserve this?" he asked.

"Nothing at all," She answered. "I just figured, as it isn't often we're both home for a meal at the same time, I might as well do it up right."

She was pleased that he appeared to be in a good mood, and she remained hopeful they would be able to talk.

"Sit down, and I'll bring you your plate," she said.

They both sat at the kitchen table and began eating. They ate in silence - the only sound was that of chewing and swallowing as he cut into his steak and threw back a beer she had brought him from the fridge.

After a while, she broke the silence and asked him how his day had gone.

"About the same as any other day," he snapped, slightly irritated.

"Oh, that's good," She responded, rushing past his irritation. "I had a good day! I'm a bit excited as I have planned a weekend getaway."

"You know I can't just leave town at the last minute," he said with more than a touch of exasperation in his voice. "You're just going to have to cancel whatever you have planned. We can't go."

"Actually, I assumed you wouldn't be able to go," She stated. "I booked it for myself."

His hand, holding a fork loaded with potato, stopped midway between his mouth and his plate.

"What do you mean you booked it for yourself?" he demanded.

"I've decided I need to get away from the everyday stuff and take a mental health weekend," she explained. "I booked a couple of nights in the mountains at a little B and B."

"What are you going to do there?" he asked, as he set his fork down beside his dinner plate.

"The same thing I always do when I go to the mountains," she explained. "I'll sleep in, take some hikes, eat some good food and do a lot of reading."

"Really," he stated.

She was surprised by the tone of his voice. She had expected him to be surprised, and maybe even a little annoyed that she had gone ahead and booked it without talking to him, but his voice sounded almost flat.

"Yes, do you have a problem with me going?" She asked, curiously.

"Oh no, you go right ahead," he said almost mockingly. "This explains so much!"

"What do you mean by that?" She asked.

"The new lingerie," he spit out. "I came across it last night when I came to bed."

"Yes, I bought that for the weekend," she said, confused. "I thought it would be nice to feel pampered, and I haven't bought myself anything new for a long time. I had some time after work yesterday, so I swung by the mall." she was beginning to feel like she needed to defend herself, but she wasn't sure precisely what she was defending herself against.

"You're trying to tell me that you're going by yourself to the mountains, for the weekend, without your husband, and you just decided to buy yourself some slinky new underwear on a whim?" he asked, his voice rising.

His meaning became clear to her, and she almost laughed out loud.

"Don't be ridiculous!" She spat out, shaking her head. " When have I ever given you any reason to be jealous, or suspicious?"

"Well, apparently there's a first time for everything," he growled.

"Stop it! You're welcome to come with me if you're so concerned about what I'm going to be doing," she snapped, becoming angry.

"That's convenient after I tell you I can't!" he snarled.

"Are you crazy? Stop acting this way!" she cried out. "I'm just taking a break and heading to the mountains; you're making this into something sick and twisted!"

"So, I should just ignore the fact that my wife bought herself some trashy clothes and is leaving town for the weekend?" He demanded.

"Trashy clothes? I bought a new pair of underwear and some lounging pajamas!" She argued, shaking her head in disbelief.

She couldn't believe the conversation had taken such an ugly turn. What had happened? He had never been the jealous type, and this was just downright unreasonable. She took a deep breath, trying to calm herself and salvage part of their evening.

"Look, Honey, all I'm doing is taking some time to get away," she reassured him, lowering her voice in an attempt to soothe his temper. "I bought the clothes as a treat for myself and no one else. Honestly, if you want to come with me, I would love it if you could make that happen."

"No. Fine. You go away for your weekend," he barked angrily, throwing down his napkin and standing up. "You go and slut around in some strange town with god knows who; I'm not going to stop you."

She sat stunned as he got up, yanked his jacket off its hook and headed for the door. She couldn't believe he had spoken to her that way. Where had all that ugliness come from? Why was he so suspicious and cruel all of a sudden? She sat among the dirty dishes and half-eaten meal as though frozen in place.

After a while, she stood up and cleared off the dishes, scraping the leftovers into the organic recycling, stacking the dirty plates and cups into the dishwasher. Then she went upstairs and began packing her bag for the weekend. She threw in a change of clothes for hiking, a nicer outfit for dinner, and her makeup bag. She hesitated when she came to the bags with her new purchases. They seemed sullied somehow. All the excitement and pleasure she had taken in buying them had been dirtied by innuendos and ugliness. To hell with him! She grabbed her purchases and added them to her bag. I'm not going to let him ruin this weekend for me! She couldn't believe that one short weekend had become so big in her life, and in her mind. She used to go on road trips all the time and never think much about it. Now here she was, fighting for two stupid days in the mountains.

The more she thought about it, the angrier she became. The shock of his outburst had worn off, and she was mad! Enough was enough. He made her life miserable when he was home and left her waiting for him when he wasn't. He barely communicated with her and shut her out of anything meaningful in his life. She was going to have this weekend if it killed her.

Once she was packed and ready for the next day, she went into her bathroom, opened up the medicine cabinet and took the vial of sleeping pills. She knew she was too wound up to sleep, and that if she didn't do something about it right now, she would be up half the night listening for him to return.

Pouring a glass of water, she threw the pill to the back of her throat and chased it down. She climbed into bed, set her alarm and snuggled under the covers, holding them close to her as though to defend her body from the unknown.

~ ~ ~

She woke up in the morning with a foggy head, her body fighting to its way to full consciousness. Shutting her alarm clock off, she rolled over and noticed that the other side of the bed had not been slept in. She paused, looking at the neatly made side of the bed. He was often late getting in, but he had never been gone the entire night before. She laid there, taking a deep breath and telling herself that it didn't matter anymore. She was not going to let him push her around. If he wanted to sulk and stay gone all night, so be it. He had probably crashed at one of his drinking buddies' houses or something. Or maybe at his office. Either way, she hoped he was happy with whatever message he was trying to send her.

Sliding her feet out of bed and into her slippers, she padded to the washroom and prepared for

work. Afterward, on her way downstairs, she picked up the overnight bag she had packed the night before and walked into the kitchen. She decided to go to a drive-through to buy a breakfast sandwich and a coffee on the way to work. She didn't want to take any chance that he would return home just as she was leaving. She didn't want to deal with him, or the situation, right now.

~ ~ ~

When she arrived at work, she quickly walked down the hall to her office and shut the door as soon as she entered. She couldn't handle talking with people today; she planned on getting her work done and getting out of Dodge as quickly as she could. Now that the day was here, she felt an almost desperate need to be in the mountains. She wasn't quite sure if she was running to something or away from something. Either way, she was gone as soon as she tied up some loose ends and got on the road.

~ ~ ~

She only had to talk to two people that morning; the first came in to make sure she was okay, as she didn't often keep her door closed for so long. Another came by to get her to sign off on their portion of yesterday's project. By lunchtime she was caught up, her emails were answered, and even her filing was done. She opened her office door, waved goodbye to the ladies in the cubicles situated just outside her office, and left the building.

She was on the road with a full tank of gas and a sub sandwich within half an hour. She cranked up the music on her stereo and began singing at the top of her lungs. Rolling down her window to feel the warm air flow through her hair, the smell of the city was thick, but somehow a welcome escape from the recycled air of the office.

She had been driving for about half an hour when she realized her cell phone was not plugged in, so she picked it up and attached the cord charger. As she did that, she noticed that the alert sign was on to let her know she had new text messages. Ignoring the distracted driving laws in effect, she opened up her message center and checked to see what messages she had waiting. She was shocked to see she had five, and they were all from her husband.

She tapped his name, and the message string came up.

"Call me."

"Don't be like this, call me."

"Are you ignoring me now?"

"Damn it, phone me already!"

"You can't just leave like this, phone me already."

She threw her phone down on the passenger seat and pounded the console beside her. Damn it! Why did he have to pull this? Why couldn't he just leave her be and let her have some time to herself? Why was it that when he wanted to talk, he wanted to talk right now? Those messages had all been left within a space of about half an hour.

How many times was she left waiting for him, her texts and phone calls going unanswered for hours? Now he wanted to talk, and he wanted it right this minute. Well, he was going to have to wait. She needed some space and some distance between them. She couldn't deal with him right now. She shook her head as she ran her hand through her hair, one hand on the steering wheel. As she looked ahead, lost in thought, she heard her phone buzz again. A short while later it buzzed again. She picked it up, and sure enough, it was her husband.

"You can't keep ignoring me."

"If you are trying to punish me this isn't going to work."

Before she had a chance to decide how to respond, the phone rang in her hand. The number that came up on the caller ID was her husband's cell. This was getting ridiculous! She was not going to answer. She turned her phone to mute and cranked up the stereo further. He was just going to have to wait for her this time.

Chapter Fifteen

Olivia

Olivia popped what she hoped would be her last day-time cold capsule as she prepared to go out on Friday night. Luckily the cold, while violent, had also been swift, and she felt almost one hundred percent better just a few days after coming down sick. The boys were off at their dads', and she was looking forward to dinner and a movie with Luke tonight; they had decided on sushi and the latest Bond movie.

She heard him walk up the front steps and opened the door before he could ring the bell.

"Well, hello!" he greeted her with a smile.

"Hi!" she responded, cheerily.

"I see you're ready to go," Luke said. "And your voice sounds even better than it did this morning, so getting back to work must have helped."

"You're right, it was the oddest cold," she answered as she turned around to lock the door. "'In like a lion, out like a lamb' - so to speak."

He opened the car door for her before going around to the driver's side. His vehicle smelled like a combination of new car, leather, and cologne. He had traded in his old car and bought this one about a week after they had started dating, and it still looked new. She leaned back and let the plush leather engulf her. He often teased her about her old car, saying she needed to upgrade, but as much as she appreciated his new car, she was happy with her twelve-year-old, paid for, old faithful.

~ ~ ~

When they arrived at the restaurant, they were taken to their booth, and she sat down across from him.

"Are you afraid of me?" he asked.

She didn't answer but looked at him with puzzlement.

"Come sit beside me," he said, patting the space next to him.

She laughed and moved into the seat beside him. He draped his arm across the back of their booth, and his fingertips grazed her shoulder. He moved in closer and whispered in her ear, "You look gorgeous tonight."

A shiver ran through her at the sound of his deep voice speaking so intimately close to her, and she went weak in the knees when he passed his lips across the thin flesh behind her ear.

A chuckle escaped his lips as he saw the expression on her face, seeming to take pleasure in her discomfort.

"You look even better when you're so obviously turned on," he chuckled.

"Never mind, look at the menu," she said with a blush.

They lingered over dinner, enjoying the food and each other's company. He talked about the beauty of his hometown, and how much he wanted to take a trip back to visit his old friends and family. They discussed the political situation and their shared feeling that it was time for a change. When they weren't talking, they sat in comfortable silence, chewing on the excellent food.

After dinner, they headed over to the theatre to watch a movie. Foregoing the snack counter, they went straight into their theatre. He walked them to the back of the room and chose two seats. As they settled in to watch the movie, he placed his hand on the inside of her leg. Tucking his fingers under her leg, he caressed her knee with his thumb. After a few minutes, he reached over and picked up her hand, placing it on his arm. They snuggled in to watch the show.

A couple of hours later, Luke pulled his vehicle up to her house. Putting it in park, he looked over at her and asked if he could come in for a bit.

"We had such a nice time tonight," he commented. "I hate for it to end."

"Of course," she said. She knew they were walking on rocky ground, but at that moment she was okay with it. One of the things they had talked about a lot was their desire to take things slowly and not let sex cloud their judgment. They had both made mistakes in the past, and they wanted to be clear-headed.

"Would you like a drink?" she asked when they were in the house.

"Just a pop would be great," he replied.

She carried her glass of wine and his glass of pop over to where he was sitting in the living room.

"Do you use your fireplace much?" he asked.

"Once in a while," she answered. "Would you like me to turn it on?"

"Sure, that would be nice," he responded.

She turned on the fireplace and joined him on the couch. He slid his arm across her shoulder and, using his hand on her neck to pull her closer, began kissing her. As always happened when he kissed her, a warmth spread across her body. But tonight, the smell of him, the hardness of his chest and the small sounds he made deep in his throat as he kissed her were so incredibly erotic, she wasn't sure how she was going to stick to the no sex rule. The sensations he brought out in her body were strong and insistent, and she felt an overwhelming need to have him consume her, to wrap her in his arms and surround her, bringing her into him.

After a short while, she gathered her wits enough to push him away.

"Okay, time out," she laughed, breathlessly.

"Don't worry," his voice was low and husky. "I'm in control."

"That's great Luke," she replied. "But I'm not so sure I am."

He gave the same kind of chuckle he had in the restaurant, seeming to relish her discomfort and the effort it was taking her to remain under control. If she didn't know better, she would think he enjoyed taking her to the edge of her will power.

"You worry too much," he said softly, moving her hair off her face and tucking it behind her ear. "I'm not going to take us anywhere we've both agreed we shouldn't be going."

"Did you just say, 'Trust me!'" Olivia asked, archly, with a chuckle and a raised eyebrow.

Without cracking a smile, he looked deep into her eyes and asked: "Don't you?" Returning his gaze, she smiled slightly and admitted that yes, she did.

"Good! Then come lie down on the rug with me and let me hold you," he said.

She felt like he was issuing a challenge to see if she truly trusted him, and so against her better judgment, they laid out on the rug in front of the fire.

He pulled her close, tucking her body neatly into his. She could feel his arousal against her leg, and again her body stirred. He tilted her chin and kissed her gently on her lips. After a moment or so, the kiss deepened. He placed his hand on her rear and pulled her in tighter against him. Oh Lord, she thought, what is he trying to do to me? He continued to kiss her, his tongue darting in and out, his hand slipping up under the back of her shirt and caressing her back. His fingertips slipped under the edge of her bra, near the back clasp, and he followed it around until his fingers were touching the bottom swell of her breasts.

Suddenly, he pushed her onto her back and towered over her, leaning all his weight on one arm. He brushed her hair away from her face again and kissed her gently, his tongue caressing her bottom lip, which he soon began to suck lightly. His free hand roamed down her body and unbuckled her pants.

"Oh no, uh-uh," she said as she tried to sit up, feeling like she was trapped in some kind of sensory overload.

"Sssshhhh," he said with a whisper. "Remember? Trust me."

"Oh Lord," she said. "Sure, trust you. Uh-huh, trust you."

He laughed as he completed unzipping her pants and pulling them down slightly. They were low rise pants to begin with, and it didn't take much for them to come half off. For a moment she felt self-conscious about her stomach and the two babies she had carried. What would he think when he saw her flawed body? Her ex-husband's disapproving face flashed before her eyes. These thoughts were soon pushed to the side as he continued to kiss her, alternating between her lips, her neck, and her ears. After a few minutes of teasing her with these light kisses, he sat up and moved between her legs. Pulling her pants down another inch or so, he pushed the crotch of her panties aside and began to kiss her there, using the same light kisses and sucking he had used on her face.

"Ohhhhhh," she gasped. "What? Don't! Ooohhhh!"

He continued as her back arched and her stomach clenched with the pleasure that came over her in waves. When her body had relaxed, and she lay panting on the floor, he returned to his position of lying beside her.

He whispered in her ear, "Don't move, just lie here. I'm going home now, and I want to know you haven't moved."

She nodded her head, her eyes closed. She wasn't sure if she just didn't want to talk or if she was incapable. But she stayed where she was, lying in front of the fireplace as he got up, put his shoes on, and walked out the front door. She wasn't sure how long she stayed there, but eventually, she heard her phone buzz. She roused herself enough to grab her cell off the coffee table.

"I was driving home, and I could smell you on my lips."

Arrrrrggghhhhh! she thought as she flopped back onto the rug. What on earth had she gotten herself into? She was supposed to be keeping a clear head. She definitely hadn't acted very rationally tonight! They couldn't keep going down this road, it wasn't helping at all. But how on earth was she going to put a stop to that, when her traitorous body obviously had other ideas?

Chapter Sixteen

She

She arrived at the bed and breakfast just before dinner time. Pulling up, she opened the trunk of her car and grabbed her bags. Her husband had continued to call and send texts every few minutes all the way here. Her nerves were frazzled, and she was ready to try and relax.

Knocking on the front door, she paused to admire the log house; its quaint welcome sign and knick-knacks lining the walkway. In the past, She and her friends had once decided that part of a proper road trip was making the place where you were staying a bit of adventure. No bland hotel room or strip motel for them when they headed out, it was always something different and unique.

"Hi!" the host greeted her enthusiastically. He pushed an errant strand of grey hair off his face, while self-consciously patting his stomach, which strained against the buttons of his plaid shirt.

"Hi!" she answered.

"Come on in," her new host instructed. "Let's get you all settled."

As he led the way to the back of the house, down a long hallway that ended with her room, she couldn't help but smile at the odds and ends hanging on the wall. Pictures from the host's vacations, souvenirs, and artifacts made way to photos of grandchildren and pets.

Looking back over his shoulder he tossed out "I'm presuming you're our guest and not the Avon lady?"

She laughed along with him, assuring him that yes, she was the guest he was expecting, not a traveling saleswoman. As he opened the door and motioned for her to enter, she felt her breath catch slightly in her throat. The room had a soaring ceiling made from the same logs as was the rest of the house, with a fireplace nestled in the corner. A huge four-poster bed reigned over the entire room, a multitude of lace and pillows piled high on its frame.

"It's absolutely perfect!" she exclaimed, entering the room and turning around in a full circle, as though trying to take it all in at once.

Her host chuckled appreciatively as though he never tired of the reaction his guests had to the room.

"The washroom is through there," he pointed to a door tucked into the corner of the room. "There are towels and everything else you should need. We would prefer that you try to come and go between six in the morning and midnight, just to keep the disruptions in the house to a minimum. Sometimes we have the grandbabies over and don't want them woken up in the middle of the night."

"Oh, you won't have to worry about that at all," she assured him. "I'm here to have some rest and relaxation, I won't be out partying."

"Alright then, here are your keys," he said, handing over a ring with two keys attached. "The round one is for your door, and the square one is the key to the house. It's often unlocked, but you have a key in case we leave for a while."

"That's perfect, thank you so much," she said, as he walked away.

Throwing her bag on the luggage rack, she walked over to the large bay window and took in the view. The window overlooked the back yard, with the mountains in the background. There was a beautiful flower garden with blooms in shades of red, pink and yellow. Large old trees bent over, dripping branches of leaves all over. She took a deep breath as if to inhale the smell of the flowers through the pane of glass. She had made a good choice when she picked this bed and breakfast.

She went into the washroom and admired the pretty bars of soap and the lacy guest towels hanging on the towel rod. She splashed some water on her face before tossing her keys in her purse. As beautiful as the room was, she was getting hungry, and wanted a feeling of being closer to the mountains than the view from her room provided.

She went for a walk down the main street, passing souvenir shops and ice cream vendors. The weather was perfect for a stroll as the day edged on toward night. A cool breeze blew down off the mountains, and she felt her spirit-lifting. There was nothing like being in the mountains to put life in perspective. The petty day-to-day issues faded when confronted with the timelessness of these rocky faces. To stand in the middle of this valley, great slabs of granite rising in all directions, was to feel small and insignificant. And in that insignificance was freedom. How many upset, unhappy women had escaped to stand before these mountains, looking for answers? In the grand scheme of things, her problems were just a drop in the vast expanse of time, and therefore what did they really matter? She found a tourist map at one of the vendors and found a bench to sit down on. Looking through the map to find a place that appealed to her for dinner, she realized that her phone was still buzzing off and on in her purse. She pulled it out.

"This isn't funny anymore, I just want to talk."

"Why are you such a bitch?"

"I hope you have fun by 'yourself.' "

She threw her phone back in her purse before she could read the rest of his messages. He was on a rampage, and there was nothing good that could come out of reading or responding; it would only upset her more. She stashed her map in her purse and began walking purposefully in the direction of a place that was named the best sushi restaurant in town. Her husband wasn't a big fan of sushi, so this was a great chance to indulge and not have to hear any griping.

Returning to her room that evening, stuffed full of sushi and sake, she poured a bath, lit the fire, and checked her phone for the first time in hours. She was surprised to see that her husband's last text had been sent right around the time she had last checked her phone. He must have decided to give up, she thought. She poured herself some of the wine she had brought with her and took it into the washroom with her. Sinking deep into the tub, she felt the warmth of the water soothe her tired muscles and nerves. As she soaked, she began to wonder what her husband was doing. Was he watching TV by himself, or did he decide to find some friends to go out drinking? She thought of him in their home, alone and upset. Maybe she had been too hard on him; going completely silent wasn't exactly fair. He was probably just concerned about her, and his constant texts and voice messages were just his frustration speaking. As she continued to rationalize his behavior, she sipped some more wine and decided to get out of the tub before she fell asleep in it.

She looked at her phone once more, and there were no further messages; not even a missed call. Guilt started to eat at her and she contemplated calling him, just to let him know she had arrived safely and where she was staying.

She punched in his phone number, and it began to ring at his end. It rang and rang before going to his voice mail. She hit the hang-up button without thinking. She sat there and wondered if he was playing some kind of game with her. If he was at home watching tv, he should have seen her calling; even if he had gone out with his friends and had the phone on vibrate, surely he would have felt she was calling? She sat there, musing about the situation, wondering what she should do. It bothered her that he seemed to have turned the tables, making her feel anxious when she hadn't been in the wrong. After a few minutes, she called him again. This time it went straight to voice mail. That meant he was either on the phone or he had turned it off. This time she was prepared, and she left a message.

"Hon, it's me. I just wanted to let you know I arrived okay. Please call me, and I will give you the name of where I'm staying. I love you. Bye."

As she finished, she threw the phone down on the bed and gave a grunt of discontent. This was supposed to be her time away, time to relax and rejuvenate. And what as she doing? She was fretting about him. Once more. She felt a sense of self-loathing for allowing herself to get caught up in this again. She should never have called in the first place. She poured herself another glass of wine and settle in the chair in front of the fireplace. Opening the paperback she had purchased at the gas station on the way up, she flipped to the beginning, determined to get her mind off her husband.

It was a struggle, but she managed to immerse herself in the murder mystery and about an hour later, she looked up at the clock. There was no way he hadn't looked at his phone by now. He was compulsive about it. So that meant he was intentionally ignoring her. Fine, two could play that game.

She helped herself to some more wine, turned off her phone, and crawled into bed with her book. She decided to take advantage of being here alone. There was no one to keep up late at night because she was reading, or become annoyed with her moving around or getting up to use the washroom. She read for another hour and then got up to use the washroom. Coming back to the bed, she plugged her phone into the charger. She wanted to go for a hike tomorrow, and she would need a fully charged phone. Hiking by yourself was one thing, hiking without a means of communicating if you had a problem was quite another.

~ ~ ~

In the morning, she put on her hiking shoes, sprayed herself down with mosquito repellent and put her phone in the pocket of her hiking pants. She stopped by the gas station on her way out to the trailhead, picked up a sandwich, some beef jerky, and trail mix before filling up her bottle of water. She drove down the highway to where the trail she wanted to hike began. Before she left her car, she checked her phone for reception and to see if there were any new messages for her.

Locking the car, she started up the trail, taking a deep breath and letting the mountain air, mixed with the scent underbrush in the trees soak into her very pores. She wished she fully understood why being outdoors could bring so much peace and rejuvenation; it would be great to figure out a way to bottle and sell it.

An hour and a half later found her sitting on a fallen log, halfway around the trail. She was eating the sandwich she picked up and sipping on more water. The sweat trickled down her back in a steady stream, and into her eyes. Finding her handkerchief in the front pocket of her hiking pants, she mopped the sweat from her forehead and tilted her head back to catch a bit of the breeze that was gently moving the treetops. Her body was tired. Tired in a good, worked-hard kind of way. She had walked down the trail at a brisk pace, barely easing up when she came to a steep section. The next half of the trail would be easier as it was more downhill. She had hiked this on previous trips, and it was one of her favorites.

A fly buzzed lazily around her head as she closed her eyes and felt her body respond to the rest. A few moments later, her head jerked up in surprise. She had nodded off and almost fallen off the log. Time to keep moving.

She did the second half in record time and was soaking in her tub with a glass of wine by early afternoon. There had been no further messages or calls on her phone, and she was beginning to get anxious.

She couldn't understand why, after trying so hard to get her to talk to him last night, that he was totally ignoring her now.

She reached for the phone and redialed his number.

"Hi," he stated.

"Oh, I'm glad you answered," she said with some surprise that he picked up. There was silence at the other end of the phone.

"I'm sorry about not responding to your texts and calls yesterday," she said. "I just felt it was best if we both calmed down a little and I cleared my mind some."

"Okay," he said in a non-committal voice.

"How was your evening?" she asked.

"It was okay," he answered. "It would have been better if I had been with you, but if you felt it was better..."

"What do you mean? Better with me? You couldn't come," she said.

"Well, I couldn't, but I made arrangements," he said. "But you didn't answer so...."

"Well then, what are you waiting for, it's not too late!" she said excitedly.

"Yes, it is. It isn't worth driving out there to turn around and drive right back."

"But you wouldn't be if you leave now. We could have a nice dinner together, go for a walk, have a nice evening, and even hang out tomorrow." She responded.

"No, it's too late!" he said emphatically.

She felt as though she was a child who had been offered candy and then had it abruptly taken away from her. On top of that, she felt like somehow it was her fault. She laid in the fast-cooling water, and the relaxation of the day seemed a distant memory.

"I'll talk to you later, I have some things I need to do," he informed her. "I'll see you when you get back."

The click in her ear seemed to echo in the tiled washroom. Her mind whirled, and her body wrestled with feelings of anxiety, disappointment, and confusion. He had been in such a rush to contact her last night. He had made it sound like he was angry with her, not that he had found a way to join her. He could have sent her a text saying he wanted to join her instead of sending angry, accusing messages. Why was their relationship so difficult?

She finished her soak and curled up under the covers of her bed, her cell phone laying close by with the volume turned on. She didn't want to miss a call if he changed his mind. She snuggled down into the fluffy, down-filled duvet, convinced sleep would come quickly after her day of fresh air and exercise. An hour later, she lay staring at the ceiling, her body crying out for sleep, but her thoughts whirling in a thousand different directions. She couldn't get the conversation with her husband out of her head. She knew she should be doing something about how unhappy she felt, but no matter what she considered, she felt stuck. She had been single before, and she didn't want to go back there, not at her age. Leaving him would also mean a substantial financial hit for her, and while not insurmountable, she hated that idea as well. But if she stayed and continued as things were, she would spend the rest of her life unhappy. She also had to admit to herself that part of it was her pride. If she left him now the people who had urged her not to marry him would be proven right. She knew it shouldn't factor into things, but she couldn't help reflecting on the comments her friends had made when they were dating, and how ardently she had defended him and their relationship.

Turning over for the umpteenth time, she punched her pillow and groaned with frustration. She could make all the excuses in the world, but the fact of the matter was she still loved him. Or rather, she loved the man he had been. But she had to admit to herself that the man he had been may never have existed. The longer they were married, the more she realized he had been acting a part when they first met. He was so attentive, so loving, and he'd made her feel like the most beautiful woman in the world. That feeling was addictive, and now she craved its return; by leaving her marriage, she faced the real possibility of never experiencing it again.

Chapter Seventeen

Olivia

Luke came by the house on Sunday for dinner with Olivia and the boys, as well as with a couple of her friends. This was the first time he would meet the boys, and Olivia was a bit nervous. She had purposefully kept Luke away from them, just as she had done with anyone she had dated. She didn't want a string of men coming through their lives like a revolving door, so it was a big step for her to arrange this dinner. For the first time, she admitted to herself how much she believed there was a future for them.

Her anxiety had brought up deep-seated emotions that she had assumed she had dealt with years ago. She was second-guessing herself and her relationship. Surely there was something wrong with him that everyone else would be able to see - after all, he couldn't be as great as she thought. She had checked and double-checked her appearance in her bedroom mirror. Turning to the side, she touched her stomach and tried to suck it in so it would lay flat. Why was he attracted to her? She wasn't one of those lean, athletic women who could eat whatever they want and still keep their figure. Next, she fiddled with her bra strap and tried to find a way to adjust it so her breasts looked perkier.

Finally, she gave up with a sigh of resignation and went back to the kitchen to start the meal.

~ ~ ~

"Need help with anything?" he asked, coming up behind her in the kitchen and placing his hands on her hips.

"Nope, I think I have everything pretty much under control," she answered with a smile, as the doorbell chimed.

"How about I get that?" he suggested as he moved towards the front door.

There was a flurry of activity as her best friends and her boys all entered the house at the same time.

"Look who we found coming home," Terri announced as she entered the kitchen. Terri was a petite blond whose small size and pixie-like features often had bartenders asking the middle-aged mom for ID.

"Hi Mom," Jonathon said as he slung his backpack over his shoulders and headed to his bedroom.

"Hey Mom," Adam mumbled as he walked past her.

Terri laughed at their apparent lack of excitement at being back home.

"Don't you love the overwhelming excitement of teenage boys?" April added with a sardonic smile. The contract between Terri and April was striking. While Terri was childlike in size, April physically dominated any room she entered. Where Terri was fair and blond,

April had olive-toned skin and a mass of black curls that she claimed were the bane of her existence.

"Have introductions been made?" Olivia asked, looking from her girlfriends to Luke, and back.

"Yes, it's all taken care of," Luke said with a smile.

"Well, why don't we sit in the living room while dinner finishes cooking," Olivia suggested, moving towards the couch. Luke sat next to her, his strong leg pressing up against hers.

"So, Luke," April said as soon as she was settled in the chair opposite them. "Tell us all about yourself."

Olivia laughed nervously as April cut-to-the-chase. Olivia could always count on her to point out the elephant in the room and tackle it. Of course, Luke didn't know that, and he looked taken aback at her forthrightness.

"Well, um," he began. "I'm an electrician, I like running and hiking..." his voice trailed off, unsure how to proceed.

"Oh April, give the guy a break!" Terri interjected, saving the moment from becoming too uncomfortable. "The man just met us, don't put him on the spot so soon!"

"You're right Terri," April responded. "I'm sorry Luke, I'll wait until I know you better before putting you on the spot."

The resulting laughter broke through the awkwardness.

"Oh gosh, I'm not a very good host!" Olivia exclaimed. "Does anyone want something to drink?"

"Wine me!" Terri declared.

"Make that two," April chorused as she turned toward Luke. "What about you, Luke?"

"No, I don't drink," Luke answered.

"Oh really?" April said, her interest piqued. "Is that by choice or necessity?"

"What do you mean?" Luke asked gruffly. "I don't have a problem with booze or anything."

"I was just curious," April said, as she held her hands up, palms out towards him in a defensive posture. "I didn't mean anything by it."

The room went quiet as Olivia left to get the wine, the women looking around uncomfortably, unsure what to say. Luke leaned forward, resting his elbows on his knees and stared at his hands.

After a few moments, Olivia came back in carrying the wine. She sat the bottle down on the coffee table and passed around the glasses. She then returned to the kitchen to get Luke a can of pop. Luke leaned forward and poured wine in the glasses and gave them to Terri and April.

"So, Luke," Terri said. "Are you into sports at all?"

"No," he answered.

"Ah," she said, a bit unsure how to continue.

"Luke prefers to be out doing things rather than sitting and watching others," Olivia said in an attempt to elaborate.

"That makes sense," Terri said. "Especially if you're into running and hiking, those are a fair bit healthier than being a couch potato!"

Just then her boys came into the room.

"When is dinner ready?" they asked.

"In about ten minutes," Olivia responded. "You can go and get washed up now."

They left the room, and the adults could hear them thumping around as they raced to be the first one to the washroom. Sipping their wine, they continued to make small talk, and there was a palpable sense of relief when they heard the timer go off in the kitchen. They all stood up and began moving toward the kitchen.

"Sit anywhere you want," Olivia said, as she opened the oven door and pulled out a chicken casserole. "Luke, would you mind grabbing the salad from the fridge?"

"Absolutely," he answered.

The boys sat down at the dining room table along with her two friends. They were chatting about the boy's classes and their annoyance with their teachers when Olivia and Luke brought in dinner.

"Oh, that smells wonderful!" April exclaimed.

"It sure does," said Terri. "What is it?"

"It's a chicken tetrazzini casserole," Olivia said. "It's one of the boy's favorites."

They were all seated and passing around the food, the boys dishing out heaping portions for themselves and continuing to talk about school.

"Who wants to say grace?" Olivia asked the boys.

"It's Jonathon's turn," Adam said.

"Jonathon?"

"'K, Bless this food and bless the hands that made it. Amen." Jonathon rushed through the grace faster than the adults had a chance to bow their heads.

"Gee, thanks Jonathon," Olivia said with a smile and a shake of her head.

They all dug into their dinner, the women continuing to engage the teenagers and Olivia watching on contentedly. After a few moments, she realized that Luke wasn't participating in the conversation.

"What about you Luke?" she asked, in an attempt to draw him in and make him feel at home. "Did you like school when you were a kid?"

"Ha! Not exactly," he said between bites. "I was a bit of a hell-raiser."

"Oh really?" Olivia said, with a smile. "Interesting!"

The rest of the meal passed pleasantly, as the adults regaled the boys with tales of their own high school shenanigans.

~ ~ ~

Once dinner was over, everyone took their dishes into the kitchen and set them on the counter. Olivia began to load the dishwasher with the dirty plates and glasses as Luke came up behind her.

"Don't waste water and energy on using the dishwasher for those few dishes," he suggested. "Here, you go and visit with your friends, and I'll wash them up."

"You don't have to do that Luke," Olivia protested. "Why don't you leave them for now and come join us?"

"No, they're your friends, and you put together a great meal for us all," he insisted. "It's time for you to relax."

Standing on her tiptoes, she reached up and kissed him before heading for the living room.

"Did we scare him off?" April asked when she saw Olivia come into the living room alone.

"I don't think so," she answered with a smile.

"I don't know," Terri lowered her voice a little. "He sure didn't like being asked about his drinking."

"Oh, give the guy a break," Olivia said. "You two can be a bit intimidating at times, you know."

"Who? Us?" April laughed, batting her eyelashes.

Terri poured more wine into their glasses, as they settled into their seats.

"I'm so full!" April groaned. "That was so good, I had a hard time knowing when to stop."

"Pasta will do that to you," Olivia agreed, as she leaned back in her seat with a deep sigh.

"The boys sure didn't waste any time leaving," Terri said. "I'm not sure how comfortable they are around Luke."

"Not surprising," Olivia said. "I'm sure the idea of their mother dating is a bit hard for them."

"You mean a bit creepy, don't you?" April said with a laugh. The women giggled at the accuracy of April's comment.

"I'm sure they'll adjust," Olivia said. "They just need to get used to the idea and get to know Luke."

"So, you two are getting pretty serious, huh?" April asked. "Meeting the kids, meeting the girlfriends..."

"I think maybe we are," Olivia said while showing her friends her crossed fingers. "But only time will tell."

"Well, keep taking it easy," Terri commented. "No need to rush into anything."

"Oh, don't worry, I am," Olivia said. "I've learned from my mistakes."

Just then Adam came into the room, asking for permission to go to his friend's home to do homework.

"Homework, huh?" Olivia asked, with a raised eyebrow. "Why do you still have homework on a Sunday night?"

"I didn't get it all done on Friday, and Alex has better notes," Adam explained in his best putting-up-with-grownups voice.

"Okay, but make sure you're home in decent time," she said. "It's a school night, and I don't want you to start the week tired."

"'K, thanks," In his haste to leave, Adam nearly bumped into Luke as he came out of the kitchen.

"Oh! Sorry," Adam mumbled.

"S'okay," Luke mumbled as he stood aside to let Adam by.

"Well, I better get going," Terri announced as she finished off the last of the wine in her glass. "I've got some projects I need to get finished tonight too."

"Yeah, it's that time," April agreed as she stood up and stretched. "Thanks so much for a great meal, Olivia."

Hugging Olivia, April turned to Luke and smiled, "It was great to meet you, Luke."

"Yeah, you too," he said.

They all moved to the front entranceway, and Luke draped his arm around Olivia's shoulder as they stood saying their goodbyes.

Later that evening as Olivia stood in the same spot saying goodbye to Luke, she had a vague sense of unease about how things had gone.

"What's on your mind?" Luke asked, sensing her mood.

"Nothing, why?" she hedged.

"Are you worried your friends don't like me?" he asked.

"Why on earth would I be worried about that?" she asked incredulously. "Of course, they like you."

"I'm not so sure," he disagreed.

"Why?" she asked

"I don't know, I can just tell," he responded. "I don't think they think I'm good enough for you."

"Why would they think that?" Olivia asked.

"Just a sense I get," Luke said. "Will it matter to you if they don't?"

"They like you, don't be silly," she answered.

"Would it matter to you if they didn't?" he pressed.

"Well," Olivia considered carefully, "It wouldn't be a deal-breaker. After all, I can think for myself, but it would give me pause."

"Okay," he said, drawing her close to him and nuzzling her neck. "I just care about what you think."

"I like you," she said with a smile.

"I think you do," he murmured, kissing her lips gently. His kiss quickly began to deepen as his tongue entered her mouth. His fingers slipped into the belt loops on her jeans, and he pulled her closer. Moving his left hand downward, he cupped her buttocks and slipped his other hand under the back of her top.

"Your skin is so incredibly soft," he whispered. "How do you keep it so soft?"

"I don't know," she said, panting slightly as he left a trail of kisses down her neck.

"And it gets softer the lower I go," he chuckled seductively as he tucked his hand in the band of her jeans. Following the band along her waist, he found the crevice between her ass cheeks and slipped one of his fingers down lower. Groaning, he used his upper body to pin her more tightly to the hallway wall.

"God, you are so sexy!" he breathed. "You have the most amazing ass!"

Laughing a bit nervously, Olivia placed her hands on his chest, trying to put even some semblance of distance between them. No matter how many times she told herself she wasn't going to let things escalate, they always ended up this way - panting and clawing at each other like two kids on prom night.

"I think maybe we should call it a night," she suggested.

"You want me to go?" he asked, as he pulled at her bottom lip with his teeth. "Are you sure?"

"Stop it!" she giggled as she playfully hit him on the chest. "Be good!"

"You're good enough for the two of us," he teased. "But I'll do as I'm told and head home."

He pulled away from her abruptly and was walking down the front stairs before she could catch her breath again. Any concerns about the evening were long gone, and she stood for several minutes, leaning against the wall and reveling in the glow of being the object of desire of a man she found almost irresistible.

Chapter Eighteen

She

She knew she had been working too hard since her return from her mini-getaway, but she couldn't seem to help herself. She stayed later and later at the office and submerged herself in her work. She realized she was avoiding her unhappiness by simply avoiding going home until later into the evening. Working was a form of escape for her; she could tuck away her growing sadness back in the corner of her mind somewhere and do what she did best. Work was something she had always been good at, and it never judged her or let her down.

She would work until 7 or 8 at night, stop by the gym for a quick work out, and then grab something easy to prepare for supper on her way home. After a quick bite, she would be ready for bed. There was no time left to try and talk to her husband, or to notice whether he was coming or going. It was just easier on her emotions, and right now she simply needed a break from the ongoing stream of dialogue in her head that never seemed to resolve or change anything.

These were the thoughts whirling around in her head as she pulled up onto her driveway and noticed that his car was parked there.

She turned off the ignition and sat looking straight ahead for a few minutes. She knew she couldn't keep avoiding him and that at some point she would have to deal with the situation. Sighing deeply, she took her purse and briefcase off the passenger seat, locked her car, and walked up the steps.

He was sitting at the kitchen table when she opened the door. He closed the newspaper he was reading and set it aside.

"Hi," she greeted him as she walked in, setting her purse and briefcase down at the front door.

"Hi," he responded. "Nice to see you."

"Yeah, things have been pretty busy at work these days," she answered.

"What's up there?" he asked.

"What do you mean?" she looked at him quizzically.

"What's up that's making things so busy all of a sudden," he clarified.

"Oh, you know, this and that, always something," she said vaguely.

"Can we cut the bullshit?" he asked.

"What do you mean?" she asked, trying a delaying tactic, so she had time to get her thoughts together.

"You know exactly what I mean," he insisted. "You've been working late, coming home late, and basically avoiding me since you returned from the mountains."

She took a deep breath and steeled herself for a conversation she knew was overdue.

"You're right," she admitted, sitting down in the chair across from him. "I've been avoiding coming home as much as possible."

"Why?"

"Because whenever I'm home, all I can do is focus on our relationship and how unhappy we both seem to be," she blurted out.

"I see," he stated, looking down at his hands, his jaw set firmly in place.

"I just don't know what to do anymore," she explained. "We rarely talk, and when we do, we argue or fight. We live in two separate worlds where we are each coming and going, we have nothing in common and do nothing together, it's like we live two completely separate lives."

"You've given this a lot of thought," he said, still staring at his hands.

"How can I not? Don't you?" she asked. "I'm miserable, and I don't think you're happy either. You are cold and aloof most of the time, or you are angry and grumpy. What am I supposed to think?"

"Huh," he grunted.

"Huh? What do you mean huh?" she asked, in an exasperated voice. "Please speak to me for a change!"

"What do you want me to say? You've basically told me I'm a horrible husband and you would rather work than be around me," he barked. "How am I supposed to respond to that?"

"I didn't say you were a horrible husband," she argued. "Please don't put words in my mouth."

"Then what else do you call the person you described?" he demanded.

"Look, it is obvious we're both unhappy," she said in a voice she hoped was calming and reassuring. "This isn't about blame."

"It sounds like it to me," he responded.

"It's about us as a couple," she reassured him. "Not about who is right or wrong."

"So, what do you propose we do about us 'as a couple,'" he asked.

"I honestly don't know," she answered. "I want us to be happy. I want things to be like they were before. Maybe we could try counseling?"

"Counselling," he repeated.

"Yes."

"Okay," he finally looked up from staring at his hands. "Okay, let's try counseling. You aren't the only one who wants things to be like they were before."

"Good,"

"But you need to start coming home on time," he demanded. "I don't like not knowing where you are or when you'll be home."

"Fair enough, I'll do that," she stated a small smile on her face. She considered pointing out that this was exactly what he had been doing for a very long time. She remained quiet, however, as it seemed like a rather petty point to make when they had just taken a step forward.

They sat in silence for a while before she worked up the nerve to ask him what had been on her mind for the past few weeks.

"Hon, can you tell me something?" she asked.

"What?"

"Why are you so unhappy all the time?"

He sat for a few moments, in silence. After a while, he took a deep breath and responded "I don't really know, I just know things aren't the same as when we got married. I feel a bit cheated."

She felt a bit like the wind had been knocked out of her. He was saying things that completely reflected how she had been feeling but had been unable to express to him. She had never considered that he, too, must think that things had changed so drastically for the worse. What on earth had happened to them?

"How do you feel cheated?" she asked.

"When we were dating you were so into me," he started. "Now, I can tell it is ho-hum. When we were dating it was exciting and passionate, and now it's, well, blah."

It stung a bit to hear him put into words such a negative description of their marriage, but she honestly couldn't disagree with his assessment. Their courtship had been whirlwind, exciting and so passionate. When they married, things seemed to turn to dust. She had expected the emotions to last forever.

"Okay, fair enough," she acknowledged. "How do you suggest we change that?"

"I don't know," he shrugged. "Maybe when you start coming home on time again, we can spend more time together as a couple. Maybe we could spice up our sex life a bit too."

"Okay," she said, biting her tongue to keep from reminding him that she had tried doing just that and that he had rebuffed her on several occasions. This wasn't the time to worry about the past, but to concentrate on the future. He's ready to work on it now, that's all that matters.

"Well, let's go on up to bed, it's getting late," she reached her hand out to him.

"Are you sure you want me to go up with you?" he asked.

"Of course, don't be silly," she smiled.

That night, their lovemaking, while not overly exciting, was gentle and tender. She went to sleep with a glimmer of hope that maybe, just maybe, they had turned a corner of sorts and their marriage wasn't over.

Chapter Nineteen

Olivia

Driving down the road, she wasn't sure why she had agreed to meet Luke tonight. Her day had been hectic, first with work, and then getting the boys ready to spend a couple of weeks with their father. Summertime was always a mixed bag for Olivia. She enjoyed her alone time, and how her schedule opened up, and she had so much time to do just what she wanted. But it also threw her routine off, and she felt slightly off-kilter when her day- to- day schedule had so little structure.

Luke had called her just after she'd finished wrestling with camping gear, and cajoling her boys into showers and clean clothes. No easy task when all they wanted to do was leave in their dirty jeans, earbuds firmly inserted in their ears, eyes glued to their screens.

"How about a movie?" he opened up the conversation.

"Oh, that would be lovely, but I'm wiped, and I just want to sit back and enjoy the silence once the boys leave," she answered as she sank into her couch. "It was a hellish day at work, and I swear getting these boys to do anything is like pulling teeth."

"Sounds like you could use some time away then," he stated.

"No, really I… Adam! Get out of that fridge, your dad is taking you both to supper first!" she shouted. "Sorry 'bout that. No, really, I'm beat."

"Too beat to sit in a movie theatre and snack on popcorn?" he asked, feigning incredulity.

"No, it's more the getting ready and getting there that's the energy sapper," she responded with a laugh. "I want to wait until my ex comes to get the boys so I can get times straightened out and by the time that happens, it will be late."

"Well, I wouldn't want to get in the way of that," Luke said. "You're a good mother, and you know best."

"Thank you," she responded with a smile.

"But I'll miss you," he purred, his voice dropping. "I'll miss the soft feel of your skin when I hold your hand, the firmness of your thigh when I move my hand there."

"Okay, okay enough of that!" she laughed. "But nice try!"

She hung up the phone with a smile on her face and shook her head. The boys were gathered at the front entryway, each of them on their phones, earbuds in their ears, and oblivious to their surroundings.

"Do you visit at all with your dad when you see him?" she asked. They continued with their phones.

"Helloooo?" she asked, waving her hands in front of them to grab their attention.

"What?" they asked irritably, almost in unison.

"Do you put your phones down long enough to visit with your dad when you're with him?" she asked again.

"Yeah, sure," Jonathon answered. "He makes us put them down for meals."

"Oh, good," Olivia with a raised eyebrow. "Nice to know you get lots of quality time."

"Yeah," Jonathon agreed as he put the earbuds back in his ears, oblivious to the sarcasm in his mother's voice.

Just then the doorbell rang. Olivia opened the door and ushered Ed, her ex, in. Her former husband stood uncomfortably in the entryway of her home, hands thrust deep into his coat pockets. She found it odd to see him looking so out of sorts. He was the type of man who physically towered over most people, with a commanding presence. His dark brown hair was cut shorter than usual, and he scratched at his neck absently as he stood waiting for their boys.

The divorce had changed their relationship from two people who had known each other since they were teens to complete strangers. Whenever she was around him, she felt herself shrink. She felt insignificant and unattractive whenever he looked her way, his eyes seeming to barely register her existence. She had always felt that she wasn't enough for him, but she could never quite figure out what she wasn't enough of. He had solidified those feelings and left her with insecurities that had taken years to deal with when he had told her that one of the reasons why he felt their marriage had broken down was because of her struggle with her weight.

Snapping out of this painful reverie, she explained what she had packed for the boys, and what they still might need for camp.

"When are you planning to bring them back?" Olivia asked.

"Well, the camp is over on the 14th, and I have to pick them up by four o'clock," Ed responded.

"Okay, but I was wondering if you were planning on spending a couple of days with them. They are going to the camp tomorrow, so you won't have much time. You're welcome to keep them longer if you want." she elaborated. It was an ongoing concern for her that her ex did not spend much actual time with his boys. They were at the age where they needed their father, but Ed seemed to feel it was time to start letting them go.

"No, I can't, I have to work," he stated in a voice that brooked no argument.

"Okay, boys! Have a fun time at camp, and don't bring home head lice or anything," Olivia instructed as she gave them each a swift hug.

"Ewwww!" They cried out.

"Just sayin!" Olivia laughed.

With a flurry of activity, the boys banged their bags around and shuffled into their shoes, and everyone left. It was quiet so suddenly that Olivia could almost feel it.

She looked at her house, with sweatshirts and dirty socks laying over chairs and scrunched in corners, and for the first time wondered if she had enough to do while they were gone. She always felt a bit lonely after seeing her ex. He always made her feel, as he had in their marriage like she just didn't matter. Combined with the suddenly empty house, she felt a wave of sadness flow over her.

Just then she heard the 'ping' of an incoming text message. It was as though she was an addict and the ping was a promise of a fix as she opened up the message.

"I'm leaving in fifteen minutes in case you change your mind!" Luke informed her.

She sent him back a non-committal "Thanks" message. She was torn between being tired and needing time to just be, and wanting her time with him to make these feelings go away. If she stayed, she would be able to rest and relax, but she would be by herself, feeling the awful sting of rejection she always felt while around Ed.

She went to the bathroom to freshen up and was in her room slipping into a fresh pair of jeans before she even admitted to herself that she had made up her mind.

She picked up her phone and sent him a quick message asking him where she should meet him.

"Don't worry, I'll swing by and get you," he responded.

"It's okay, I'm already leaving. I have some things to pick up first," she shot back. She was surprised that she had just told him what amounted to a lie, but for some reason, it was necessary to her that she remain somewhat in control of her evening. If she tried to explain that to him, he would just try and talk her out of it, and she wasn't up to that right now.

Arriving at the theatre, she spotted him right away, his broad shoulders, square jaw and the way he stood - as though he was completely comfortable in his own skin - seemed to set him apart from the crowd.

"Hi there," she called as she walked up to him.

He slipped his arm around her waist and pulled her close.

"I thought I wasn't going to get to see you tonight," he observed. "I'm so glad you saw the light."

Her mood began to lift as she felt his arm around her, holding her close as though to make sure anyone who saw knew for sure that she was with him. She couldn't help a fleeting thought that her ex-husband never made her feel that he was proud to be with her.

"I've got our tickets," he said. "Do you want some popcorn?"

"No, I'm fine, thanks," she responded. "Just a diet pop will be great."

Luke made his way to the very back of the theatre, below the projection room lights. They settled in just as the trailers started. For the first time, Olivia wondered what movie they were watching.

About a half an hour in, he set aside his popcorn and placed his hand on her leg. They spent a lot of time in the movies, and this had become their go-to position. He began rubbing her leg gently, up and down from her kneecap to her thigh.

"Aren't you glad you decided to come?" he whispered in her ear.

"Mmmmm," she responded with a smile, keeping her eyes looking straight ahead.

His hand continued to rub her leg, each time going slightly higher. Up and up it went with each stroke of her leg. She was beginning to wonder when he would stop and whether she wanted him to or not. Finally, his hand reached her crotch and lingered there. Instead of an up and down motion down the length of her leg, he began an up and down motion with his hand lightly touching her crotch.

She glanced around furtively to check if anyone could see them. There was no one behind them or on either side of them. The people in front were too busy laughing at the comedy to pay them any mind. She slumped a bit further down in her chair, which caused him to chuckle knowingly under his breath.

What the heck was wrong with her? They were acting like horny teenagers, unable to control themselves. But even knowing that, she let him continue rubbing. Every so often he would let his hand drift back to her knee, as though he knew it made her wonder if that was it or if he was going to make his way back up.

The charged sensations running through her body left her thrilled and a bit breathless. His touch was not heavy or rough, but fleeting and gentle. The small finger on his left hand barely touching her but rubbing up and down gently. It was just enough that she was utterly aroused but nowhere near close to having an orgasm.

Well, she thought to herself, this was sure better than sitting at home and feeling like a failure. But how on earth was this going to help them remain clear-headed?

After a while, she was not sure how long, she placed her hand over his when it reached her knee, effectively stopping him. She glanced sideways at him and mouthed, "Behave yourself!" She smiled slightly. He leaned forward and whispered, "All you had to do was ask," sitting back in his chair, he had a knowing smile on his face; he knew she hadn't wanted him to stop.

Afterward, they drove their cars to her house for a drink. Settling in on the floor, she passed him his can of pop while she set her glass of wine down next to her.

"You chose a good movie," she said. "It was very funny and light; just what I needed."

"I'm glad," he said.

They sat in companionable silence, with Olivia leaning up against Luke contentedly. After a while, she noticed he had been staring off into space with a distracted look on his face.

"Hey, penny for your thoughts?" she asked.

He continued to stare out into space, before giving her a small smile.

"Nothing really, just missing my Mom and thinking about the past," he said.

"Tell me about it," she urged.

"Not much to tell really, you already know my Dad died when I was little," he stated, taking a quick swig from his can. "My Mom raised us along with my Granny and Uncles and Aunts."

"That's a whole lot of years all rolled up into a sentence or two," she pointed out. "Tell me more."

"What else is there to tell you?" he asked. "They did their best, and I turned out okay, I guess."

"Hmm," she non-committally, thinking that if she kept quiet, he might open up more. The silence hung in the air for a few minutes, with Luke staring off at nothing, his mind obviously caught up in another time and place. The sounds from the music she had chosen on the stereo played softly as she waited.

"You don't want to hear about it," he finally stated.

"How do you know I don't want to hear about it?" she persisted. "I want to know all about you."

"You don't need to know everything about my past, it's the now that's important," he insisted.

"But the past influences the now, it made you what you are now," she stated quietly. She held his hand and rubbed his fingers lightly, trying to encourage him to open up to her. After a couple of minutes, she realized that he had bowed his head and his shoulders were quietly shaking. She was taken aback at the abruptness and depth of emotion which had taken over him but pleased that he was letting her in.

"Why did he do that?" he gasped. "Why? Why did he do that?"

"Why did he do what?" she asked. "Who are you talking about?"

He took a couple of deep breaths and tried to pull himself together. "It doesn't matter, I'm screwed up, that's all, just a screwed-up mess."

"Don't be silly, you aren't screwed up," she argued, trying to reassure him.

"It's just, I was molested when I was a kid," he blurted out. "It was a family friend. He was a monster, and he took advantage of me."

She continued to hold him, running her hands over his head and down his back, making murmuring sounds of encouragement and comfort.

"It's okay, it's okay," she insisted. "You're not screwed up, he was."

"I wish that were true," he sighed deeply. "I'm damaged because of it."

Olivia didn't know what to say. This sudden revelation had taken her aback. It was one thing to hear that something this awful had happened to someone she knew, but the emotions he was expressing as he explained it to her made it feel like it had happened to him yesterday.

After a few moments, he raised his head and gave her a sheepish look.

"I'm sorry, I don't know where that came from," he murmured. "I don't usually talk about it, but you're so easy to talk to."

"You can talk to me about anything, anytime you want," she reassured him. Looking at him, she caught a glimpse of the hurt little boy he would have been so many years ago. Her heart swelled with compassion, and she realized she was falling deeply in love with this man.

Chapter Twenty
She

She was fighting tears as she left the therapist's office. She knew the first visit had been rocky, with her husband sitting quietly most of the time, but she had hoped the second one would be better. In the end, she spent the entire appointment crying into a tissue as she poured out her hurt and disappointment to the therapist. Her husband had never even bothered to show up. The therapist reassured her that it wasn't unusual for men to get scared when it came down to dealing with issues in their marriages, but she couldn't help but feel deserted.

After their talk several weeks ago, she'd had a renewed sense of hope that their marriage may be salvageable. It had taken a couple of weeks to find a time that worked for him to have their first session. While they waited to see the therapist, she'd made an effort to be home on time, to prepare him nice meals and adopt a light and pleasant attitude. After all, she couldn't expect him to do everything - making a marriage work takes two. Unfortunately, he still treated her in a dismissive way, not seeming to care overly about her feelings or making her feel appreciated.

Now, he had just not shown up. How much more of this could she take? She drove back to work with a throbbing headache and a dull ache in the pit of her stomach. She was walking down the hallway toward her office when Wanda appeared.

"Hi, I was wondering if..." her colleague's voice trailed off. "Are you okay? Did something happen to your dad again?"

"No, no, he's fine. I'm fine," she said, hurrying past Wanda and into her office. Setting her purse down on her desk, she hung her coat up before turning around to face Wanda again.

"I'm sorry, but you don't look fine," Wanda insisted, her hands on her hips.

"I know, it's just a bad day," she responded. "Really, I'll be fine, I just need to clear my head a bit and get some work done."

"Work can wait!" Wanda declared. "You have been moping around here all week, and now you come in here looking like you lost your best friend."

"I'm sorry, okay?" she retorted defensively. "I had a bad appointment, and now I just want to work."

Wanda's body relaxed as she realized she had been too harsh. It was obviously not a topic for discussion right now.

"Well, you take your time," Wanda relented. "Make some coffee, close your door and take a moment."

"I know, I will," she said. "I promise."

She took a deep breath and exhaled noisily once Wanda had left her office. For heaven's sake, her marital problems were now showing up at work. The one place that was supposed to be her refuge. She needed to get it together, and fast. If only she could talk to someone about her problems. She didn't want to involve her colleagues in her personal life, and she didn't have anyone else except maybe her sister. What had happened to all her girlfriends? They used to be so close, sharing all the ups and downs of being single. She had slowly drifted away from them when she had started dating her husband, and at the time she had thought that it was just natural. As she sat thinking about it, she realized that maybe it wasn't a simple case of growing apart. Her girlfriends were never overly fond of her husband, right from the beginning. They tried to hide it, but she could tell. And so, she recalled, could he.

They'd spent so much time together in the beginning that she had just found it easier to beg off a girl's night out or an invitation to an event, rather than justify 'girl time' to him. At the time it had only made sense; she had spent years forging relationships with her girlfriends, and now it was time to put her focus on her relationship. But she wondered now why it was that she hadn't tried harder to blend the two parts of her life better.

Calling up those girlfriends now, after so much time, and expecting to be able to talk to them with the same kind of closeness and candor they had shared in the past just didn't seem possible or fair. She would appear to be running back because she needed something from them.

"Oh, Lord!" she cried out, laying her head on her arms, stretched out on the desktop. She felt so alone and trapped. When she and her husband had married, she'd thought it meant she would never have to be alone again. How ironic that she now felt more alone than she had ever felt in her life!

She lay stretched out on her desk for a few minutes more before she sat up and took a deep breath. Enough with feeling sorry for herself! She had work to do, and she could figure the rest of this out later - sitting and moping in her own misery wasn't going to solve anything.

~ ~ ~

Hours later, the tantalizing aroma of frying seafood met her nose as soon as she opened her front door. She couldn't help but feel her heart leap, as he had always cooked when he was happy, and whenever he was in a good mood, he was always much more open toward her and willing to talk.

"That smells amazing!" she exclaimed as she walked into the kitchen. "What are you cooking?"

"Some fried calamari, mushrooms, and onions topped with a salad," he answered. "Go wash up, and we'll eat."

When she came back into the kitchen, he had pulled down plates and cups from the cupboard and was setting out a bottle of wine. She noticed he had a tumbler of clear liquid sitting on the counter, a half-melted ice cube floating in the middle of it. As she picked up the plates to set on the table, he reached into the freezer and pulled out a bottle of vodka, which he poured into his glass, topping it off.

Her earlier thoughts about how things were when they had first started dating came back to her. She reflected on what a contrast the amount he drank now as compared to when they met. This was just another thing that had changed drastically. For the first time, she let herself acknowledge that the bottle in the freezer was nowhere near the first one that she had found there. The truth was, the bottles in the freezer were just another thing she tried not to think about too much.

"You're looking awfully deep in thought," he commented, taking the plates from her and setting them on the table.

"I was just wondering what happened to you this morning," she responded. She hadn't intended on jumping right into things, but the words were out before she had a chance to decide whether it was wise or not.

"When this morning?" he asked, rearranging the cutlery around their plates.

"The counselor?" she asked. "We had an appointment."

"No, we didn't," he stated with confidence.

"Yes, we did," she disagreed with a tinge of impatience in her voice.

"Don't be silly! We didn't book the second one because we weren't sure if we liked her," he argued.

"What? We booked the second appointment right there in the office after the first one!" she stared at him incredulously.

"Yes, but I assumed you canceled it after I told you I didn't feel she was right for us," he responded patiently.

She couldn't believe what she was hearing. After their first appointment, she had asked him how he felt it went and he'd said that he wasn't sure he'd liked her. She had explained that it might take a bit of time to develop some trust, and that wasn't unusual. That had been the end of the conversation. Why would he have assumed she had canceled it based on that?

"No, I didn't cancel it," she answered through gritted teeth.

"Well, sorry then, but I can't be expected to show up to something I knew nothing about," he stated emphatically.

"But you did know about it!" she felt as though she had entered some alternate universe where she thought she was speaking English, but he was hearing a different language.

"Look, let's not fight," he placated her, taking her by the elbow and leading her to her chair. "Have a seat, let's have a nice dinner and enjoy each other's company."

She sat down, caught between confusion, anger, and a desire to let it all go and just enjoy herself for a change. She chose the path of least resistance and reached out to pour herself some wine.

"So, how was your day?" he asked.

"Fine," she answered, deciding not to tell him about how hard she had found it to recover from her solo counseling session.

"Good, you're good at your job," he said. "How many years have you been working there now?"

"About eight years," she answered. "Or maybe it's nine now?"

"You've given them a lot of your time and energy over the years," he commented. "Have you ever considered looking at something else, just for a change?"

"No. Why would I?" she asked, slightly confused as to where this line of questioning had come from. "It pays well, I enjoy it, and I'm good at it."

"Of course you are, but don't you find life a bit boring if it's the 'same ole same ole' all the time?" he asked.

"No, not really," she answered.

"I'm not sure I could last at any job that long," he commented. "I think the longest for me has been four years."

"Yes, but you have the type of job where you can work just about anywhere," she explained. "My job is a little bit less so, as I have become more focused over the years."

"True," he said.

They ate their dinner in silence, savoring his cooking. He didn't cook often, but when he did, he had some amazing recipes. Afterward, they both sat back in their chairs, her with a glass of wine in her hand and him running his finger along the rim of his drink.

"So, I've been thinking," he broke the silence.

"About what?" she asked, feeling an odd, indescribable sense of unease.

"Maybe what we need is a change of pace," he suggested. "to help our marriage and bring back a sense of adventure."

"What would that look like?" she asked.

"Well, I thought maybe we should move," he said.

"Move?" she asked in a shocked voice. Somehow that wasn't even on the list of what she had expected him to say. "Why would we move? We love our house!"

"Oh, the house is nice," he agreed. "I don't mean change houses, I mean move to another city."

"What city? Why?" she asked.

"We've talked about eventually moving back to my hometown," he pointed out. "When we were dating you said it was something you would consider."

She sat in stupefied silence. She vaguely recalled conversations when they were dating about his desire to go back home, but it had never been anything more than talk. Until now.

"You seriously want to move across the country?" she asked.

"It would be an adventure!" he exclaimed. "As you said, I can find work just about anywhere, and it just might be the boost we need."

He reached out and placed his hand over hers. Looking earnestly into her eyes he said,

"Don't you want to go on an adventure with me?"

She gazed off into space, completely oblivious to her surroundings and the persistent ringing of the phone on her desk. Wanda was walking by and noticed the vacant look on her face and heard the phone. She popped her head in and waved her hands to attract her attention.

"Where were you?" Wanda asked with a laugh.

"What?" she asked, her reverie broken. "Oh, nowhere important."

"Well it must be important for you to not hear your phone ringing," Wanda pointed out just as the ringing stopped.

"Oh crap!" she exclaimed. "That was probably a supplier I've been waiting to hear from!"

After finishing her work for the day, she sat in her car in the parking lot, once again staring out into space. The bombshell her husband had dropped the other night was still on her mind. What was he thinking? Running away wasn't going to solve any of their problems, was it? It was crazy to even consider it. But he had made it sound so logical, so normal. As though people just up and moved across the country every day. He had seemed so surprised that she wasn't on board.

And it wasn't that she wasn't on board, she had just been blindsided. She didn't know if she was on board or not.

While moving seemed impulsive, part of her couldn't help wondering if it was a good idea to start all over again. To get away from everything and everybody. If she was a hundred percent honest with herself, she had suspected for a while that there just might be somebody in his life they should be running away from, but she didn't want her thoughts to go there.

However, starting all over again? In a different town? A new job? New friends? Although, she had to acknowledge to herself that she didn't have many friends to lose at this point. Once they had married, she had drifted away from her girlfriends. Either he didn't like them, or they didn't like him; either way, it was easier to just move on.

She wasn't concerned about a new house or a new town - that she did see as exciting and a bit of an adventure. But what about her family? What about her kids? Her husband seemed to have forgotten that she had children from a previous marriage. Certainly, they were living their own lives and seemed to be happy with their father, and perhaps they weren't as close to her as they had been when they were younger, but did he expect her to just leave them and move hundreds of miles away?

She shook her head in frustration. No matter which way she looked at it, she just couldn't see this as being the answer to anything.

Chapter Twenty-One

Olivia

Olivia floated through the next week as though she didn't have a care in the world. Things that used to bother her and cause her stress didn't seem so important. Life seemed so much sweeter now that she had someone who doted on her and who made her feel so special. They had only been dating for a couple of months, but it had been a whirlwind of emotions. It was so new that there were still times when she would look over at him when they were out for dinner or out for a walk, utterly amazed that he was there with her. She could hardly believe that her single days might be over for good.

Sitting in her living room on a Monday night, they talked more about their histories and past relationships. She was surprised to learn that he had been in quite a few and yet had never settled down.

"The closest I came to it was my last girlfriend," Luke explained to her. "But in the end, I'm glad we only lived together because she was a disaster."

"What do you mean by disaster?" Olivia probed. "What was wrong?"

"She drank too much, she would get drunk and yell and scream," he said. "One time she insisted I drop her off on the side of the road because she was so upset about an argument we were having."

"Wow, that doesn't sound very good," Olivia responded. "How did things end with you two?"

"Oh, I ended up leaving," he said. "But tell me more about you - I can't believe you have only had one serious relationship and that was your ex-husband."

Olivia was disappointed that he had changed the subject, as she was interested in learning more about his past relationship, but she was also trying to respect the signals he was sending her that made it clear he didn't want to re-visit that time of his life.

"Well, you know, I'm a bit picky," Olivia said teasingly. "I only want the best."

"Then what are you doing with me?" Luke responded in kind.

Later that evening, after her sons had returned from their friend's house, they all sat around the table and nibbled on a pizza Olivia had ordered.

"You aren't a real talkative bunch, are you?" Olivia asked, after long moments of silent chewing. Luke smiled slightly, and her boys simply shrugged. No matter how much time the three of them spent together, they didn't seem able to connect. Luke was awkward and tongue-tied, and the boys acted uncertain of what to say. Luke was convinced they didn't like him, but Olivia always reassured him that it was more about the fact they didn't know how to handle their mother dating. After all, he was the first male she had brought into their lives since her divorce.

"What's happening at school these days," Olivia asked, hoping to fill the silence somehow.

"Not much," Adam said as he helped himself to another slice of pizza. "Same ole, same ole"

"Well, I'm glad you feel able to confide in me," Olivia teased.

"Well, I don't know," Adam mumbled in a tone in his voice that told Olivia he didn't appreciate being put on the spot.

"Do you have any homework tonight?" Olivia tried another angle.

"I don't" replied Jonathon.

"I have a little," said Adam.

"Then when you're finished here, head up to your room and get it done Adam," Olivia instructed before turning to Jonathon. "Can you give me a hand putting things away in the kitchen?"

"I can help do that," Luke insisted. "You relax and let Jonathon and I take care of it."

Olivia was pleased that Luke seemed to be making an attempt to spend some time with her son and so she smiled gratefully and thanked him.

Jonathon and Luke proceeded to clear the plates and the empty and half-empty pizza boxes off the table.

"Hey! Don't take the pepperoni, I'm not done yet!" Adam protested.

"Get a move on," Jonathon taunted, giving his brother a slight shove on the shoulder. "We don't have all day, dude!"

"Yeah, yeah," Adam responded, swatting at his brother's hand. Within seconds, the boys were wrestling in a half playing, half-serious way. Adam had his younger brother Jonathon in a headlock when Olivia threw down her napkin, shaking her head.

"Okay, that's enough you two!" she said sternly. "Knock off the wrestling before someone gets hurt!"

The boys reluctantly separated but weren't finished sending jabs each other's way. Laughing, Jonathon used his foot as a hook and tried to bring his brother to the ground by pulling Adam's feet out from under him. Adam responded by running to the other side of the table and taunting his brother.

"Boys!" their mother exclaimed with exasperation. "Enough!"

"Okay, Okay," Jonathon assured her. "We'll behave, right Adam?"

"Yeah, yeah, sure we will," Adam laughed while moving to the other side of the table, his eyes kept firmly placed on his brother. At the same time, Jonathon was slowly walking around the table, as though stalking his Adam.

Luke was watching the interaction, slowly shaking his head and smiling slightly, as though to say that boys were a pain sometimes but, boys will be boys. Just then, Jonathon moved quickly to gain distance on Adam and was almost entirely behind Luke. Caught up in the moment, Jonathon reached up, and with a mischievous grin, quickly yanked on the small hair at the base of Luke's head.

Reacting as though on instinct, Luke abruptly swung around, his arm drawn back, and his fist raised in Jonathon's direction. The room went silent. Adam stopped in his tracks. Jonathon stared at Luke with his eyes wide.

As though waking from a dream, Luke quickly put his arm down and blinked rapidly.

"I'm, um, I'm sorry," he sputtered. "But you can't do that Dude, you shocked me."

"Yeah, okay, right," Jonathon said as he backed away from Luke. "Sorry man."

Olivia felt the blood drain from her face, but she was rooted in place with her breath caught in her chest and her thoughts racing. What the hell just happened?

Jonathon quickly left the room, and Adam was not far behind him, mumbling about having to get his homework done now. Luke was still, not moving from where he stood.

"What," Olivia said in a daze. "What was that all about?"

"I don't know, he just surprised me," Luke answered. "I reacted without thinking."

"But he is just a kid," Olivia insisted. "He wasn't going to hurt you."

"I know, but as I said, I just reacted," Luke tried to explain. "He surprised me, and it did hurt when he pulled."

"Okay," Olivia agreed hesitantly. She picked up the boxes which had been abandoned on the table and began taking them into the kitchen. Luke reached out and touched her arm as she walked by.

"I really am sorry if I scared you or the boys," Luke stated.

"I know. It's okay," Olivia said quietly, continuing to the kitchen.

Later that evening, the boys had called out from their bedrooms that they were turning in for the night and Olivia had gone in to say goodnight. They had long outgrown the tucking in ritual of their youth, but she wanted to make sure they were okay.

"Is your homework all done Adam?" she had asked.

"Yup, all done," Adam responded.

"Good." She hung around his doorway for a few more minutes. "Are you okay? You know, about tonight?"

"Yeah, sure," Adam replied, barely looking up from his computer game.

Heading towards Jonathon's room, she knocked and entered. Her youngest was flopped on his bed, earbuds in his ears and playing on his game. She flickered the lights off and on to get his attention.

"Yeah?" he exclaimed, taking the earbuds out. "What?"

"Just wanted to check in on you and make sure you're okay," Olivia explained.

"Yeah, sure," Jonathon shrugged.

"I mean, are you okay after what happened tonight?" Olivia asked.

"Yeah, I'm fine," he said, not making eye contact.

"Are you sure?" she asked.

"Yes Mom, I'm sure," he spat out in an irritated tone. "Now just go back to your boyfriend and don't worry about me."

She backed out of his doorway, unsure what to think. Teenagers were hard enough to read at the best of times, and this was uncharted territory for her. She honestly didn't know what to think. When Luke raised his fist, she had felt like her world stopped. But he was so contrite afterward, and really, it was an instinctive response on his part. It wasn't like he intended to hurt him or anything.

Heading back to the living room, she sat down beside Luke on the couch.

"Everything okay?" Luke asked.

"Sure, they're fine," Olivia responded with a slight smile.

"Good," Luke looked relieved. "You know I would never hurt them, right?"

"Of course, I know that," Olivia answered. "I have no doubt."

"Good, I'm glad you trust me," Luke said, putting his arm around her. They settled in to watch a TV show; the mindless sitcom they watched was just the reprieve from her emotions that Olivia needed.

Luke caressed her shoulder with his one hand while holding her other hand. After the show was over, he looked down and asked, "What size fingers do you have?"

"What size fingers?" she asked, confused by this line of questioning.

"Yes, what size of ring do you wear?" Luke answered.

"Oh! Um, I'm not sure, a six and a half I think," she stated, uncertain where he was going with this question. "Why?"

"No reason," Luke answered and flipped the channels on TV. "But I was wondering something."

"Yes?" Olivia asked.

"I'm not asking mind you, but I'm curious about something," Luke mentioned hesitantly. "If I was to ask you to marry me, would you say yes?"

Olivia stared at him in surprise. This was definitely not the conversation she thought they would have tonight.

"Um, it's a bit early in the relationship to be talking about marriage, isn't it?" she asked.

"Yes, I know. As I said, I'm not asking, I'm just curious," he reassured her with a smile. "So, what would you say?"

"I don't answer questions that haven't been asked," Olivia responded coyly. "but seriously, it's way too early to be talking marriage, we've only been dating a couple of months."

"I know, but it's been on my mind," he said. "You are an amazing woman, and I'm falling for you so hard."

Olivia was unsure what to think. It was way too early to be having this conversation, but on the other hand, the fact he had been thinking about it was a thrilling idea. This handsome, intelligent and sexy man was considering asking her to marry him! She wasn't sure what she had done to deserve all of this, but she was determined to enjoy it. Any uneasiness or misgivings she had about the incident around the kitchen table earlier this evening were pushed aside. There was so much good in this man and their relationship, why let something that wasn't a big deal get in the way?

Turning toward him, she put her hands on either side of his face and drew him down to her. Their lips met, and as usual, the sparks flew. There was just something about the two of them together that was so intoxicating. She leaned back on the couch as he pressed forward, nibbling at her lips, his tongue darting in and out. His hand ran down the side of her body. Pausing near her breast, his thumb skimmed over its fullness, and she caught her breath. As his hand moved to the top of her jeans, his fingers slid under her waistband.

"Uh uh!" she protested quietly, pulling away slightly. "The boys are home, and I don't want them to walk in on their mother making out on the couch."

"Are you sure?" he asked seductively as he nuzzled her neck and nipped at her earlobe. "I was just starting to have fun."

Laughing, she pushed him further away.

"That is quite enough out of you tonight Mister!" she joked. "Now cease!"

Standing up abruptly and pulling her off the couch to join him, he started to walk toward the front door, her hand in his.

"I guess I best get going," he agreed. "Time for you to get to bed and stop tormenting me with your bod."

"Ha!" she laughed. "Me, tempting you? You're a fine one to talk!"

Slipping into his shoes, he drew her up against him once more.

"Promise me you'll get some rest tonight?" he asked. "You have a lot on your plate, and you need to take care of yourself, or you'll have me to answer to."

"Of course," she answered. "I always do."

The kiss he gave her was deep, tender, and full of promise. She never ceased to be amazed at how well her body fit into his and just how right it felt.

"Okay, I'm leaving now," he said as he pulled away slightly. "But remember, one day I'll ask you for real, and you need to be ready to answer because I'll only ask once."

With a small smile, she watched him close the door, but as she locked up the house for the night, a sense of unease settled over her. Heading into the kitchen to tidy up the last bit of supper, she mused as to why she was feeling so uncomfortable; it was like a nagging sense that she was missing something.

She realized that his talk of marriage, while flattering and more than a little exciting, was part of the problem. Things were moving so fast that she felt like she hadn't had any time to sit back and process what was happening. He was taking their relationship to the next step when she was barely used to where they were now. While she liked knowing that he wanted to see her all the time and that even being ill wouldn't keep him away, on some level she felt like she had no control over things. Even his comment about only asking her to marry him one time made her feel that if she wasn't ready when he was, she could miss her chance. It never occurred to her that by throwing her mind into turmoil about marriage, he had completely overshadowed his earlier behavior with her son.

In exasperation, she threw down the cloth she was using to wipe the counter. Why was she looking for trouble? Couldn't she just enjoy the relationship for what it was and not over-analyze it to death!

Chapter Twenty-Two

She

Picking up the telephone, she was surprised to hear her friend's voice for the first time in a long, long time.

"What are you up to?" her friend asked. "I've been thinking about you a lot lately."

"It is great to hear from you!" she responded. "I've been thinking about you too, life has been busy, you know."

"Yes, I do know, but we really should try and get together soon," her friend said. "We've let too much time pass; maybe we could go for lunch sometime next week?"

"That would be awesome," she answered. "What about Wednesday at the Thai restaurant we liked?"

"Wednesday is good, but that Thai place shut down months ago,"

"Oh really?" she said. "That's too bad, I liked it there."

"How about we try something new? There is a great sushi place just off Hudson Street that I've had my eye on for a while." her friend suggested.

"It's a date then, lunch on Wednesday at the new sushi restaurant," she said, a smile on her face for the first time in days.

It was nice to have something to look forward to that would take her mind off the emotional rollercoaster she was on right now. It would do her good to get out and chat about girl things with her friend. She just hoped the topic of her marriage wasn't brought up; she just didn't want to deal with having to admit things were not going well.

Later that day, she was surprised when she received a phone call from the car dealership where they had purchased her car. They wanted to let her know her truck was ready to be picked up.

"I'm sorry, there's been a mix-up," she explained. "I don't have a truck."

"But didn't you order this year's Ford F-150 Lariat?" the salesman at the other end of the phone asked her.

"No, I absolutely didn't," she said with a laugh. "You must have your files mixed up, I haven't been into your dealership in months, not since my last oil change."

"Hmmmm.... That is odd," he mumbled to himself. "It says here your husband was in on the 23rd to order it."

"My husband?" she said, stunned.

"That is what it says," the salesman confirmed.

"Oh no! I hope I didn't spoil a surprise," the man said worriedly. "Oh crap, there is another phone number on the order sheet, and it looks like a cell phone."

After confirming that the cell phone number was indeed her husbands, the salesman continued to apologize for ruining any surprise her husband had planned for her, explaining that he had simply pulled up the name on his computer and it must have used her phone number from their past purchase.

"It's fine, really," she reassured him. "Just phone him on his cell please."

She hung up the phone and sat there, bewildered. When had he decided to purchase a truck? It certainly wasn't as a surprise for her, as he knew she didn't care for trucks and never even drove his. Her excitement over meeting with her old friend next week was now overshadowed by concern and worry. What was he up to? Why hadn't he kept her informed on such a significant purchase? And where was he getting the money for it?

She didn't dare phone him at work, in case they got into an argument, and she made things far worse. Resting her forehead in her hand, she sighed deeply. What on earth was going on now? She had been avoiding talking to him about his desire to move as she knew it wasn't going to help their situation, but he seemed so excited and convinced this was the change they needed.

Cleaning off her desk for the evening, she left for home, knowing it was time for another talk with her husband.

Unfortunately, the talk she was convinced they would have to have that evening never happened. The house was empty when she returned from work, and her husband didn't make it home until she was almost ready to go to bed. She was tired and didn't want to engage with him, so she gave him a peck on the cheek and went to bed. She didn't even bother asking him where he had been all evening. It was apparent from the smell of alcohol on his breath that he had been out with friends and she wasn't up to probing him for details.

Crawling into bed, she reached over and shut off the bedside lamp just as he entered the room. He undressed in the dark and then slipped in next to her. Snuggling up against her back, he wrapped his arms around her and cupped her breast with one hand.

"Hey, remember when we talked about spicing up our sex life?" he whispered in her ear.

"Hmm," she said.

"I was thinking, have you ever considered getting a piercing?" he asked as he nuzzled the nape of her neck.

"A piercing?" she asked, surprised. "What kind of piercing?"

"They say that it can increase your pleasure when you have sex," he answered. "Honestly, the idea of it is pretty hot."

She laid still, surprise washing over her. She'd thought when he'd mentioned spicing up their sex life that he was talking about role-playing or something. She never considered he might mean poking holes in her body.

"Um, I would have to think about that for a bit," she hedged. "I've never thought about it before."

"Give it some thought," he said. "Maybe it's time to try something you've never considered before."

He continued to kiss her neck, and she tried not to let the uneasy feeling she had in the pit of her stomach stop her from enjoying her husband in a rare good mood. She turned over, so she was facing him.

"What made you think of a piercing?" she asked. "I didn't know you were interested in them."

"A friend of mine was talking about it. Apparently, it really makes sex hot," he said, running his hand up and down her arm. "She said the orgasms are out of this world."

"Your friend is a woman?" she couldn't hide her surprise. "What on earth were you discussing orgasms and genital piercings with a woman for?"

"Oh relax, it was just a conversation," he said with an annoyed tone.

He slipped her nightgown off her one shoulder and began to sprinkle kisses all over her. She felt uneasy, although she tried to push her thoughts and feelings aside and just enjoy the moment. His mouth found her nipple, and she moaned gently as he sucked on it. No matter what else seemed to happen, the chemistry between them in bed was always incredible. It wasn't something she could ever figure out, as it wasn't that the sex was any different than the sex she had with her first husband; there was nothing unique or kinky about them in the bedroom, in fact, her husband seemed to be content with fairly conventional couplings. But she couldn't seem to get enough of him, and no one could turn her on faster.

Sighing deeply, she ran her fingers through his hair. Questions about piercings and the ordering of trucks were pushed to the back of her mind, to be dealt with tomorrow.

Chapter Twenty-Three

Olivia

Olivia was excited about their evening out. They were going to a colleague's barbeque, and she was looking forward to showing Luke off to her workmates. Although she had told some of the people at work that she and Luke were dating, they hadn't had a chance to meet him yet. Tonight would be a chance for everyone to get to know him. The only thing dampening her excitement was an undercurrent of unease with the way he had reacted when he met her friends and even her sons. He tended to get quiet and sometimes even a bit defensive. She didn't understand why, he had nothing to be concerned about as he was attractive, intelligent and interesting. She knew her friends from work would love him if he would just relax and show them the side of him that she saw.

He pulled up in front of her house right on time and Olivia grabbed the bottle of wine and plate of appetizers she had prepared for the barbeque. Placing them in the back, she slid into his vehicle. She reached over and kissed him hello just as he hung up his cell phone. He looked a bit unhappy, and she wondered if maybe he had received some bad news. When she probed a bit, she learned that he had a bad day at work.

"What happened?" she asked.

"Nothing really, just some guys that work there can be a bit of a pain," he answered vaguely. "It just gets in the way of work sometimes when you have to watch your back all the time."

"What do you mean, watch your back?" she asked.

"Oh, just the usual worksite stuff," he answered. "Sometimes people just want to stir up trouble if they don't like you and will pin anything they can on you."

Olivia was a bit surprised to hear him talk about his work in such a negative way. He usually spoke quite favorably of the men he worked with, and in fact, had taken her to dinner at one of his colleague's houses a week or so ago. They had a lovely visit, and Luke seemed to enjoy their company. To hear that he was having problems was surprising news to her.

"Don't worry about it hon," he reassured her. "I'm a big boy, I can take care of myself."

"Okay," Olivia responded reluctantly. "But who were you talking to on the phone?"

"That was my Mom," he murmured.

"Was it bad news? You seemed unhappy talking to her," Olivia probed.

"Oh, nothing really," he answered with a sigh. "She's upset because my brother and I aren't talking, and she wants me to call him."

"I didn't know you weren't talking to your brother!" Olivia exclaimed. "When did that happen, and why?"

"My brother's a piece of work," Luke responded. "He stole some money from me, and my Mom doesn't seem to think I should be upset. But then again, she thinks he can do no wrong."

Olivia sat back in her seat in surprise. This was the most information he had given her about his family interactions. Of course, he had told her how many siblings he had, and how much family meant to him, but he had never talked about their actual relationships.

"He stole money from you, and she thinks that's okay?" Olivia asked.

"Oh, she doesn't think him stealing money is okay, but she thinks I should just forgive him and move on," Luke explained. "But it isn't surprising, she never sides with me."

"That is terrible, Hon," she said, her hand reaching out to rub the back of his neck as he drove. It hurt her to think that his family might not be as loving and supportive as she had assumed. There was no opportunity to pursue the conversation, as they soon pulled into her colleague's driveway and their conversation ended.

"Well, well, well! So you're the guy Olivia has been keeping all to herself," piped up one of her colleagues as she and Luke sat down on lawn chairs.

"Yup," Luke replied with a small smile.

"It's great to finally meet you, Luke," Wanda threw out the greeting with a smile in Luke's direction. "Don't mind this crew, they've had a few beers, and they aren't responsible for what they say."

"No problem," Luke reassured her.

"Don't let them intimidate you, Luke," Wanda's husband joined the conversation as he came back from the house. "They're all really just a bunch of teddy bears."

"All good," Luke replied.

"So, Luke. I'm thinking you know all kinds of things about Olivia that you can share with us," someone else spoke up.

"What do you mean?" Luke asked.

"You know, secrets she wouldn't tell us… you know! The good stuff!"

Luke looked uncomfortable at being put on the spot. He held onto his pop can with both hands, elbows resting on his knees.

"Nope, sorry, I don't," he answered.

"What are you guys yattering about?" Olivia chimed in, "I have nothing to hide, you know that!"

The good-natured banter continued for a while until the group became distracted by another person's arrival. Olivia was glad that Luke had managed to hold up under the well-intentioned onslaught. He was quiet but didn't look too uncomfortable with her workmates.

That evening, Luke pulled up in front of her house. Turning off the ignition, he turned to her.

"Did you have a nice time?" he asked.

"Yes, I did. It was nice to have you in my world for a bit," she answered. "My work is important to me, and I'm glad you had an opportunity to meet my work friends."

"I'm glad you had a nice time," he said.

"Did you?" she asked.

"I always enjoy myself when I'm with you, you know that," he answered as he pulled her toward him.

"Do you now?" she asked playfully.

"I could give you some proof," he said, as he grabbed her hand and moved it toward his crotch. Laughing, she pulled her hand back, reminding him that her children were asleep in the house mere feet away from them.

"I'm not sure I want them looking out and seeing their mother in a car playing catch and grab with a man." she joked.

"Oh come, on," he moaned. "There's always some reason why it's not a good time."

"Not the right time, not the right place...." she droned as she reached over and opened the car door.

"Aaaargh!" he joked, as he leaned his head back on the headrest of his car.

Coming around to his side of the car, she stuck her head in the open window.

"You'll be just fine," she said. "You're a big boy - you can take it."

"Says who?" he asked, turning to look at her.

"Says me, that's who" she answered as she planted a kiss on his lips.

She was smiling as she put her key in the front door lock. It had been a lovely evening, and although Luke had not seemed overly comfortable at the barbeque, he had held up well, and there were no awkward moments. She ignored the unease she felt, the little voice inside her asking her if maybe it was a bit unusual to be worried that her date might make people uncomfortable because of his awkwardness. Was it normal to worry that your date might become defensive and uncomfortable in a typical social situation?

Chapter Twenty-Four

She

She was looking forward to lunch with her friend today. It had been so long since she had spent any time with her and she was at a loss as to exactly how long it had been. She did know it had been way too long and, in some ways, she felt awkward and uncomfortable. She knew she had dropped the ball in their relationship, but she didn't want to let that stop her from seeing her and extending a hand of friendship.

She pulled up to the sushi restaurant on Hudson's at noon on the dot. She was lucky to find a parking spot, as the lunchtime rush was in full swing. She punched her license plate number into the parking machine, grabbed the receipt and headed toward the restaurant.

Despite the time that had gone by since they had last seen each other, it was like it had been only days. They were soon chattering away, laughing over sushi and a bottle of Malbec. During a lull in the conversation, her friend asked her the question she had been waiting for since lunch started.

"So, how is the hubby doing?" It was apparent that she was asking to be polite.

"He's just fine," she answered with the same small, tight smile in return. "He's keeping busy with work."

"Great," her friend responded. Taking a deep breath while patting her lips with her napkin, she went on, "Listen, I feel bad that we've just lost touch."

"I know, don't worry about it," she responded. "I know it was on me just as much as you, and I've missed you."

"I've missed you too," her friend responded. "That's why I called - I couldn't let any more time go by."

"I know I haven't made things easy," She continued. "I felt like I had to choose between my husband and my friends."

"Don't worry about it," she was reassured.

"No, I need to say this," she insisted. "I should never have treated you like that, and the fact that I felt the need to choose, should have warned me that something was definitely not kosher."

"Oh?" her friend responded quizzically.

"Yes. I should have protected all my relationships better," she said. "But I was so wrapped up in having found someone that I lost sight of how important all my relationships were."

She reached across and placed her hand over her friends. Her friend responded by placing her hand on top of hers.

"Thank you for saying that," her friend said. "Now, let's put that all behind us."

"Sounds like a great idea to me," she responded with a smile. "Let's see if this place has any decadent desserts!"

Chapter Twenty-Five

Olivia

Olivia was tired after a long day of running against the clock, trying to meet the usual deadlines. She just wanted to soak in her hot bath, sip on a glass of wine, and let the tension leave her body. So many hours of being hunched over her keyboard had left a tight knot in her shoulders.

Luke had to work a bit later tonight than usual, so she was able to stay at her office and get some of the odds and ends tied up so she would be good to go tomorrow. Or at least until the next deadline, she chuckled to herself.

She had a quick sandwich, as she couldn't be bothered with making a proper meal, and anyway, the boys were at their Dad's house tonight. Something about an important baseball game on TV. Pouring her tub, she added some foaming bath oil to the water and swirled it with her hand. She took a sip from her wine and sighed deeply. Life was good. So good that some days she wanted to pinch herself to see if she was dreaming. Luke coming into her life had awakened a whole new side of herself that she had never experienced before. She felt beautiful and sexy for the first time in, well, forever. She looked forward to seeing him and realized she was looking hopefully into the future for the first time in years. Although she had always enjoyed her work, there was just no replacement for feeling loved.

Sliding her robe off her shoulders, letting it pool on the floor at her feet, she stepped into the hot bath. She sank deep into the water and let out a contented sigh. The warmth sunk into her body and seemed to go right to her bones. She closed her eyes and rested her head on the back of the tub. The phone rang.

"Aaargh!" she exclaimed, as she reached for her cell phone that was sitting on the stand beside the tub. She never felt comfortable ignoring the phone when her kids weren't at home. You never knew when they will decide they need you and she wanted to be there for them.

"Yes?" she answered, not looking at the caller ID.

"Well, that didn't sound like a woman who appreciates a phone call," Luke responded with a chuckle.

"Oh, sorry hon," she said. "I thought maybe it was the boys, and I just settled into a hot bath."

"It's okay, I forgive you," he teased. "So, a hot bath, huh?"

"Yes, it was a long day at work," she answered, ignoring the sexy tone he took on when mentioning her in a bath.

"Are you in there now?" he asked, his voice lowering and causing goosebumps to rise on her warm skin.

"Yes, I am," she answered. "It feels great."

"I bet it does," he said. "Do you have bubbles in the tub?"

"Yessss," she replied coyly.

"Is your skin warm and slippery?" he asked.

"I assume so," she answered.

"Check and see," he instructed her. "Run your hand along your thigh."

She giggled a bit as she followed his directions, running her hand up and down her thigh, the warm water and bubbles causing her skin to feel warm, soft, and slick. She tapped on the speaker button on her phone and set it beside the tub. She took another sip from the wine glass in her other hand.

"Move your hand over your stomach," he continued.

Moving her hand, she felt the flatness of her stomach. She was quite proud that even after two kids, there was only a slight mound leftover from her pregnancies. The warmth of her skin, the slippery feeling as her hand moved over her stomach, and the sound of his thick, sensuous voice caused her to moan slightly.

"It feels good, doesn't it?" he asked with a chuckle.

"Yeah, sort of," she said teasingly.

"Now move your hands up to your breasts," he said. "Move them over your nipples."

She followed obediently and sighed deeply as he continued to purr directions in her ear.

"Are your nipples hard yet?"

"Yes," she gasped.

"Squeeze them, just a little bit," he told her. "Roll them between your fingers gently."

Oh lord, she thought, what kind of insanity was this that she was enjoying so much? She didn't consider herself a prude, but it seemed so decadent and kinky somehow to be listening and waiting for his next instruction.

"Put the phone on speaker," he demanded. "You need to move both your hands up and down your thighs, feeling the slickness of the soap as it skims over your body."

Her breathing was becoming heavier as she anticipated his every word. Her body was beginning to ache and throb.

"Put your hands on the inside of your thighs now," he instructed. "But only your thighs, don't touch anywhere else until I tell you."

"Okay," she answered quietly, her breath becoming ragged.

"Up, over your stomach again, and then down to your pussy," he crooned.

She moaned as she followed his every word. It was as though he was right there in the room with her, watching her. The sexual tension was like nothing she had ever experienced, and he was just on the phone.

"Rub up and down," he said. "Are you turned on, Olivia?"

"Yes," she answered simply and honestly.

"Feel your clit, is it hard?" he asked.

"Yes"

"Rub it gently."

"Yes, mmmm."

"Are you going to cum for me, Olivia?" Luke asked.

"I think," she almost stuttered. "I might!"

"Then stop."

"What?" she asked in disbelief.

"Do as I say and stop," he spoke firmly.

"Okay." she obeyed.

"Now put your fingers inside you," he continued.

She obeyed as she slid further down into the tub, lifting her one leg and draping it over the side of the tub. The combination of a long, tiring day, a glass of wine, and his sexy voice purring in her ear had left her with no resistance at all. She was ready to do his bidding.

"Move in and out," he said. "Close your eyes and pretend it's me, I'm over top of you, and I'm moving in and out."

"Oh shit," she said, her breath heaving now.

"I'm giving you all you need and all you want," he said. "Now keep your fingers inside you but use your thumb to rub your clit."

She obeyed and almost immediately she felt a tremor build up and spread throughout her body. Her back arched and she gasped with pleasure as an orgasm rolled over her.

"Oh God! Oh God!" she cried out. She heard him chuckle softly on the phone and that only amplified the sensations as they coursed through her body.

"Good-night my dear," he said softly, and he was gone.

Olivia lay in the tub, panting as she recovered from one of the most intense orgasms she had ever experienced. She couldn't believe he was able to do that to her and not even be in the same room. And then he just hung up!

"Oh, Lord love a duck!" she exclaimed with a giggle as she sunk into the tub, submerging her head.

Chapter Twenty-Six

She

Isn't this just hunky-dory, she thought to herself. Now she had three things to think about; genital piercings, moving out of province, and a mystery truck. Each thing left her feeling anxious and uncertain. If she was honest with herself, she didn't want any kind of piercing. But she also wanted to please her husband, and he was trying by thinking of different things they could do. But why did it have to be something painful and permanent? She was no further ahead in deciding on the move either. It seemed like such a random answer to their problems, but again, at least he was trying. And the truck? Oh lord! she thought she was not looking forward to bringing that up with him. She'd had the best of intentions last night, but she hadn't wanted to ruin the mood. And now it was a brand-new day and another day of worrying.

He was coming to pick her up from work today and take her for lunch, just like they used to do when they were dating. He had taken an extra-long lunch break to make it work, and she was grateful. How could she ruin it by bringing up these topics? But how could she continue to ignore them?

"Your husband is here," the receptionist said when she picked up her ringing phone.

"Tell him I'll be right there," she responded, taking her purse out of her office drawer and heading towards reception.

Greeting him in the front foyer, she was pleased when he reached out to give her a big hug and then waved goodbye to the receptionist as they left the building. He appeared to still be in a good mood, and she felt herself relax a bit. Maybe they had turned the corner on whatever had been happening in their marriage.

He opened the truck door for her and then went around and let himself into the driver's side. She reached forward and turned the radio down a bit before settling back, ready to enjoy her husband's company. Maybe talk about the truck could wait until another day.

She did not have to bring up the topic of the truck after all. While they were digging into their pizza, he casually mentioned that he would be later getting home from work tonight as he had to stop by the car dealership. He was bringing home his new truck.

"What new truck?" she kept her voice non-committal as she carefully set her pizza down on her plate.

"My new truck," he answered, as though she should know what he was talking about.

"You have a new truck?" she asked.

He looked over at her, blankly, as though he was not at all engaged in the conversation happening at their table.

"Yeah, I'm sure I mentioned it to you."

"No, I don't think so," she stated. "I think I would recall discussing something as important as the purchase of a vehicle."

He set his pizza down on his plate, wiped his hands on his napkin, and took a swig from his mug of beer.

"Yes, I bought a new truck, I figure if we're going to make some changes and have a fresh start, now is as good a time as any."

She wasn't sure how spending money on a truck would help their marriage, but she took a deep breath and tried not to escalate the situation.

"Okay, but how are we going to afford a brand-new truck if we're considering giving up our jobs and moving to a different city?" she asked, trying to sound reasonable rather than accusing.

"Don't worry about the money," he reassured her. "I can cover it."

"What do you mean you can cover it?" she asked, more puzzled than ever. "I know what's in our accounts, and I don't think a new truck is in the budget."

"I have some money," he insisted. "Don't worry about it."

"You have some money," she stated, as though the words weren't quite sinking in. "What do you mean, you have some money? We have joint accounts, I know what we have."

"I have a bit of money set aside," he explained patiently.

"Where did this money come from?" she asked.

"I said, don't worry about it," he replied. "I've been saving some money."

She sat there, dumbfounded and unsure what to say or how to respond to what she had just learned. When they married, they had decided that they would have joint accounts, and all the money would be pooled. He was insistent that, as a couple, there should be no separate accounts but that what was his was hers and vice versa. This revelation that he was saving money for himself unbeknownst to her set her back on her heels. Apparently, purchasing a truck wasn't the first thing he had done without her input or awareness. What else had he not bothered to tell her? She didn't dare ask him any further questions, as she knew it would wreck the rapport they had established over the last week or so.

"And anyway, a new truck will ensure we have reliable transportation, especially if we decide to move somewhere far away." he reasoned.

"Where did you have in mind?" she asked casually. "I don't think you ever really suggested anywhere specific"

"Well, you know I've always wanted to move back home," he said. "Maybe this would be a good time; your kids aren't kids anymore, and we have no real reason to stay here."

"Hmmm... that would be quite a change."

The idea of moving across the country to settle down and start over in a place she had no ties to, didn't exactly thrill her. He would know people and be able to re-establish relationships fairly fast, and he had his family, no matter how rocky those relationships were. But she didn't know a soul and had only met his mother once. It hadn't left a very good impression on her, and she couldn't see her mother-in-law jumping in to help her feel at home. She had already lost most ties with her friends, and she didn't see her kids all that often, now that they had moved away from home. All she had was her work and her work friends. Could she just give that up and move to try and save her marriage?

He reached out and placed his hand over the top of hers. Looking into her eyes, he gave her a smile that she remembered from the early days of their relationship. Looking deeply into her eyes, he caressed her hand with his.

"You are so incredibly amazing," he said. "I don't know what I was thinking - I haven't been giving you enough attention, and you deserve to be treated better."

Her breath caught in her throat, and she felt the old familiar rush of emotion come over her. She felt a combination of amazement and gratitude. This was the man she knew and fell in love with so many years ago. Maybe there was a way to salvage their marriage, after all! She just needed to be flexible and open to what he was suggesting. It wasn't too much to ask of her, was it?

Chapter Twenty-Seven

Olivia

Olivia was in the middle of editing an article when her office phone rang. Picking it up, she was pleased to hear Luke's voice.

"Why hello there!"

"Why hello there you," he responded. "What are you up to?"

"Oh, you know, working hard," she leaned back in her chair and stretched the tense muscles in her shoulders.

"Glad to hear, it means you're staying out of trouble," he teased.

"Always," she responded.

"You didn't sound like you were staying out of trouble last night when you were moaning in your bath,"

"Oh, you never mind!" she answered with a laugh and a tinge of embarrassment.

"I'm sorry, did I embarrass you?" he teased.

"No, I'm just at work," she said.

"Okay, I won't keep you long," he said with a laugh. "I just wanted to know if we could have dinner at my place tonight?"

"That would be good, are you cooking?"

"Of course! I wouldn't invite you over and expect you to cook for me. So, I'll see you after work?"

"I'll be there," she said, hanging up the phone.

She was still smiling to herself as she went back to her work, although she was finding it harder to concentrate than before Luke phoned. He had a way of unnerving her but in a good way. His voice had brought back memories of the night before, and she turned slightly pink as she recalled the effect he'd had on her.

She had been working for about an hour when she heard the text notification ping from her phone. Picking up the phone, she realized it was from Luke. It was a short text, but it made her catch her breath a little.

"Do you like gold or platinum?"

She hesitated before she answered.

"I like both, but I sometimes have an allergic reaction to gold. Why?"

"Okay, thanks – go back to work now!"

She sat staring at her phone. What was he up to? He hadn't brought up marriage other than in a casual way since he the night he had asked her if she would say yes to a proposal. That was only about a month ago, and now he was asking her about her metal preferences? As much as she was thrilled with the way their relationship was progressing, it was way too soon, and she was worried he was planning to ask her for real. What would she do if he did?

She was staring off into space, pondering those questions when someone knocked on her door.

"Flowers for you!" the receptionist exclaimed.

"Wow, thank you, I wonder who they're from?"

"Well duh, they're probably from that hunky man of yours," the receptionist laughed.

Reaching into the beautiful arrangement of red roses for the card, she opened it and walked towards her desk, shielding it from the receptionist's inquisitive look.

"For the love of my life, my beautiful, squeaky clean Olivia."

She smiled and gave a quick giggle before she turned around and thanked the receptionist.

"Are they from him?" she asked Olivia.

"Yes, they're from Luke," she answered with a smile.

Sitting down at her desk, she fired Luke off a text thanking him for the flowers. Then she went back to work, her concern over his possible intention to propose relegated to the back of her mind.

After work, she drove over to Luke's house for dinner. She enjoyed spending time at his home, as it allowed her to see him in his surroundings. She liked the way he moved easily around the kitchen, preparing dinner for them. She sat at the table and sipped on her glass of wine, feeling content and happy.

Later, they curled up on the couch to watch a mindless sitcom. Lying out on the couch, her head resting in Luke's lap, she laughed at the antics on the show. Luke was playing with her hair and caressing her in a distracting way, but she managed to ignore it for the most part.

"Hey!" he said, looking down at her.

"Yes?" she asked, taking her eyes off the tv and looking at him.

"Kiss me," he said.

She smiled and reached up and kissed him. Not a peck on the cheek - just a sweet, comfortable kiss that lingered.

"Is that the best you can do?" he asked.

"Excuse me?" she responded with a smile.

"Give me a real kiss," he instructed.

"You're the boss!" she laughed.

He used his hands to help raise her head closer to his, and they exchanged a deep and passionate kiss. The memories of how intensely erotic he had made her feel when she was in the bathtub were not far from her mind. As a result, it seemed to take very little for her breath to increase to a rapid rate. He effortlessly lifted her and set her on the rug. With the sound of the TV playing in the background, he began kissing her neck.

Pressing her into the floor, he shifted his weight half onto her. Looking into her eyes, he moved her hair off her forehead.

"You are so damned sexy," he whispered. "I want you!"

She placed her hand at the back of his neck and drew him down to her. His free hand wandered over her body, stopping first at her hip and sliding his hand under the waistband of her jeans, before moving around to her back, to caress her back, and ass. Pulling her closer to him, she could feel his hardness press against her leg. The smell of his cologne, mixed with his own body's scent, wafted toward her, and she felt her self-control slipping. Not slipping by mere inches, but by feet, and rapidly.

"God, I want you!" he repeated.

His hand had now moved towards the front of her body and was working its way under her shirt, along her stomach and up and under her bra. Her nipples were firm and pointing as his fingers teased them. Lifting her shirt, he moved to suck on her nipples, causing a shot of desire to go from the middle of her out to her fingertips.

"Oooooh," she moaned.

Undoing the buckle of her jeans, he slowly unzipped them and slid his hand down her stomach. She arched her back as he sunk his fingers into her. Time stood still, and all the promises of no sex and keeping a clear head were gone. She craved more of him, more of his smell, more of his touch. She wanted to get closer to him, as close as she could get. She wanted to melt into him like one candle melting into another. She wanted to be consumed and engulfed by him.

Their kissing intensified, becoming more aggressive and intimate with each passing second. Suddenly, he stood up. Reaching his hand in her direction, he said gruffly.

"Come with me."

She grabbed his hand, stood up, and walked with him to his bedroom. There, he quickly removed his shirt and reached over to remove hers. She began undoing his jeans, all the while raining kisses along his chest and flicking her tongue across his nipples. She knew he had a nice physique, but she was in awe of the sight of him without his shirt. Large, firm biceps and defined pecs on a chest that tapered down to his waist in a perfectly proportioned 'V' took her breath away.

Suddenly, she felt a wave of insecurity wash over her. What if she wasn't what he'd thought she would be like? What if she paled in comparison to his previous lovers? She'd had two children, what if she wasn't as tight as he expected? And she had cellulite; she wasn't a young woman.

Then, she looked up at him. The desire she saw reflected at her put all her concerns to rest. Whatever she looked like, she was enough. For the first time in her life, she was certain she was enough.

Slipping out of her jeans and panties, she stood before him. The look on his face was all she needed to know that tonight they would-be lovers. There was no turning back for either of them.

He pushed her back on the bed, her legs dangling over the side and stood over her as he took off his jeans and underwear. She gasped a bit when she saw him. Up to now, she had felt him pressing up against her - his hardness was felt only through his jeans. Tonight, for the first time, she was able to see what she had previously only felt and it took her breath away. She had never been one that believed that size mattered but seeing him standing in front of her with an erect nine inches, she knew she was going to put that theory to the test.

Moving her legs apart, he sunk to his knees and buried his head between them. She felt his tongue lapping up the wetness that was coming from inside her. She felt him slip his finger inside her at the same time and she wiggled with pleasure.

"Oh, that is going to be a tight fit for sure," he said, partly to her and partly to himself. That comment was too much for her, and she knew she needed him inside her, quickly!

"Come here," she demanded as she put both hands on his head to guide him up to her. She plunged her tongue deep into his mouth.

"Can you taste yourself?" he asked when she had finished kissing him.

"Oh God, yes!" she answered.

He pushed her further up the bed, so her feet were no longer over the edge. He rested with his elbows on either side of her. She felt the tip of him as he began to enter her, and she took a sharp breath. He was right, it was going to be a tight fit! It had been years since she'd had sex. The last time had been with the boy's father. But tight fit or not, it felt incredible.

Just then, he moved and placed his arms behind her knees, bringing her legs to rest on his shoulders. He plunged into her in one fluid motion, and she felt like her world stood still. He began to move rhythmically, pushing the full length of himself into her. She could feel as he went as far as her body was able to accept him.

She was soon distracted from her amazement at how their bodies fit together by the sounds that were coming from Luke. He was making guttural noises deep in his throat and crying out with each thrust. The noises were turning her on even more, and she felt an orgasm rise within her body. Just then, he reached out and slid his hand between them, touching the center of her.

Together, they reached a climax that left then breathing raggedly. Luke collapsed on her and lay there, inert. Olivia struggled to catch her breath under the effects of her orgasm and his weight.

Eventually, he raised himself on his elbows and looked down on her with a smile.

"Oh wow!" he said.

She laughed at the simplicity with which he stated his satisfaction. She couldn't have described it any better herself.

"You are amazing," he raised himself a bit more and sucked on her nipple.

"You aren't so bad yourself," she laughed.

He was still inside her, and they laid there for a while, enjoying the after-effects before she began to notice that he seemed to be hard again. She wasn't sure until he started moving slowly in and out of her.

"What the-" she asked incredulously.

"That is what you do to me," he said, huskily.

She laughed in delight as she threw her arms around his neck, prepared for a very long night.

Chapter Twenty-Eight

She

When she came home from work the next evening, she was surprised by the smell of frying mushrooms and onions that greeted her as she opened up the door.

"What's this?" she asked as she walked into the kitchen to set her purse on the counter.

"What?" he answered. "Can't a man make dinner for his wife?"

"Oh, far be it for me to interrupt a cooking man," she said with a laugh.

"I poured you some wine, sit down and get comfortable, it's almost ready."

She sat down at their kitchen table, appreciating the time he had taken to set out a placemat, cloth napkins, and their good dishes. She could get used to this kind of treatment. He came out of the kitchen and set her plate down in front of her, and she took a deep breath in, taking full advantage of the decadent aromas coming off her plate. He had made some savory rice and topped it with his special recipe of fried squid, made in a sauce of mushroom, onions, and brandy. She'd been skeptical the first time she tried it, but it was now one of her favorite special occasion dishes.

That evening, after the dishes had been cleared and washed, they sat together on the living room couch, her sipping her wine and him from his glass of vodka. She still couldn't understand why he would want to drink vodka straight, but she had learned not to say anything to him.

"So, how was work?" she asked.

"It was okay," he answered. "The usual."

"You don't talk much about work, so I don't know what the usual is," she pointed out.

"I don't talk about it because I can't be bothered it's like being in high school with all the drama, gossiping and back-stabbing."

She was shocked at how he was describing his work environment. He had never talked negatively about it before, in fact, he had often spoke highly of his co-workers.

"I didn't know things were that bad!" she exclaimed.

"Nothing I can't handle," he reassured her. He set his glass down on the coffee table and reached for her, pulling her legs up over his so she straddled him.

"Enough talk," he murmured. "How about a bit of us time?"

"Oh really?" she teased. "Us time, huh?"

"Uh-huh," he said as he ran his hand up the inside of her leg. She moved her legs closer to him so she could feel his hardness pressing up against her. Her heart began to beat faster, and she felt a flush rise up her neck. It felt so good to be back in sync with each other again.

He reached up and undid the zipper of her pants, the whole time never taking his eyes off of hers. She was the one who finally broke eye contact and sighed quietly when he slipped his fingers under her panties and towards her center.

"Does that feel good?" he asked.

"You know it does," she answered.

"I love watching you when you're turned on," he said. "Your face is so expressive."

"Yeah?" she said, her breathing coming faster as he moved expertly over her body.

"Yeah," he said. He pulled down on her pants and soon she was sitting on his lap, naked from the waist down. He quickly undid his zipper, and she mounted him right there.

"Oh God!" she moaned, as she felt him slide into her.

"You like that, don't you?"

"Uh-huh," she answered, distracted by how her body was reacting to him. He grabbed her by her upper thighs and drove her onto him harder and harder, his body almost rising from the couch to meet hers. She used her knees to brace herself and gain momentum. Just when she thought she was going to climax, he reached out and used his thumb to rub her clitoris and her body began to tremble violently.

"Oh, dear God!" she exclaimed, as one of the strongest orgasms she had ever experienced washed over her. Just as she was catching her breath, he pulled her up and off of him. Turning her around, he bent her over the furniture and entered her from behind.

"You love that, don't you?" he asked, through clenched teeth as he reached for her hair, pulling it back with enough pressure to lift her head. "Don't you?" he insisted when she didn't respond.

"Yes, yes, I love it," she answered, just as he climaxed into her.

They stayed half standing, half lying over the couch, as they caught their breath. Finally, he pulled himself into a completely upright position and grabbed his jeans.

"I'm going to shower off, you want to join me?" he asked.

"Sure," she said as she gathered up her clothes. She was always amazed at how he was able to recover from such mind-blowing sex so quickly. He could have just as easily been asking her if she wanted fries with her meal.

In the shower, they lathered up and washed off while exchanging quick kisses and playful touches.

Later, she was blow-drying her hair and watching him out of the corner of her eye as he pulled on a pair of pajama bottoms.

"It feels good to really connect again," she commented.

"Yeah, sure,"

"Seriously, you were amazing," she said.

"Thanks, you too," he responded with a smile. "Although, I still want to get you to the point you become a squirter."

"A say what?" she asked.

"You know, a woman who squirts when she has an orgasm," he answered, nonchalantly.

"Um, I don't think that's how a woman's body is made," she disagreed. "They don't have an orgasm like a man."

"Some women do," he insisted.

"Oh really?" she said, with a raised eyebrow and a teasing tone. "And how would you know that?"

He chuckled at her reaction, and she was pleased he didn't take her teasing seriously.

"A buddy of mine sent me an email once," he explained. "I opened it, and before I knew what it was, I realized it was a video of a woman squirting."

"Your buddy sent you a video of it?" she asked, incredulous.

"Yeah," he said. "So, I know it's possible."

"Huh, well, there you go," she said distractedly. Why was it he always mentioned friends who had no names and she had never met? Uneasiness welled up inside of her and she tried to shake it off. They'd had a wonderful evening and connected in a way they hadn't in a long time. There was no point in ruining it by analyzing everything. What did it matter if he had creepy friends who sent him pornographic videos? Even as she thought that she wondered, What kind of man sends another man that type of material?

Chapter Twenty-Nine

Olivia

She was in the middle of making supper when the phone rang. It was Adam, telling her that his father was going to pick him up from school to take him to his baseball practice.

"Do you have your equipment with you?" she asked.

"No, Dad says we can swing by the house to pick it up after we grab a bite," Adam informed her.

"Okay, have a nice time," she said and then hung up.

Just then Jonathon walked in the door, threw his backpack down on the counter and opened the fridge.

"How come we never have anything good to eat?" he lamented.

"What do you mean? I just bought groceries yesterday!" she answered.

"Yeah, but not good food!" he insisted.

"There are kids in the world starving; you'll be just fine," she reassured him. "Why don't you just grab an apple? It won't be long until supper."

"Yeah, maybe we should send some apples to the starving kids," he said playfully.

"Don't be cheeky," she laughed back at him.

As he bit into his apple, she looked at him, and a small smile curved her lips. She couldn't get over how much Jonathon looked like his father. When she had started dating Ed, he was only a few years older than Jonathon was now. It amazed her how time had flown by, and how young they had both been when they started dating in school.

"What are your plans for tonight?" she asked.

"I'm gonna go to Justin's," he answered through bites of the apple. "He has a new guitar I want to check out."

"Do you have any homework?"

"Nope, teachers have a professional development day tomorrow, so we're free,"

"Well, make sure you're in before your curfew whether there's school or not, you need to keep to a routine."

"Okay," he answered as he went to his room and grabbed some sheets of music.

"Wait, aren't you having some dinner?" she asked, as he slipped into his runners and headed to the door.

"Nah, Justin always has snacks. I'll grab something at his house," he said.

Well fine then, she thought to herself. Luke and I will just have more for ourselves! He was due to arrive shortly, and she removed all but two plates from the kitchen table. Opening a bottle of wine, she poured herself a glass. If she was honest, she was just as glad the boys weren't going to be here tonight. It was two days after their evening at his place, and she had only talked to Luke on the phone but had not seen him face to face. She preferred for them to be alone when that happened.

It was so awkward to be dating as a woman with kids who were almost grown. She wasn't always sure how to act, and the latest turn in their relationship left her wondering if things would be a bit uncomfortable between them.

She shouldn't have worried. When she answered Luke's knock, he met her with a kiss and a bouquet in his hands.

"Those are gorgeous!" she exclaimed. "You didn't have to!"

"Of course, I didn't," he said. "But I wanted to."

She walked into the kitchen to search out a vase for the arrangement. Luke followed her in and exclaimed.

"Wow, it smells great in here!"

"Thanks! I had a bit of a creative streak, and felt like cooking today," she said with a smile. "Sit down and prepare to be impressed!"

After dinner, they went outside for a walk.

"That was a great meal, but I'm stuffed," Luke said. "This walk will do us good."

"It would be great to go for a run, but I don't think that's a good idea after that meal!" she joked.

They walked in companionable silence for a while, heading toward the nearest park and strolling down the pathways.

"This is nice," Luke observed with a small sigh. "It's a beautiful evening."

"Yes, it is," she was content just to be holding his hand. They wandered until the mosquitos became unbearable, and then they headed back to her house. She was pleased that they were just as comfortable with each other as ever. She wasn't sure what she had expected, but this was her first real adult relationship that included sex. She had been so young with her first husband that it seemed like a lifetime ago; a lifetime that had a totally different set of rules.

When they returned to her house, she assumed he would be going home, as it was getting late and he began his shifts very early.

"No, I think I'll come in for a while," he said. "The night is young."

They chose the floor in the living room as the perfect place to snuggle. He was leaning over her and began to kiss her. It was not his usual passionate kiss but rather gentle, light ones. Then he pulled himself away and sat up beside her.

"So, remember when I asked you if you would marry me if I asked you?"

"Yes, I certainly do," she answered.

"Well, if I asked you will you marry me?"

"I told you, I don't answer questions that haven't been asked," Olivia said with a laugh.

"You don't understand. Will you marry me?" he insisted.

It took Olivia a moment to realize he wasn't fooling around. She sat for a moment and just stared at him. She had known he was way ahead of her on the marriage road, and she had known this was a possibility, but she still couldn't quite believe that after four months of dating he was proposing to her.

"Ummm, I... Ummm," she stammered.

"Remember what I said, you better be ready to answer because I'll only ask once!"

"Ummm, ah... yes, I mean YES!" Olivia squealed as Luke slipped a ring on her finger.

She threw her arms around his neck, laughing almost hysterically. Luke held her tight, and wrapped his strong arms around her. The sense of love and acceptance she felt from him flowed through her anew.

"Have you even checked out the ring yet?" he asked eventually, laughing.

She glanced down at her hand for the first time and let out a gasp. It was a large, sparkling solitaire diamond.

"Wow, you did good, Luke!" she gasped.

"So that means you like it?" Luke joked.

"I do, I really like it," she smiled, as she sat back on the rug.

"I decided on platinum," he explained. "There is no way I want to take a chance that my ring would give you a rash."

"You made a good call, it's just perfect," she exclaimed. "Thank you!"

"No, thank YOU! I know you would prefer to wait, but I wanted to get my ring on your finger as soon as possible," he said with a smile. "We don't have to get married right away."

"Yes, we need to still take some time," she agreed. "We can spend the next few months getting to know each other more and then get married."

She couldn't believe it. If someone had told her a couple of years ago that this day would come, she would have thought she was daydreaming. The man of her dreams, who made her feel so wanted, sexy, and loved, actually wanted her for his wife. He was everything she could have imagined.

To hell with it being too soon, to hell with playing it safe and keeping her head clear. She was so madly, passionately, head over heels in love with this man, there was no way she wasn't going to throw caution to the wind.

Chapter Thirty

She

She was going through papers that had accumulated over the past year or so, hoping to distract herself by taking on a project she had been avoiding for months. Things had been going well between her and her husband, but she still felt like she was walking on eggshells. She didn't want to bring up the topic of them moving because, if she were honest with herself, she would have to admit she had no interest in giving up her job and moving across the country. Some part of her hoped if she just left it alone that the idea would lose its appeal for him. He had talked about moving home before, although not with this much conviction and excitement. It had always been something he was hoping to do someday.

She had separated the papers into three piles, one for shredding and disposal, one for filing, and one she needed to act on, somehow. She was smiling to herself because the piles seemed to represent the different issues in her life when she came across a paper that gave her pause. She sat back in her chair and frowned as she read the piece of paper. It was a single sheet with a business card stapled to it on the upper right-hand side. It appeared to be post-operative instructions on the proper treatment after a vasectomy. The business card was for a local doctor, although one she had never heard of, or used, before. Why on earth would this be mixed up in their household papers? Her mouth had become dry, and she had a queasy feeling in the pit of her stomach. This must belong to her husband, but that didn't make any sense! She had a hysterectomy several years before they married. Why would he have information on getting a vasectomy? She reassured herself that there must be a perfectly acceptable reason for it, although even if there was, why had she not heard about this before now? Hell, she hadn't even noticed him limping around, either. The fact that he hadn't come looking for sympathy after something like that seemed a further suggestion that he had deliberately hidden this from her. How could she not consider his intentions suspicious in this case?

She would deal with this later when she could calmly ask her husband about it. She carefully set the paper to the side and continued working on the stack before her.

Later that evening, she was setting dinner down in front of him when the phone rang. He quickly grabbed it and walked into the other room. She could hear him talking, but couldn't make out the words. Not that she was trying to eavesdrop she reassured herself, she was just curious.

"Who were you talking to?" she asked him, a few minutes later when he walked back into the kitchen.

"Just someone from work," he answered. "This smells wonderful!"

Deliberately, she pushed the uneasy feeling she had about confronting him aside. She needed to get a few things out in the open and ask for some explanations. She couldn't keep functioning with an ever-growing list of topics she couldn't talk to him about. It was now or never.

"So, I finally got some of the paperwork cleared out today," she started.

"Oh good, if we're moving, we'll need to make sure we've gone through everything, and only kept what we really need," he commented.

"When I was going through the papers, I came across some information on post-operative care after a vasectomy," she began. "Do you know why we would have that?"

"Oh, that's months old, you can throw it out," he said, as he dug into his dinner.

"But why was it here in the first place?" she pressed.

"It was probably from months ago when I had my vasectomy," he answered.

She sat there, stunned. So, the paperwork was his. He had gone and had a vasectomy without talking to her. Why would he do this when there was no chance of her getting pregnant anyway?

"You had a vasectomy?" she asked, incredulous.

"Yes, a few months ago," he responded.

"But," she shook her head in confusion. "Why would you have a vasectomy?"

"We weren't getting along very well, and it's something I always assumed I'd do anyway," he explained. "Before we got married, I mean, I always assumed I would get a vasectomy because I've never wanted kids."

"But I don't understand," she pursued. "I get that you don't want to have any kids, but it isn't possible anyway with my hysterectomy."

"I know, but as I said, we weren't getting along," he answered calmly, as though that explained everything.

She sat back in her chair, her brow furrowed in confusion.

"What does that have to do with anything?" she asked. "What does it matter if we were getting along or not?"

"I don't know, why are you making such a big deal about this?" he said. "It isn't as though we had planned on having any kids, what difference does it make?"

"That's not the point," she said.

"Then what is the point?" he asked quietly, as though daring her to push the issue.

"Why did you have an unnecessary medical procedure and not even tell me about it?" she asked, determined to get to the bottom of it.

"I told you," he said, with a patient sigh. "I always assumed I would get a vasectomy and when we weren't getting along, it seemed like I might as well get it done."

They sat at the table, staring at each other. She was perplexed and upset; he was becoming exasperated at her apparent inability to understand what he was telling her. Finally, she asked the question that had been circling in her mind ever since she'd found the paperwork.

"Did you intend to leave me?" she asked. "When things were rough, did you get a vasectomy because you were planning on leaving?"

"I wouldn't say I was planning on it, but yes, the thought that we wouldn't last went through my head," he admitted. "Don't tell me it didn't cross your mind?"

"Yes, I was worried," she admitted. "But I still didn't go and secretly have an unnecessary medical procedure because of it."

"It wasn't secretly," he explained. "I just didn't mention it because we weren't talking much."

He made it sound so reasonable, as though it was the most natural and obvious thing to do when you are going through a rough time in your marriage. But it left an uneasy feeling in the pit of her stomach. There was nothing to say to him, as he had an easy answer for everything, but she was left with a sick queasiness that just wouldn't be calmed.

Was she ever going to feel settled and content in her marriage? Even when he was communicating, and they were spending time together, things kept coming up that blindsided her peace. Whatever happened to the calm life she had anticipated when they married?

Chapter Thirty-One

Olivia

Her boys had taken the news of their engagement in stride. In fact, Olivia wasn't all that sure she knew what to think of their reaction.

"Oh, okay," Jonathon said. "Congrats."

"Yeah, congrats," Adam echoed.

"Does this mean we're going to have to move?" Adam asked.

"Um, I don't know for sure," Olivia replied. "We haven't gotten that far in the planning."

And they were off to their rooms. She wasn't sure what she'd expected from them, but this seemed to be almost anti-climactic. Surely the news of their mother getting married should have elicited more of a reaction?

Oh well. It was hard enough to know what teens were thinking, never mind male teens, she decided. She was sure though, that she would receive a more excited response from her friends, and she couldn't wait to tell Terri and April. Her friends had been with her on this single's journey for years, and they would appreciate how excited she was to be engaged to the man of her dreams.

"Wow, that was quick!" Terri responded. "Are you sure you aren't moving too fast?"

It wasn't quite the response she had hoped for, and she sat there for a moment, unsure what to say.

"I mean, I'm happy for you and everything," Terri continued. "It's just very sudden."

"I know, but it isn't like we're going to run off and get married tomorrow," Olivia explained. "We're not in a rush to hit the church just yet."

"Then why the rush to get engaged?"

Olivia wasn't quite sure how to make her understand that Luke was anxious to 'get his ring on her' and that was really the only reason. It didn't change anything, they still wanted to spend time getting to know each other better. His reasoning had seemed sound last night, in the heat of the moment. When she thought of telling her friend the reason, it sounded almost possessive, like he couldn't wait to brand her.

"Can you just be happy for me Terri?" she asked.

"Yes, of course, I am!" Terri suddenly seemed to realize she was not giving her friend the reaction she wanted. "Now let me see the ring!"

The awkward start to the conversation soon passed, and before long, April joined them.

"Sheesh, this place just keeps getting busier and busier, doesn't it?" April said as she pulled up a chair. "Good thing for them that they have the best Thai in the city, or I would suggest we find a new place to hang out!"

Terri looked at April with a smirk on her face that said, "I know something you don't!" and she squirmed in her chair in anticipation. She seemed intent on making it up to Olivia for her less than enthusiastic first reaction to her news.

"What's going on?" April asked, looking from one of her friends to the other.

"Oh, nothing much," Olivia said as she waved her left hand around the table.

"What are you doing Olivia?" April asked, confused as she watched her friend make odd hand gestures.

"Oh my God!" she squealed when her eye caught sight of Olivia's ring. "Will you look at that rock!"

They laughed and giggled as they sipped their wine and nibbled on spring rolls. Her friends peppered her with questions, for many of which she didn't have an answer. She didn't know when they were going to actually get married, she didn't know where they would live, it was all very new, and they were not in a rush.

"Of course, you aren't in a rush," April exclaimed. "Only four months of dating and you land a rock the size of Gibraltar."

"It's beautiful, isn't it?" Olivia smiled as she moved her hand side to side, causing the light to grab the facets of the diamond and sparkle.

"Yes, it definitely is," Terri agreed, as she grabbed Olivia's hand to take a closer look. "What does his family think of this?"

"I'm not sure yet, he was going to call them tonight and let them know,"

"He isn't very close to his family, is he?" April asked. "What about close friends? Does he have any around here?"

"He has friends," Olivia answered, feeling defensive for reasons she couldn't quite put her finger on. "But friends aren't as important to men as they are to women."

She didn't want to try and explain to them how most of his friends had been at work, but lately, he seemed to have had a falling out with them.

"Well, here's to Olivia and Luke," Terri cheered as she raised her wine glass. "May you be happy for many, many years to come!"

"Here, here," they chimed as they clinked glasses and took a sip.

They spent another hour or so talking about wedding possibilities; a destination wedding was out because Olivia wanted her family there and she knew they couldn't afford to take off to parts unknown. A traditional wedding in a church with all the pomp and circumstance seemed a bit overblown considering she had been married before.

"I'm not thinking I can pull off a white frilly ballgown concoction," Olivia laughed.

"What does Luke think?" April asked. "This will be his first wedding, maybe he wants the big to-do."

"Hmm," The truth was she had no idea what he was thinking of for a wedding. He seemed so intent on them becoming engaged that they had never discussed what would happen afterward.

"Well, there's lots of time for all the planning and details," Terri said, coming to Olivia's rescue whether she realized it or not.

"To happily ever after!" April offered up a toast.

"Here, here!" they all responded, clinking wine glasses once more.

Chapter Thirty-Two

She

She was walking through her days in a cloud. Even at work, her colleagues had to repeat things to her because she had somehow zoned out and missed relevant information. Since she had confronted her husband about the vasectomy, she just wasn't sure what to think. He seemed confused as to why it was an issue for her, and she was beginning to think she might be a bit unhinged. But no, his behavior lately had been odd, even if he was now talking to her and spending time with her. She'd thought the issue was just his moodiness and the time spent away from her, but now she wasn't so certain.

The incidents were piling up, and she didn't like what they were telling her: He spent a lot of time away from home. He was a man with a strong sexual appetite, but when they were having trouble, he hadn't come near her for weeks. He'd had a vasectomy even though she was sterile. A vasectomy! A woman at work was talking to him about female genital piercings and their effect on the quality of sex.

Could he have been having an affair? It was something she had tried not to look at too closely before. She wasn't stupid, she knew the signs, but she hadn't wanted to consider it might be a possibility. Was that why he wanted to move away? To make a clean and fresh start? And if that was the case, was it worth bringing into the open now? He seemed committed to working on their marriage. What good would it do to bring up the past?

These were the thoughts that she chased around in her mind hour after hour. But she came to no easy solution or way to go forward. It was, quite simply, crazy-making thoughts she mused. But then again, his had been crazy-making behavior.

For now, she decided to just leave things. While she definitely didn't want to move, and she certainly didn't want to subject herself to a piercing, she would continue to put the past behind them and not let it ruin their future.

Pulling up on the driveway, she took her briefcase from the backseat and walked into the house. It was uncharacteristically quiet. It looked as though her husband was late from work. She picked up her phone and fired him off a text, asking him if he was up for going for a run before supper. It had been a while since they had gone together, but there was a time when they both looked forward to going for a run and touching base with each other at the same time.

She opened the freezer door and pulled out a frozen lasagna. She didn't feel like preparing dinner tonight, so this would have to do. Then she went upstairs to change into her running clothes before lying down on the bed and closing her eyes for a few minutes. It had been a long time since she'd woken up early for work this morning. A few seconds of rest would do her good.

Chapter Thirty-Three

Olivia

Two nights after his proposal, they were out for a run on the trails by his house. They were jogging in companionable silence, listening to the birds chirping and the sound of someone mowing a lawn in the distance.

"Where will we live?" she asked.

"What? When?" he answered. "When we get married?"

"Yes, when I told the boys, they asked if they would have to change schools and I didn't know what to say to them," she explained.

"I don't know, what do you think?" he responded.

"I can't see you fitting in my house," she answered with a smile. "But for that matter, I can't see the boys fitting into yours."

"Okay, so we buy a different one that will fit us all," he agreed.

"Could we buy a house that's in the school zone the boys are in now, so they don't have to move?" she pressed.

"I don't see why not," he replied.

"Okay, good."

She wasn't sure why, but it felt like an odd conversation. There was an undertone that she couldn't quite put her finger on. She felt almost embarrassed or inappropriate talking about their future. She wasn't sure why, after all, he had done nothing but talk about their future since they started dating.

"I was thinking that maybe we could get married in about 8 months," she pursued the line of conversation. "That way we will have known each other for a year in total."

"Yeah, that sounds good, whatever you want," he murmured.

They ran some more, around bends in the trail that would take them to the next set of park benches, and then up short hills that tested their leg strength. Olivia was beginning to pant more than usual as she tried to keep up to Luke's stride. Luke seemed almost unaware that he was pulling ahead of her inch by inch.

She was struggling to keep up with him and also struggling with her emotions. She couldn't understand why she felt uneasy, but he seemed so distant. Finally, when they reached the crest of one of the last hills, she spoke up.

"Okay, you have to slow down, I can't keep up," she said, gasping as she bent over with her hands on her knees.

"Oh shit, I'm sorry," he stopped automatically and came back for her. "I didn't realize I was going that fast."

They stood there for a few moments while she gained her breath back before they resumed their usual pace.

"Have you had a chance to call your mom yet," she asked him.

"Yeah, I did last night," he answered.

"And?" she probed.

"She said "congratulations,"

"Oh, okay, it doesn't sound like she was overly excited?"

"Well, you know," he responded, as though she should understand exactly what he meant.

"No, I'm sorry, I don't know," she asked curiously.

"I've been engaged before, and so she's happy, but she isn't the excitable kind of mother," he explained calmly.

"You've been engaged before?" she stopped straight in her tracks.

"Yeah, I thought I told you," he said as though it must have slipped his mind.

"No, I don't think so," she said. "I think I would have remembered that. Who were you engaged to?"

"I told you about my psycho ex?" he asked. "It was her, we were engaged for the last couple years we were together."

"Oh. Why didn't you get married?" she asked.

"At first there seemed no real rush, and then, as I said, she went psycho," he explained. "Do you know if there are any steaks in the house for a barbeque?"

Olivia was not sure how to take this revelation he had so casually made to her. He obviously didn't think it was a huge deal, but it changed how she viewed them in some small way. She wasn't sure exactly how, but she felt like something had changed. Maybe because the story she had been telling herself about them, and the story he played into was that she was the first real big love of his life. That she was extra special and was the one who was finally able to earn his heart. To find out that he had been engaged before called that all into question.

They made the remaining portion of the run in silence and soon found themselves back where they started, at his house.

"Some old friends of mine from back home are in town today and are coming over, and I'm going to do up some steaks," he announced as they were stretching. "Can you come by and say hi?"

"Umm, sure," Olivia replied, unsure if she was being invited to the barbeque or to just stop by later. "What time?"

"Oh, any time after about 7:30," he told her.

"I'll be here with bells on!" she answered lightheartedly, in an attempt to dispel the tension she felt.

"Okay hon," he leaned forward to give her a quick peck on the lips. "I'll see you later."

He left her standing on the driveway, uncertain of what had just happened. He was usually so insistent that they do everything together and be around each other as much as possible. This was the man who'd insisted on showing up when she'd had that awful cold, who checked in on her when she was out with friends without him. Now he was having a barbeque and casually asking her over later, as though she were an after-thought.

She jumped in her car and went back to her house, trying to reason things through as she drove. There was absolutely nothing wrong with him having friends over without her; why was she making such a big deal about it? He had been in a quiet mood today, that was all. She couldn't expect him to be 'up' all the time. And what did it matter if he had been engaged before? She was engaged to him now, and they were planning their future together, that is all that mattered. It didn't matter that they hadn't made any concrete plans; that was at her insistence. But no matter how much she reasoned with herself she couldn't get rid of a vague sense of uneasiness that was nestled deep inside her.

That evening, she pulled up to his house and walked up the front steps. She could hear laughing in the backyard, so she changed directions and went to the back of the house.

Luke was sitting on a chair around the bonfire, and at first, she didn't see the bottle of beer in his hand. Only as she approached and placed her hand on the back of his neck did she notice. She bent down and placed a kiss on his forehead.

"Oh, hi hon!" he exclaimed. "These are my friends from way back."

He introduced her to the three friends who were in town for work, and she smiled and said hello to everyone. She then opened up a lawn chair and sat down next to Luke. She wasn't included in the reminiscing, but she understood that they had a shared past that she knew nothing about. Maybe this would be a good time to learn more about him.

"Remember when we were out at Jordie's house, and he set fire to his garbage," Carl, Luke's friend said. "And he was so drunk he didn't realize we were in the house?"

The group roared with shared memories, and Olivia smiled indulgently.

"I don't know, that still doesn't beat the time at Debbie's house," Murray, Luke's light-haired friend said. "Remember when she and Luke were in the back making out and…"

"I think we can hold off on that story," Larry, the final friend of Luke's interjected.

"Oh, I don't know, this sounds kind of interesting," Olivia laughed.

"No, I think we can move on," Luke said.

They all started to laugh at Luke's obvious discomfort but Olivia found it endearing. It was sweet that he wanted to protect her. They both had a past, and that was okay with her.

"Okay, fine," Murray said. "But can we talk about the time we tried to sell blotters to that guy who ended up being a cop?"

They all laughed except Luke, who just smiled and looked uncomfortable. Olivia looked a bit confused. She wasn't sure what a blotter was, but if selling it to the police was a bad thing, then she wasn't sure she wanted to know more. Or did she?

Afterward, Luke walked her back to her car. He wasn't completely steady on his feet, and she was surprised to realize that not only had he decided to drink but he appeared to have had quite a bit.

"Thanks for coming over," he leaned her up against her car. "The guys liked you."

"Good," Olivia responded. "Luke, what's a blotter?"

"Ooooh, nothing for you to worry about," he answered as he closed his eyes and rested his forehead on her shoulder.

"I'm not worried, I'm curious," she insisted. "you can either tell me yourself, or I'll look it up online."

"Okay, Okay," he said reluctantly. "Blotters are square pieces of paper that have acid on them."

"You tried to sell acid to cops?" Olivia asked, trying to wrap her head around what she was hearing.

"It was a long time ago. I haven't done that kind of drug for years," he reassured her.

"But if you were selling it, you weren't just doing it," she pointed out.

"Yes, but if you're going to afford to do it, you need to sell it," he explained patiently.

"Of course," she shook her head bemusedly, as though it was the most logical explanation in the world. "Well, I best get going now."

She opened the driver's side door and slid into her seat.

"Take care and drive safely," he said as he shut her door.

She drove home in a bit of a daze, stunned and unsure of what to think about this new insight into her husband-to-be.

Chapter Thirty-Four

She

She awoke with a start. The room had darkened considerably, and she could just make out the shapes of the furniture around her. She had no idea what time it was or even how long she had been sleeping. She got up quickly, patting her hair and rubbing the sleep out of her eyes while she walked to the dining room.

The rest of the house was just as dark as her bedroom and somehow seemed twice as quiet. She glanced at the digital clock on her oven and discovered it was already 9:30 in the evening. She had slept for hours! She quickly picked up her phone to find out what had happened to her husband. He had probably answered her text, and when she didn't reply, he had assumed she wasn't interested. Or worse yet, that she was upset at him and ignoring him on purpose.

When she punched in her passcode, she was shocked to see there were no messages. He had never replied to her inquiry regarding going for a run. And he wasn't home, hours after his work would have been done. Had something happened to him? Was he okay? She quickly punched his name in her contact list and heard the phone ring. It rang several times before being picked up by his voice mail. She left a message, telling him she was worried about him and could he please phone to let her know what was going on.

Her heart was pounding. At one time he had done things like this regularly, but not now. Now they were in a good place, and he was happy to be at home. Wasn't he? But what could have happened to keep him away from home and not answering her phone calls or texts?

She dialed his number again. Again, it rang several times, but only his voice mail responded. Now she was becoming anxious. She didn't have any of the phone numbers of his friends from work, and he didn't have any other friends aside from them. How should she even begin to find out if something was dreadfully wrong?

She sat down at her computer and started googling hospital emergency numbers and placing calls. With each phone call, she learned he had not been admitted. At least not under his name. But what if something had happened and for some reason, he had no ID on him? She tried not to think about that, and she sighed a breath of relief with each negative response she received.

Having gone through all the hospitals in town, she sat on the couch, head resting on the back of it, eyes closed. She didn't know what else to do but wait. It was almost eleven now and she had exhausted all ideas. The only thing left to do was to go out looking for him, but that made no sense whatsoever. What if he returned and she was gone? No, if she left, she would just spend the whole time wondering if he had come home while she was gone.

She was pacing up and down her living room an hour later when she heard a key in the front door lock. She stopped, her heart picking up pace as she watched him walk through the door.

"Oh, thank God you're okay," she said, as she flung herself towards him, wrapped her arms around him and began to sob uncontrollably.

"What on earth is wrong?" he asked, surprised.

She took a few minutes to collect herself as it sunk in that he was, in fact, alive and well but that he didn't seem to realize how worried she had been.

"You didn't answer my text," she sputtered. "I phoned you and no answer."

"You know I get caught up sometimes and don't pay attention to my phone. It must have been turned on silent. "

"But it's been hours!" she protested. "You should have been home hours ago -I thought you were in an accident or something."

"Well, I wasn't," he stated with annoyance. "There is no need to make a federal case out of me taking a few hours to myself."

She stood stock-still in the hallway as he brushed past her and into the kitchen. He opened the fridge door and pulled out a beer. Chugging it back, he walked towards the living room and turned the tv on to the sports channel.

What had happened, she wondered. Were they back to this now? She thought when things were on track that they had put this behind them. But he seemed to think it was perfectly reasonable to come and go as he pleased, not caring if she was worried. Well, she wasn't going to let that happen without a fight.

Walking into the living room, she picked up the remote and snapped off the tv.

"We need to talk about this," she stated firmly. "I have had the fright of my life, and you don't seem to even care."

"What am I supposed to do?" he responded belligerently. "I can't control how worried and freaked out you get over little things."

"Little things? You disappear for an entire evening with no word of where you are, not answering texts or phone calls from your wife and that is a little thing?" she asked incredulously.

"So that's the kind of marriage you want, is it?" he asked, his voice rising.

"What do you mean? What kind of marriage?" she asked.

"The kind where I'm at your beck and call," he replied with a snarl. "You want to know where I'm every second of the day and night."

"What?" she asked, amazed. "All I'm asking from you is that you show me some respect and some common courtesy!"

"No, all you're asking from me is that you own me!" he yelled. "You knew I wasn't a stay at home kind of guy when you married me. You knew I didn't want a cozy little home with a measly little wife and matching his and her towels, so why are you complaining now?"

She stepped back as if slapped. So, this is what it was really about. They were finally getting to the root of the problem. He felt trapped and hadn't wanted to marry her in the first place.

She'd thought they had put that all behind them, but apparently it was still there, bubbling up when she least expected it, long after she thought it was tucked away safely in the past.

Chapter Thirty-Five

Olivia

Holy crap on a cracker!" Wanda screamed when she saw Olivia's ring. "Looks like someone had to sell the farm to buy that puppy!"

Olivia laughed at the overblown reaction of her colleague. She had come in this morning and said nothing about her engagement. She was wondering how long it would take someone to notice her ring. It hadn't taken the always perceptive Wanda long to pick up on things.

"It is nice, isn't it?' Olivia smiled. "He did good!"

"He sure did, hon," Wanda agreed. "You're a lucky lady."

"I know," Olivia agreed, with a pleased smile. It was nice to talk to people who were happy for her, no questions asked.

"So, when is the big day?" Wanda asked.

"We haven't set a date, but it will probably not be for months," Olivia responded. "We have only known each other for four months so we figure it wouldn't hurt to not rush the wedding."

"Smart thinking," Wanda agreed. "No point hurrying into anything."

They had a conversation about the odd reaction her sons had to her engagement news, and Wanda expressed her opinion that boys are just weird, no matter what age they happened to be.

"Do you have any ideas for the honeymoon," Wanda asked.

"I haven't given it any thought at all actually," Olivia answered honestly.

"That's the best part of wedding planning," Wanda insisted. "Before you get into all the nit-picky stuff like who sits next to who at the reception, or what kind of favors to put at the plates, do the fun stuff, like decide on your honeymoon."

"That's probably a good idea," she laughed. "Do you have any suggestions?"

"As a matter of fact," Wanda said. "I've always thought Greece would be an amazing honeymoon."

They went through the pros and cons of various honeymoon destination spots, the most significant sticking point seeming to be that Olivia had traveled to many of those places on her own already. She wasn't interested in being a tour guide for her new husband but would prefer it if they discovered a new place together.

"Thanks for all the suggestions," Olivia said at the end of the conversation. "I'll chat with Luke and see if he has any ideas."

On her way home from work, she stopped by a travel agent and picked up many books and brochures. While planning an actual wedding seemed very daunting, maybe they should start with something easy, like choosing a honeymoon spot. The very idea of being Luke's wife and taking off to some exotic destination caused a thrill to course through Olivia. She could barely believe this was actually happening!

At home, she laid the pile of material from the travel agent on the kitchen table and started heating some leftovers for dinner. She checked her phone to see if Luke was trying to contact her, but there were no texts or missed calls. He usually contacted her shortly after work, and they made their plans for the evening.

She still hadn't heard from him at 6:30 when she had finished her dinner. It wasn't like him not to contact her, but she reassured herself that there was no way she could expect him to continue with the steady stream of sweet electronic cards, flowers, texts, and phone calls forever. They had stepped from courtship to planning a wedding, and things were bound to change a bit.

She picked up her phone and dialed his number. He answered on the third ring, and she could tell by the reception that he was on his Bluetooth and driving.

"Hi, you!" she greeted him.

"Hi, you too!" he replied.

"What are you up to tonight?" she asked.

"I'm heading to a friend's house for dinner."

"A friend from work?" she inquired, as she didn't know of any other friends that were on a close enough basis for dinner plans.

"No, just a friend," he answered noncommittally.

"Oh, okay," she said, unsure whether she should ask more questions or just let it go.

"What are you doing?" he asked.

"I was going through some brochures I picked up," Olivia told him. "They're from a travel agent and are from places I thought might be interesting for a honeymoon."

"That sounds like fun, you'll have to show them to me soon," he agreed.

"Yes, it will be fun," she agreed. "Have you thought at all about where you might want to go?"

"Honestly, I've never given it any thought," he responded.

"Okay, well then we can look at them and go from there," she said.

There was awkward silence as they both sat on the phone. Olivia wanted badly to ask him where he was going tonight, but she felt ridiculous pushing any further. She wasn't the jealous type of person, and she certainly liked her independence, but for some reason, this was bothering her. He had spent four months pursuing her with cards, texts, phone calls, gifts, and non-stop attention, but the last couple of times they'd talked or were together, he seemed to have put up some kind of wall; but she couldn't quite put her finger on what it was all about.

"Okay, well, I'll let you go," she said. "Will I hear from you tonight?"

"That depends on how long I visit," he responded. "Let's say not and if we do it's a bonus?"

"Yeah, that sounds fine," she answered, although she knew she would miss his goodnight phone call. She had gotten used to being talked to sleep most nights and hearing his deep, husky voice in her ear. Oh well, in a few months she would be able to listen to that voice beside her every night she reassured herself.

Hanging up the phone, she looked down at the honeymoon brochures and once again thought of how nice it would be to jet off to some remote beach, sip exotic drinks and make love under the undulating ceiling fan in an exotic hut somewhere.

Determined not to let doubts creep in and dampen her happiness, she decided to use the spare evening to clean out her fridge and tidy up the house. It would also be an excellent opportunity to spend some time with her boys. Who knew, maybe she would get lucky and convince them to help her so she could do both at once!

Chapter Thirty-Six

She

She had decided to take a few days off work and go to the mountains. She needed some time to evaluate her life and decide what she was going to do. After their fight, she knew their problems ran much deeper than she had thought. So deep, in fact, she was beginning to think that their marriage wasn't salvageable.

Her husband hadn't put up any resistance or concern about her leaving for a few days. He seemed almost oblivious to her. He was back to coming and going without telling her where he was, or when he would be home. Some nights he came home at two am and crawled in the bed next to her. She laid there and pretended to be asleep. She just didn't want to deal with him.

The concerns she'd had before about what he was doing seemed naively simplistic now, as he was almost openly flaunting the fact that he had a life that she knew nothing about. Some nights when he came home, he smelled of smoke, alcohol, and perfume. When he was home, he would be on his phone, texting to someone for hours. There were times now when the phone rang, that he would look over at her, pick up his phone, and move to a different room, as though challenging her to question him.

The obvious disintegration of her marriage left her with an odd mix of despair and relief. She couldn't believe it had come to this; living in different worlds and antagonistic towards each other. But at the same time, she felt a sense of relief to realize that she wasn't crazy. She hadn't been imagining what had been happening between them, no matter how much he'd denied it at the time.

The question now was, was she finally ready to do something about it?

Chapter Thirty-Seven

Olivia

A few weeks went by, and Olivia and Luke concentrated on spending more time with her boys. They'd both decided Jonathon and Adam did not know him well enough, and it was vital if they were going to be married, that everyone was comfortable with it. It wasn't always easy as the boys often had other ideas and their plans rarely included hanging out with the old folks.

It was on one of the nights that the boys had left for a friend's house that Olivia decided it was time to make some decisions.

"Okay, you were in a big rush to get engaged," she started. "Now let's set a date even if it is months away so I can start planning."

She pulled out her iPad and tapped on the calendar icon. She tapped her way through a few months until she came to February of the next year.

"I'm thinking of a winter wedding, a year from the month we met," she said.

"Sounds good," he replied, rubbing her leg absently as they sat on the couch.

"What about the 19th?" she asked.

"Yup, works for me," he responded.

"Why do I get the feeling I could say I want to be married on Groundhog Day and you would say it works for you?" she asked, laughing.

"Because it doesn't matter to me," he told her. "I would be just as happy to grab a flight to Las Vegas and tie the knot this weekend."

"That's sweet, but there is no way I'm going to get married without my family present," she said.

"Yeah, I know."

"Do you care where we get married?" she asked. "We should probably decide and find a place. It is early, but places get booked up fast."

"Seriously, it doesn't matter at all to me," he said, hooking his hand around her thigh and pulling her closer to him. "Why don't you put that stuff away and come show me some attention."

She laughed as he pulled her down onto the rug, spread her legs and rested himself on his elbows, perching over her. He began to kiss her passionately, and she melted into his arms. Whenever she wondered if he was maybe not into planning their wedding, he could always reassure her this way that he was still interested in her. His hand strayed to her mid-drift, and he caressed her side as his other hand moved down and cupped her buttocks, drawing her to him.

Damn it, she thought. He had a way of distracting her by making her turn weak in the knees. They hadn't slept together again since their first night and she was amazed at their restraint. Although they had already had sex, she didn't want it to be the focus of their relationship, and she would like their honeymoon to be a time of abandon and exploration, not just the same old, same old. It might be an old-fashioned way to think, but she wanted to hold off a bit and make things extra special for them.

"Luke, Luke!" she said as she pulled away from him. His hardness was still pressed against her leg, and she was having a hard time staying focused.

"Stop, we're supposed to be planning our wedding!" she insisted. Her words were hampered though, by her giggle as he nestled his lips at her ear and began nibbling.

"Yup, lets plan," he said, but his actions showed otherwise. He had moved his knee between hers, parting them, so he and his hardness rested between her legs.

"Aaaargh!" she moaned. "What are you trying to do to me!"

"Do you really need to ask?" he teased.

She was soon lost in his kisses and her growing passion. The boys wouldn't be home for hours, she thought to herself, what would it matter if they spent the next few hours in her room? He would be gone before they were back.

"Come with me," she stood up and reached her hand down to him.

"Are you sure?" he asked, as though he hadn't spent the last several minutes trying to get her to this exact point.

She shook her head and moved backward, towards her bedroom. With a smile on her face, she beckoned him to follow her.

In her bedroom, she stripped down quickly and reached for him. He was already almost naked, and she pushed him down onto the bed.

"Lay there, do as I say, and don't say a word," she demanded.

"But-" he interjected.

"But nothing, hush!"

He chuckled under his breath, and she spread him out on her bed. Straddling him, she couldn't help but notice his huge erection. She smiled to herself as she started by kissing his fingers. Then she sucked them. After she was done with all his fingers and his hands, she moved down his arm, peppering him with kisses. When she was done with his arms, she began kissing his chest. Rolling his nipples between her teeth gently, she heard him moan, and she chuckled quietly.

She kissed his cheek and ran her tongue up and down his torso. Inching downwards, she began running her tongue along his hip bone. By this time he was starting to writhe in pleasure. She ran her tongue further down his leg, straddling it as she moved. She used her hands and nails to lightly scratch a trail behind her as she worked her way downward. Luke began arching his back and moaning louder with pleasure. She had awakened all his senses.

Eventually, she made it to his feet, and she drew each of her toes into her mouth and sucked gently on each one. Luke made a half moan half giggle sound, as though he wasn't sure whether he was turned on or if he was just being tickled.

Olivia couldn't get enough of this man - the smell of him, the taste of him sent shots of pleasure through her. If only they could stay like this forever.

Working her way back up his legs, she lingered near his thighs, teasing and tantalizing him, making him want more. Her tongue flicked, he strained, she retreated. The sense of power was intoxicating, and she was surprised by how much she was enjoying it.

She laid kisses around his groin, never hitting the spot he really wanted, but teasing and tempting him. He writhed on the bed, caught between pleasure and pain.

Finally, when she felt she had teased him enough, she took him in her mouth. He gasped as he felt her tongue close around him. She began moving up and down, sliding her tongue along the length of him. He reached out to place his hand on the back of her head, and she swatted him away.

"Uh! Uh! Uh!" she admonished him. "I told you, lay still and do as I say, nothing more."

His hand flopped back on the bed, and she continued sucking on him. Taking the full length of him into her mouth was almost impossible, but if she concentrated, she could almost make it happen. She just needed to relax the muscles in her throat and ease him in slowly. After a while, she lifted her head and proceeded to place kisses along his stomach and up to his face. She placed a leg on either side of him and slowly lowered herself onto him. As she took him inside of her, she felt as though nothing in the world could be more right. She felt herself stretch to accommodate him and soon she was using her legs to hold her entire weight as she eased up and down over him.

He threw back his head and made the same noises in his throat that he had their first night together. The very sight of him experiencing such pleasure was enough to take her over the edge. Her orgasm shot through her just as he came into her.

In the aftermath of their lovemaking, they laid exhausted on her bed, his arm flung over her stomach and her lying on her back, gasping for breath.

"Well, this beats planning a wedding, doesn't it?" he asked teasingly.

She laughed weakly in response. Laying there, spent and content, it was easy for all the things that had been nagging at her to disappear. Life with Luke felt so incredibly right.

Chapter Thirty-Eight

She

The mountains once again helped her regain some semblance of peace. The only place available on such short notice was a second-rate motel on the main street, but even that overlooked the majestic peaks. She had only to look out her motel window to take them in.

When she arrived, she was exhausted from her day and the hours-long drive. She bought a salad at a fast-food restaurant and brought it back to her room to eat while looking out the window. She went to bed shortly after but slept fitfully most of the night.

The next morning, she awoke early and packed up her hiking boots and bear spray. Stopping by Denny's, she picked up a bite to eat and read the morning paper. As she finished her cup of coffee, she looked around the restaurant. There were older couples, some families, and some young couples. She noticed that the older couples seemed more interested in the meal set before them than with each other. The families appeared to be having anything but a relaxing time, and she smiled at the memories they brought back. She recalled when the boys were young, and they'd decided to take them on holiday. There was always drama over where they ate when they woke up, and who got which bed. Somehow the family trips had always seemed like a better idea in the abstract than in reality.

The young couples looked entirely into each other -giggling over jokes only they would understand and exchanging knowing looks over their coffee cups.

She felt a streak of pain go through her, as the breakdown of her marriage had hit her anew. Was she destined to be alone forever? She remembered what it was like to be single and she didn't want to go there again. But there was no way she could stay in a marriage that made her feel so insignificant and rejected. It was as though any ounce of self-respect and self-esteem was being sucked from her, bit by bit. At some point, there would be nothing left.

As much as she hated to admit it, she was also embarrassed to have to tell her friends and family. It was one thing to be divorced once, but twice? Once you could blame on the situation or the other person, but twice? That meant you needed to start looking at yourself, she reasoned; either at how you handled relationships, or how you picked your partner. She knew deep down that those who knew her well wouldn't judge her, but she couldn't help feeling that somehow, she was defective in a fundamental way.

Chapter Thirty – Nine

Olivia

Olivia was doing up her running shoes, preparing to go for a run when her phone rang.

"Hi, Olivia," Luke greeted her.

"Hi, Hon," she responded.

"Look, I'm running a bit late right now, if you want to go ahead and do your run without me, I'll understand."

"How long will you be?" she asked.

"About an hour and a half," he answered. "I'm tied up here at work."

"I didn't know you had to work this weekend," she said. "How about I come to your place so we can go for a run as soon as you are home?"

"Sounds good, see you there at around one," he confirmed.

She thought it was a bit odd that he was working on a Saturday morning, but she was looking forward to having an extra hour or so to tidy up her house. Dating Luke had not been great for the cleanliness of her house, she noted.

An hour later, she was on the road to his house, a change of clothes and her running bag in the seat next to her. She pulled up on his driveway and picked up her bag. Grabbing the spare key from under the welcome mat, she let herself into the house.

Heading towards the bathroom, she noticed that he seemed to have purchased new scented candles that were perched on the pony wall between the kitchen and living room. Odd, she thought briefly, most men aren't into buying scented candles. She used the washroom and sat in the living room and waited for him to come home.

It was two hours after she last talked to him that he showed up. He walked to his room to change and she followed him into the bedroom. As he pulled his jeans off, she couldn't help but notice how absolutely perfectly his body was formed. His boxer briefs showed off his legs and the perfect roundness of his ass.

"What are you staring at?" he teased, breaking her out of her reverie.

"Nothing, just wondering when you'll finally be ready," she shot back. "I'll wait for you at the door."

She could hear him laughing as she walked down the hallway.

They began their run at a nice slow pace, warming their muscles up and easing into the exercise. By the middle of the run, they were going as fast as they knew was optimal to maintain a steady pace back to his house.

They didn't talk much on the run, except to point as they changed direction or to warn the other one that a bike was coming up behind them. Olivia felt it was a companionable silence, one that existed between two people who didn't need to fill in every moment of silence with chatter.

They made it back to his house in good time and were stretching when she asked him what his plans were for the evening.

"I don't know, probably hang around here, get some things done."

"Oh, okay," she said. "Are you planning to come to my place at all today?"

"Um, no, I don't think so," he responded, not meeting her eyes.

A feeling of unease passed over Olivia. She wasn't sure whether she should press him to find out if something was wrong, or if she should just leave it.

"Okay," she agreed. "Then I guess I'll see you tomorrow."

"Yeah, I'll let you know tomorrow if I'm coming over."

It was Saturday night, so she was a bit surprised he didn't plan to spend it with her and to make it sound like Sunday wasn't a given either caused her more than a little surprise.

"I don't understand," she said, a confused look on her face.

"I just," he seemed unsure how to express himself. "I just think I would, you know, like a bit of time to myself."

"Oh!" she exclaimed. "Well, of course, if you need a couple of days to yourself, all you need to do is say so."

"Well, it's not just that," he continued hesitantly. "It's just, I've been feeling a bit closed in lately."

"Closed in?" she asked.

"Yes, we rushed into this relationship so fast that I feel like I need to step back," he stated.

"Step back? What does that mean?" she asked.

"I just don't know if this is working for me," he admitted.

"Working for you?" she repeated.

"Yes, I mean, doesn't it seem like we spend an awful lot of time together? Don't you ever feel, you know, a bit suffocated?" he spilled out in a rush.

"Um.. well, yes we do," Olivia said, unable to fully comprehend what was happening. "But that's a pace you've pushed, right from the start."

"Yes, but now I just feel like it's too much too soon," he was speaking quietly, not meeting her eyes.

"So, let me get this straight," she said. "Are you not wanting to see me this weekend, or are you breaking off our engagement?"

He looked at the ground and shuffled his feet as he swayed back and forth.

"Luke," She pressed. "What's going on?"

"I don't know," he groaned. "I honestly don't know. I just don't feel right about things right now."

"You don't feel right about us?" she asked, a cold ball forming in the pit of her stomach.

He hesitated a few moments before answering.

"I'm sorry Olivia, I don't know what to say," he said.

"But I don't understand, YOU are the one who was pushing ME to get engaged," she exclaimed, confused and not quite able to process what she was hearing. "You're the one who wanted to spend all our time together; whenever I tried to pull back, you pushed forward."

"I know," he agreed. "I don't know what to say."

"Well, I think I'll go now," she told him, as a sense of surrealism crept over her. "When you figure out what it is you want to say, let me know!"

She grabbed her running bag and jumped in her car. Driving back to her house in a daze, she still couldn't understand what had just happened. They had been happy, he'd proposed, she'd accepted, and now? He wasn't feeling right about them? At what point did he not feel right?

By the time she reached her house, she was trembling and had trouble fitting the key in the lock. She felt like the ground beneath her was unsteady, and she walked carefully, placing one foot in front of the other slowly. She was floating, untethered in a black void, the air she was breathing seemed to have had much of the oxygen drained from it. Like an addict whose last hit had just worn off, her stomach clenched, and she began to shake. She realized she was standing in the middle of her living room and she looked around in a daze. What had just happened? She picked up her phone and punched in Terri's phone number.

"I don't know what to do!" she cried out as Terri answered her phone. The shock wore off at the sound of her friend's voice, and she collapsed onto the floor. Sobbing out the details, she managed to explain to Terri what had happened.

"What does he mean, he isn't feeling right?" Terri asked, confused as well.

"I don't know, he just kept saying he didn't feel right about things," Olivia responded. "I have no idea what he's talking about."

"Okay, take a deep breath," Terri told her. "I'm coming over."

"No, it's okay," Olivia resisted.

"No, I'm your friend, and you need a friend right now," Terri insisted.

Olivia reached for a tissue and wiped her face with it. She couldn't believe this was happening, she didn't even know WHAT was happening. She just knew that everything was crumbling down around her, and she didn't know why. What had she said? What had she done? She didn't think she had pushed the wedding planning too hard, she just wanted to set a date and a venue. And after all, he was the one who wanted to get married so badly.

A half-hour later, the tears were still flowing when she heard a knock on her front door. She opened it, and Terri stood there with a bottle of wine in one hand and a box of chocolates in the other.

Olivia broke out in a laugh that was soon stifled by a sob. Terri wrapped her arms around her and held her close, while at the same time managing to shut the front door behind her.

"Let's go sit down, hon," she said, leading Olivia back to the living room.

"I just don't understand what's happening," Olivia cried. "Everything was perfect, I thought. He's the man of my dreams and everything was going so well!"

"I know hon, I know," Terri reassured Olivia as she poured her a glass of wine.

"He's the one who was so gung-ho to get married, he's the one who was so insistent on pushing for an engagement," she sniffled. "Now he says he feels like he's suffocating? He's the one who set the pace of our relationship! This makes no sense!"

"I don't know what to say to you Olivia," Terri answered. "I don't know for sure if this is the case, but some guys just like the chase."

"What? What kind of twisted thing is that?" Olivia wailed. "He's a grown man for God's sake, he's too old to play games!"

"I know," Terri agreed. "I don't know, I'm just grasping at straws because I hate seeing you in so much pain."

"This just makes no sense," Olivia repeated. "Nothing changed except that he asked me to marry him."

Olivia sat in the living room and sobbed in her friend's arms. She had never felt so bereft and abandoned before. If only she could figure out what she had done, so she could fix it. What was so different between now and a month ago? Or even weeks ago? They talked for hours, coming to no understanding or conclusion about what happened.

"This is it," Olivia concluded.

"What do you mean?" Terri asked.

"I will never feel this way again," Olivia responded.

"You will find someone to love, I know you will," Terri reassured her.

"Maybe, but I will never feel as wanted and needed as he made me feel," Olivia explained, "I may love again, but I will never feel as loved."

By the time Olivia fell into bed, exhausted, she had moved through a wide array of emotions; from shock, disbelief, and sadness, to numb anger that he would discard her with so little explanation.

Chapter Forty

She

After she finished her breakfast, she jumped in her car and drove to the trailhead. She decided she wanted to do a particularly strenuous one, one that required her attention, so her mind wouldn't stray and obsess. The trail she chose had a series of steep inclines and several switchbacks. She pulled out her backpack, double-checked the water was there, along with some trail mix and her bear spray. Unscrewing her walking stick, she began walking.

It was several hours later before she finally took a break. She was more than halfway done, and it was time to gather her breath. She sat down on a log and pulled the water and the trail mix from her bag. The hike was just what she needed, she thought to herself, as she leaned back and closed her eyes against the bright sun. It wasn't that she was able to entirely forget her problems, but at least when she was here, she could set them to the side for a while and not focus on them quite so much.

She munched on the trail mix while watching a squirrel scamper among the intricate series of fallen trees and branches that covered the ground. Oh, to have that simple of a life, she mused. The thought came unbidden; oh well, they probably still had to worry about their nuts too! That ridiculous notion caused her to giggle so hard that she nearly choked on her trail mix! The more she realized how silly she must look, the more she laughed, and every time she thought about how her worrying about her husband cheating on her was similar to the squirrel worrying about its nuts, the more hysterical she became.

Chapter Forty-One

Olivia

She rolled over in her bed, and, trying not to wake up, she pressed her eyelids closed tightly. She didn't want to face the day. She had been up late last night crying and trying to figure out what had happened. Luckily, she had managed to pull herself together when the boys returned, at least long enough for them to get themselves settled into their rooms for the night.

She hadn't heard from Luke at all, not even a text. She wasn't sure what to do. She still had his ring, and she didn't know if he wanted it back, or what. She felt so alone and rejected.

She pulled herself out of bed when she realized there was no way her brain was going to turn off long enough for her to go back to sleep. Stepping under the shower, she let the water cascade over her. She turned the temperature up as hot as she could stand it, and let the stinging needles attack her skin. After about 15 minutes of this, she shut the taps off and stepped out, grabbing a towel and wiping herself dry.

She hadn't realized how much time she had spent thinking about Luke, spending time with him, or texting, or talking on the phone to him. Only now, when the day opened up wide and yawning before her did she truly feel his absence.

"Oh, God," she cried out as she sat down on the side of the tub. What was she going to do? She had never truly fallen head over heels in love before. How was she going to live without feeling that overwhelming sense of love and appreciation? She felt an ache in the middle of her very being for the return of that feeling. Would she ever experience it again?

After a few more minutes, she gathered herself up and, returning to her bedroom, and slipped into her clothes. She felt like she was walking around with a heavy burden on her shoulders and in her heart.

She was in a daze for the rest of the morning as she tidied up the house, ran the vacuum over her rug, and took something out for supper. Just then, her phone dinged, letting her know she had received a text. Her heart leaped. But it was just Terri, checking in to make sure she was okay.

"I'm fine," she texted her friend. "I'll survive one way or the other."

"Any word from him?"

"Nothing," she answered.

"What are you going to do today?" Terri asked.

"I don't know, mope and clean my house," she answered.

"That doesn't sound like much fun, want me to come over?"

"No, I'm not great company right now, and I just need to deal with things," she responded.

"Okay, well if you need anything, you call okay?"

"Absolutely."

After making herself some lunch, she sat down at the kitchen table to read the paper. She found it hard to concentrate, but she knew she needed to try. The constant questions that were rolling around in her head right now were crazy-making, and she had to find a way to get her mind out of the continuous loop of "Why?".

It was about one-thirty when she heard her phone again, signaling an incoming text. She smiled at the thought of how lucky she was to have friends who were so concerned about her. Looking at her phone, her heart skipped a beat as she saw it was from Luke.

"Can I talk to you?"

"Okay,"

Moments later, her phone rang, and she picked it up right away.

"Hello,"

"Hello,"

She waited as the silence on the other end stretched out. She waited for him to say something. If he felt the need to phone her, it was up to him to say something.

"I, um, I've been working around the house," he commented, his voice low and quiet.

"Yeah?" she responded. As much as she had wanted to hear from him, she wasn't about to make this easy on him. He had dropped a bombshell on her and then left her with no answers.

"Yeah, but I can't stop thinking about you," he said.

"Oh?" she stated, noncommittally.

"Yeah, I'm just walking around my house, sick to my stomach," he explained. "I can't get you out of my mind and keep wondering what I've done."

"I see," she replied.

"Yeah, I think I made a big mistake Olivia, I'm so sorry, but I don't know what I was thinking, I guess I just got scared," the words tumbled out of his mouth in a rush.

"What do you mean?" she asked.

"I mean, can you please forgive me? You're one of the best things that have ever happened to me, and I need you in my life."

Olivia's legs went weak, and she quickly sat down on the nearest chair. This was what she had been hoping and praying would happen. It was all a mistake, and he still loved her. This was what she wanted, but she felt a twinge of anger that he would hurt her so badly, with no explanation.

"What happened?" she asked.

"I told you, I don't know," he answered. "I can't explain it, I just started getting anxious and feeling like the walls were closing in around me."

"But Luke, you're the one who decided we needed to get married," she probed. "any walls you felt closing in, were built by you."

"I know, I know," Luke groaned. "I should never have pushed you so hard."

"How about we set the engagement aside for right now and slow things down a bit?" Olivia suggested.

"Okay, whatever you want," he said. "As long as you can forgive me."

"Yes," she whispered, determined to wipe away the brief spark of anger and not drive him further away. "I can forgive you."

"Good, then please open the door and let me in," he said.

She jumped up and went running to the front door, tore it open, and there he stood. It was apparent he had just showered, and as she reached out to him, she was surrounded by his scent.

She began to cry in his arms, and he rocked her back and forth.

"There, there," he crooned. "It's okay, it's all okay."

"What the hell are you trying to do to me," she exclaimed, hitting him lightly on his chest. "You scared me to death!"

"I know, I know," he said. "I don't know what got into me, you're the perfect woman for me; I think I just got scared."

She grabbed his head between her hands and kissed him passionately. She wanted to consume him, take him into her so he would never leave. He backed her up against the wall and slipped his hand under her top. The kiss deepened and became almost aggressive as they tried to get closer and closer to each other, as though to obliterate the twenty- four hours they had spent apart.

"Where are the boys?" he gasped.

"At their dad's" she responded, in between kisses.

He threw her down on the floor and unbuckled his jeans, all the while looking her in the eye, as though searching down to her very soul. She quickly undid her pants and slipped them off. He grabbed her legs roughly and entered her immediately. The abruptness of it caused her to catch her breath in pleasure. The more carried away he seemed, the more wanted she felt.

Plowing into her, he grabbed her hips and pulled him toward her, as though wanting to penetrate her even deeper. He let out several long guttural sounds. Reaching down, she touched herself and almost immediately bucked beneath him, letting out a loud moan. As they both finished, he flopped down on top of her, breathing loudly.

It took them a few minutes to recover and collect their clothing. She felt a bit silly as she couldn't believe they had been so carried away that they couldn't make it to the bedroom. She was a grown woman, a mother of two who just had sex on the floor in her front hallway. She started to giggle at the absurdity of it.

"What's so funny?" Luke asked.

"Oh nothing," she answered. "You just bring out something very primal in me."

Chapter Forty - Two

She

She slept in the next day and woke up bleary-eyed and lethargic. She couldn't seem to shake the sick feeling rolling around in the pit of her stomach. So much water was under the bridge, and she knew it was for the best that it was over, but that didn't keep the tears at bay, and it didn't make her feel positive about her life.

She knew money wouldn't be a big issue; she made a decent salary and could take care of herself. There was no real reason for there to be a big fight over money as they were pretty much peers in that regard. Indeed, no one would be looking for support of any kind as they didn't have children together.

She tried to reason herself into a better mood by reminding herself that not much would change. Her husband never socialized with her co-workers, so that wouldn't be different, and he didn't have any friends that she would miss either.

When they married, they had blended their households, including furniture, so they would just take away what they had brought with them. At least, she hoped so. She felt so drained and empty, she didn't think she had anything left in her for a fight of any kind.

After getting up to use the washroom, she rummaged around in her bag and pulled out a novel she had wanted to read for the last several months. There was no point in hurrying home, so she might as well try to relax and lose herself in someone else's story. The novel was a thriller, and she was soon engrossed in the plotline. She surprised herself when she finally looked up and realized it was almost noon. It had been easier losing herself in the book than she had anticipated, and she already felt better for it.

Jumping out of bed, she quickly showered and threw her clothes back in the bag. She shoved her book into her purse and left her room. Heading towards the main street, she stopped in at a coffee shop, purchasing a latte and a scone for lunch. She sat in a corner, alternating between munching on her scone, reading a few lines of her book, and people-watching.

She began to wonder about the emotional landscape of the people around her. Was that man sitting by himself in the back suffering from a marriage breakdown too? And what about that couple, snuggling together on the side – were they as blissfully happy as they appeared? Or did they harbor deep, dark concerns that they pushed to the side whenever they threatened to surface, intruding on the life they hoped they were having?

She knew there was a time when that had been her. Smiling, and loving, and pushing things aside. The good had seemed to outweigh the bad for so long, that it had been easy to choose not to look too closely at the bad. Until the scales tipped.

The thing was, she could have understood if the scales had slowly tipped in one direction, but it seemed as though they were tipping back and forth erratically, with no notice.

Chapter Forty-Three

Olivia

"So, did he tell you why?" April asked. Her friends were shocked by the news that their friend was back with Luke so quickly. They had come over to her house to sip on some wine and get the low-down.

"He said he doesn't know exactly what happened, just that he got cold feet and felt like things were moving too fast," Olivia relayed what Luke had told her

"And that's okay with you?" Terri asked incredulously.

"Of course, it isn't okay with me, but it isn't for me to say what someone else should be feeling," Olivia tried to explain.

"I get that, but I'm worried about you," Terri insisted. "You were so heartbroken, and I don't want to see you get hurt."

"I know, but we have put this behind us," Olivia responded.

"I still don't get how he could have felt like things were moving too fast for him when he was the one pushing things along," April stated, with a shake of the head.

"I think he just got swept up in the momentum of everything," Olivia found herself parroting Luke once again.

"Well, it's obvious that he really loves you," Terri reassured her. "He dotes on you and has since the day you met; I guess it was just something he needed to work through."

"Uh-huh," April grunted in a less than convincing manner.

"You can be skeptical if you want," Olivia said as she reached out to give her friend a hug. "But this has shown me how much I really do love Luke and want to marry him when the time is right for both of us."

"Just be careful, okay?" April asked.

"You know I will," Olivia answered.

Terri picked up the bottle of wine and topped off everyone's glasses. They made a toast to the future and turned their conversation to lighter topics for the rest of the evening. After her friends had left and she was taking the dirty glasses to the kitchen, Olivia reflected on how lucky she was to have such loving and supportive friends. They may not always understand or agree with her, but they were there for her no matter what.

The phone rang just as she was turning out the lights, and it brought a smile to her face. She and Luke had decided that, in the interest of slowing things down, they would not see each other tonight, but she knew that would be him, phoning to see how her evening had gone.

"Hello," she chirped.

"Hi," he responded. "Did you have a nice evening?"

"I did," she answered. "We drank wine and chatted for hours."

"Nice," he said. "Do they hate me now?"

"No, they don't hate you," she answered. "They're a bit confused, but they don't hate you."

"Oh," he said. "So, do you want to do something tomorrow night?"

"I'm sorry, I promised the boys I would take them to a movie," she answered, regretfully. "There's that new one that they've wanted to see for a while, and I keep putting it off."

"Okay, I see," he stated quietly. "I'll talk to you later then."

"Wait!" she exclaimed.

"What?"

"Why are you hanging up, are you upset or something?" she asked.

"No, it's all good," he reassured her. "Go and spend time with your boys, family time is important."

"Yes, it is," she agreed. "What are you going to do?"

"I don't know, probably just stay home and watch some TV," he said. "But I should get going, I still have some work to do before I hit the hay."

"Okay, well, thank you for calling," she said, a bit uncertainly.

"Goodnight,"

She stood there, staring at the phone as a feeling of dread washed over her. What had just happened? He had asked for more space and to slow things down, and that's what she was trying to do. But he was acting like she was rejecting him. She walked into her living room and looked out the curtains into the night. Staring at the stars, she felt frustrated that she couldn't seem to figure out what it was he wanted. Her stomach began to churn with anxiety and the familiar feelings of fear washed over her. One minute he wanted to be closer, the next thing he was acting as though she was crowding him. As she paced around her house, she thought back to their conversation about their relationship. She went over and over what he had said, and tried to get a better understanding of what was happening. Finally, she threw down the phone in frustration and went to her bedroom to get ready for bed.

She was just settling in when she heard a text message come in on her phone. Glancing at it, her heart picked up its pace a bit as she noticed it was Luke.

"Are you in bed yet?"

"Just crawled in," she typed back.

"I'm sorry for being an ass."

"What happened? What was wrong?" she asked.

"I don't know, it just seemed like you were more than happy to just continue on with your life without me. You have your friends and your kids, what do you need me for?"

"Are you serious?" she responded incredulously. "You know I love you and want to spend the rest of my life with you, but you're the one who wanted space."

"I know, but it doesn't feel very good," he responded.

"I agree, but this is what you wanted," she said.

"It just seemed like things were moving so fast - you were talking about dresses and locations and honeymoons and tuxes. I thought we would get engaged and then talk about getting married in a few years."

"You neglected to mention that part to me."

"I know, I didn't realize that's what I thought until it was happening."

"Well, I'm in no big rush to get married, I've told you that all along, so we're good."

"Well, either that or we just elope and don't fuss with all this other extra stuff."

Olivia felt like she was getting mental whiplash. One minute, things were going too fast for him, and then he was talking about eloping.

"That would really be rushing things, wouldn't it?" she asked.

"Yeah, I guess, but then it would be done and over with, and there would be none of this back and forth."

"So, the two choices are to either hurry up and get it over with, or wait years?"

She waited for a while as he prepared to send her his response. She couldn't quite wrap her head around why eloping seemed like a good idea to him but just planning a regular wedding wasn't. One minute she felt like she had it figured out, and the next minute she was confused again. After what seemed like several minutes, he sent another message.

"I don't know, I just want to be with you."

"Then why don't we just let that be enough for now?" she answered.

"Sounds good."

"Goodnight, Luke"

"Hey, Olivia?

"Yes?"

"What are you wearing?"

She giggled as she slipped down deeper into her bed and continued to text.

Chapter Forty-Four

She

It wasn't until she was back at her car that she realized someone had been trying to contact her. The erratic cell coverage in the mountains meant that messages or notifications could come in hours after they were sent.

She checked her voice mail, and she had two messages. As she listened to the first one, she couldn't believe her ears. It was her husband, asking her to come back so they could talk. The second message was also him, this time sounding upset that he couldn't reach her.

"I don't know if you are ignoring me, or what," the message said. "Maybe you're walking in those damn mountains and not getting these messages, I don't know. Who knows? Maybe you got eaten by a bear. Just please, please call me back so we can work this out."

She sat back against the seat of her car, the air conditioner blowing ice - cold air towards her face. She was so shocked to hear from her husband like this. Not that him texting her was a new thing, or leaving a message for her, but they had barely talked for days. They both knew it was over, why was he reaching out now?

She felt a cold ball grow in the pit of her stomach. This was feeling all too familiar.

Chapter Forty-Five

Olivia

After spending the evening taking the boys out for pizza and then to the movies, Olivia was glad when it came to a close. It had been a long day at work, and she was looking forward to some time just to herself. It was hard not seeing Luke every night, but she was determined to give him whatever space he needed to figure things out.

As she removed her makeup in front of the bathroom mirror, she fired off a text to him to let him know she was home. She was hoping they could make arrangements to go out tomorrow night as she was missing him terribly. It seemed so strange to think that a few short months ago, she had an entire life that had nothing to do with him. Now it was hard to imagine her life without him in it.

She brushed and flossed her teeth while keeping an eye on her phone, waiting for him to respond to her text. She slipped into her pajamas and brushed her hair, then walked towards her closet and chose an outfit for work the next day. She was beginning to wonder what was taking him so long to respond. Usually, he answered her texts right away, and she had told him she would talk to him around this time.

After she had done everything she could to prepare for the next day, she crawled into bed and plugged her phone in, setting it on her nightstand. She was trying not to worry, or project too much into him not responding, but she could feel the anxiety rising within her. While she waited, she checked her email and answered a couple of them, deleted others. She began unsubscribing to the backlog of emails soliciting her for products and was halfway through her work emails when Luke texted her.

"Hey, what's up?"

"Not much. Just finished getting ready for work tomorrow and climbed into bed."

"Okay, well I just got home, and I have an early morning at work, so I'm going to hit the hay."

"I thought you weren't doing anything tonight?"

"I just went out for a bit," he typed.

"Oh, okay, did you have a nice evening?"

"Yeah, it was okay, you?"

"Good, the boys enjoyed the movie,"

"Good,"

"Did you want to do something tomorrow night?" she texted.

"Yeah, sure."

"What would you like to do?" she asked.

"I don't know, why don't you come here, and I'll cook dinner?"

"That sounds lovely."

"Okay, talk to you later,"

The next night, she raced home from work and jumped in the shower. Using her favorite scented shower gel, she lathered up and shivered with excitement as she ran her hands over her body. She couldn't wait to see him tonight, it felt like it had been forever, even though it was only a couple days. The depth of the pleasure she felt anticipating spending time basking in his attention was almost as intense as the feelings of loss she felt when she thought she might be losing him. She jumped into a matching bra and panties set, and a pair of her best-fitting jeans. Choosing a top carefully, she settled on a plain cotton blouse with buttons up the front that fit her perfectly in all the right places. Adding one of her new, funky necklaces that she had picked up at a flea market and spritzing herself liberally with perfume, she donned her knee-high boots and slipped out the door. She had left the boys with a pizza and strict instructions to get to bed no later than ten.

As she navigated traffic, she couldn't help but reflect on how her life had changed. She had never felt so much excitement and anticipation for a date in her life. Of course, in many ways, she supposed it wasn't really a date. She was going to her boyfriend's place to have dinner. Is that what one called the person you used to be engaged to but were now only sleeping with? A boyfriend? Well, whatever it was, she was looking forward to the evening.

When she arrived, he was sitting in the living room, a glass in one hand and the remote in the other. She was surprised to see that a bottle of booze was sitting on the counter.

"Hey, are you drinking?" she asked.

"Well, hello to you too!" he retorted.

"Hello Luke," she greeted him again, as she reached down and kissed him. "Are you drinking?"

"Yes, yes I am," he responded. "Do you have a problem with that?

"Of course not, I'm just surprised, that's all," she answered. "I drink so why would I have a problem if you do?"

"Good,"

It wasn't quite the start to their evening she had imagined, but she decided to ignore that and move forward.

"What's for supper?" she asked.

"I don't know, I thought maybe we could order pizza," he mentioned.

"Okay," she responded, although she had been under the impression he was going to be cooking. "Pizza it is."

He grabbed his phone and punched a number in that he appeared to have memorized. Once he had finished ordering, he turned to her and asked if pepperoni was okay with her.

"Sure, I like any pizza as long as it doesn't have anchovies," she answered with a laugh.

"It'll be here in about 30 minutes," he informed her.

They sat on the couch, watching a show that was on the TV. Olivia wasn't sure what show it was, as she was too busy trying to get a sense of what kind of mood Luke was in. He seemed remote but there was nothing she could put her finger on. He had said he would make dinner and instead ordered pizza, but so what? He had ordered the pizza without asking what she wanted, but that was no big deal, right? He was just so quiet, and she had anticipated he would be as happy to see her as she was to see him.

Trying to capture his attention, she snuggled down next to him, placed her hand on his knee and kissed his neck. She was shocked when he pulled away.

"Look, this isn't a good time," he protested.

"What isn't a good time?" she asked, confused.

"Now isn't a good time," he stated.

"What do you mean now isn't a good time?" she pushed. "I thought we were having a nice evening together."

"Well, there was a misunderstanding," he said. "I have plans later tonight so let's just wait for the pizza."

Olivia sat in amazed silence. What had happened? She knew they had made plans for the evening and now he was saying he wasn't even going to be home? She didn't know what to say to him. Her face began to burn, and she wished the floor would open up and swallow her. How had she gotten it so wrong? But she knew she hadn't, and his behavior didn't make any sense.

"What is happening Luke, why are you being like this?" she asked.

"Like what?" he asked.

"We had made plans to spend tonight together," she said. "I didn't imagine that, why did you make other plans?"

"Something came up," he insisted. "Look, if this is the way things are going to be, then maybe we need to just move on."

The air left her body, and she felt the world around her shift. This couldn't be happening. Not again. What had she done wrong? Myriad thoughts were whirling around in her head, but she sat quietly on the couch, staring at him in disbelief.

He sat back on the couch and took a long drink out of his glass. She noticed that the ice in his glass was barely melted and she wondered how long he had been drinking. She looked around at his living room, immaculate except for the wet glass ring on his coffee table and the newspaper spread out beside it. She felt surreal, as though the world had visibly slowed down.

Just then, the doorbell rang, and he jumped up to greet the pizza delivery boy. Paying for the pizza, he dropped it on the coffee table and went into the kitchen to get napkins. When he came back, she was standing at the front window, looking out. He sat down on the couch and pulled a slice of pizza out of the box. She turned and looked at him, amazed that he was so calmly going about life. Did he not realize what he was doing to her?

"Luke, what's happening?" she finally managed to say. He looked at her for a while, and then sighed deeply and set his slice of pizza down.

"Look, I don't know what's happening, I just know I made plans for tonight, I'm sorry if you misunderstood and thought we had plans for the entire night. I thought we were having a bite to eat," he stated.

"But we haven't seen each other in a few days," she pointed out. "I was looking forward to spending the evening with you; I thought you felt the same way."

Luke looked at her and shrugged his shoulders as though in resignation.

"We don't seem to have had the same expectations for the night then," Luke responded.

She swallowed the lump she felt in her throat and closed her eyes to force the tears back. What had happened to their wonderful night? What was happening to them?

"It would appear we have had some miscommunication," she agreed after a while. "I will just be going now."

"Aren't you going to have some pizza first?" he asked.

"No, I'm not going to have some pizza first," she answered, her voice rising.

"Come on, Olivia, don't get mad," Luke said.

"I'm not mad, I'm disappointed," she answered.

"You sound mad to me," he countered.

"Okay, yes I'm mad!" she retorted. "I'm mad that I feel like you're jerking me around! One minute I'm the love of your life, the next minute you want your space, then you don't want to get married and then you want to elope!"

He stood gazing at her for a long time. He looked as though he was trying to figure out what to say but had no idea what words to use.

"I'm not jerking you around," he finally answered. "I don't know why I feel this way, one minute you ARE the love of my life but then the next day I do need my space."

"You're messed up!" she cried out.

"I know," he said.

They stood staring at each other, at an impasse. After a while, Luke reached out and gathered her in his arms. She felt his muscular chest under her hands, and a sob broke free from her body. How could she live without this man? How could she continue living this way though? Never knowing what he was thinking or what mood he would be in, from one day to the next? Finally, she pulled herself away.

"So, is this it then?" she asked.

"I think so," he answered. "I tried. I thought if we slowed down, then I would feel better about things, but it hasn't helped."

"Okay, I'm going then," she said as she turned and walked out the door.

Chapter Forty-Six

She

Pulling onto the driveway, she thrust the car into park, leaned back in her seat and looked at their house. Some of the lights were on, including the front porch light. Small moths and various insects surged around the light, bouncing off of it, only to rush headlong at the tantalizing glow once again. The house looked so ordinary. So, every-day. How many times over the years had she pulled up to it just like this? Coming home late from work, arriving from a night of visiting friends, or hauling the kids back from a game when they were still at home.

This house had seen her through some ups and some downs. Maybe it was time to move on, start over entirely from scratch; a new job, a new town, and a new life. Time to throw it all out and begin anew.

Pulling herself out of her reverie, she reached into the backseat and located her purse. She walked up to the front door with carefully placed steps. She wasn't exactly taking her time, but she wasn't hurrying either. She wasn't sure what she was going to come face to face with when she opened the door, and she wasn't sure she was ready for whatever it was.

As she stepped into the front hallway, she set her bags down and hung up her coat. The scent of cooking meat met her, and she inhaled deeply.

"There you are," her husband said, walking towards her with a smile. "I have supper ready, so throw your bags in the bedroom and come and get it!"

She smiled weakly at him and took her bags towards their room. How could he act like nothing was wrong? Like everything was okay? As she was mentally shaking her head, a thought came to her that she couldn't remember ever having before. Did it matter? She almost stopped in her tracks. Did it matter why he did what he did? Why was she making herself crazy trying to make his behavior rational?

She felt winded at the thought. She had spent so much time trying to untangle his actions and his motivations, that the idea that maybe there was no real answer struck her as almost unbelievable. What if she had been trying to make sense of something that didn't make sense? What if it wasn't her problem to try and figure it out?

As she returned from their bedroom, she walked in a bit of a daze. It seemed so silly that she was only now considering this option. Maybe his behavior and the way he treated her just didn't make sense.

Sitting down at the kitchen table, he reached over and grabbed her hand.

"Honey, I know things have been rough," he started. "Things have been a bit rocky, but I love you, and I know you love me so let's just put it all behind us, okay?"

She was still reeling from her revelation, and she wasn't sure what to say to him. So, she smiled, squeezed his hand and started eating. That seemed to satisfy him, and he smiled and dug into his dinner.

"Why don't we go to a movie tonight?" he asked. "There's a new comedy that just opened, and I thought it would be nice to have a bit of a date night."

"Okay, that sounds good," she agreed, reasoning that if they were sitting quietly in the dark for most of the evening, she would have some more time to figure out what exactly she was feeling and what she was going to do.

That evening, as they entered the movie theatre, she went to the kiosk to purchase their tickets while he went to pick up some popcorn. She was waiting for him at some tables when he approached.

"Hope you're okay with chocolate-covered peanuts with the popcorn," he asked with a smile.

"Works for me," she answered.

They were walking towards the line of people waiting to be let into the theatres when he suddenly dropped his head to the right and looked almost over his shoulder.

"What's wrong?" she asked him.

"Nothing, nothing, just an itch," he said quickly, transferring his popcorn to his right hand and raising his left to scratch his neck.

Despite his explanation, it was apparent to her that he was trying to hide his face from someone. He kept scratching his neck and averting his face from the people on his left side. A movie had just let out, and people were streaming past, except for a couple of groups of people who were lingering and chatting. Slowly, the line they were in began to move forward as the attendant ahead of them started tearing tickets.

How odd, she thought to herself. She wasn't surprised that he was hiding, but she was surprised that she noticed. How many times had something like that happened in the past, and she had turned a blind eye? It was so obvious that he was trying to avoid another theatre patron, and while it made her stomach feel slightly queasy, she realized she wasn't surprised or even upset. She felt as though she saw things, and him, clearly for the first time in a long, long time.

They settled into their seats in the theatre, and soon the movie began. He reached over and took her hand, casually resting it on his knee. There was a time when she had enjoyed nothing more than snuggling up with her husband and watching a movie. Tonight, she felt distant, as though she was observing them dispassionately. After a few minutes, she removed her hand from his under the guise of using it to grab a handful of popcorn. She laughed at the appropriate times during the movie, but she was distracted by the thought that kept running through her head. What if it didn't matter why he was the way he was?

Chapter Forty-Seven

Olivia

Running her fingers up and down the stem of her glass, Olivia stared into the deep mahogany-colored wine. It was still early in the evening, but already she was looking forward to being able to make her excuses and go home. It was hard to pretend that everything was okay when she felt as though a brick was lodged in her stomach. Every song that came on over the loudspeakers made her cringe. She wasn't sure why, but the songs seemed hollow, and lacking in-depth, even those that talked about love appeared to be a pale version of what she was experiencing.

"Hey, Olivia!" April shouted across the table. "Penny for your thoughts!"

Olivia forced herself to smile and raised the glass in April's direction, as though to say that her thoughts weren't worth that much. She knew she wasn't exactly the best company tonight, but she also knew her friends understood and would forgive her. While she was sure they were losing patience with the on-again, off-again relationship she seemed stuck in with Luke, they tried to give her space to deal with it the best she could. The problem was, she was losing patience with herself. It seemed that no matter how many times they went back and forth, she still held on to hope.

Hope that one day he would wake up and return to the loving, caring and attentive man she thought she had fallen in love with. At least she hoped that the man she fell for was the real Luke and that he was just going through some issues that he needed to sort out. It seemed inconceivable that the man she fell in love with was the illusion.

Picking up her purse, she stood up from the table and slowly started to weave her way to the washroom. Everyone seemed to be having such a good time that she felt like a fraud for even being there. Why was she bothering to pretend that she was having a great time?

In the washroom, she glanced at herself in the dimly lit mirror, and absent-mindedly fixed her hair and re-applied her lipstick. In the relative quietness of the room, she heard her phone buzz. Her heart skipped a beat, and she felt the adrenaline begin to course through her veins. Could it be him? It had been a few days since she had left his house, heartbroken again. Her friends were confused and upset that their sensible, capable, and practical friend was acting so irrationally.

She forced herself to finish fixing her makeup and patting her hair before she reached for her phone and checked to who had sent her the text message.

He had typed nothing more than "Hi." She stared at the message for a while, unsure of what to do. She knew that logically she should put her phone away, ignore the message and go back to her friends. Her heart beat loudly in her ears as she considered what to do. The problem was that she could no more ignore him than she could decide not to breath for a few minutes.

"Hi" she typed in response.

She waited expectantly for his response. Just then the bathroom door banged open, and Olivia jumped guiltily. A woman she didn't know smiled at her and entered a stall.

So, this is where it's at, she thought to herself. A grown woman feeling guilty and sneaking around. She knew that if her friends knew she was texting with him again, they would not be happy. They would let their unhappiness be known through their concern for her. They had watched her get her heart broken over, and over again. She knew they didn't think he was good for her, and she cared enough about what they thought to not want them to think badly of her.

"What are you doing?"

"Out with some friends," she responded.

"Okay, I'll leave you alone then."

She stared at the words on the screen, her whole being screaming for just one smell, on sound, one taste of him.

"No, it's okay, I was just thinking of going home."

"I miss you."

"I miss you too," she said, and then held the phone close to her chest. This was ridiculous. If he didn't want her, why did he keep reaching out? Why didn't he just leave her alone? She drew in a deep breath, to steady her nerves a bit.

"Can I see you? Can we talk?" he texted.

"Okay"

"When will you be home? Can I come over?"

"I'll be home in about half an hour."

She left the bathroom and found April, to let her know she was going.

"Why?" her friend shouted over the music. "Stay and have some fun!"

"I have a bit of a headache," Olivia said, trying not to dwell on the fact that she was lying to one of her closest friends. She felt even worse when April threw her arms around her and gave her a big hug.

"Call me tomorrow, okay?" April asked as Olivia waved good-bye.

~ ~ ~

She was sitting in her living room, trying to steady her nerves when the doorbell rang. She stood up, ran her hands down the front of her jeans and walked towards the front door. Luke stood on the other side, looking uncomfortable. He walked into the house when she gestured for him to enter.

They were both quiet until they were sitting on the couch, then he turned to her and ran his hand over the back of her head.

"You look so pretty tonight," he commented.

"Thank you," she responded with a small smile. She didn't want to, but she could feel herself getting sucked into his vortex. The combination of his intense eyes freshly applied cologne, and the outline of his chest in his form-fitting t-shirt made her feel like all her resolve was melting away.

She quickly stood up, crossed her arms across her middle and walked a few paces away.

"Why did you want to see me?" she asked him.

"Why do you think?" he responded. "I missed you."

"Okay, but why?" she pressed. "A few days ago, you were done with this relationship, and then, once again you contact me."

"I can't help it. I just can't seem to stay away," he softly murmured, sounding like a forlorn little boy.

"You can't keep doing this," she insisted. "You need to decide what you want, once and for all."

"I know I want you," he said.

"You do today, but what about tomorrow?" she pushed. "You change what you want faster than some people change their socks; you need to make up your mind."

"You're right," he said. "I know that right now, I want to spend the rest of my life with you."

"But as soon as I start planning a wedding, you bolt," she observed.

"I know, and I can't explain it," he sighed, running his hand through his hair in frustration. "I wish we could just get married right now."

She stood there, trying to understand the conflicting emotions that she was experiencing. She was excited at his presence, hopeful at his declaration of love, and frustrated at his explanation about his behavior. She was terrified that he would stand up and walk out.

Suddenly, he stood up and came towards her, turning her around to face him. He placed his hands on her face and drew her close to him.

"That's it," he said with a smile.

"That's what?" she asked.

"Let's get married, now," He was smiling as though he had just found the perfect solution to a complex problem.

"What?" she asked incredulously.

"Let's go and get married now," he said, with a huge grin on his face. "Obviously the issue is the planning and getting cold feet. I know I want to spend the rest of my life with you, so let's do it."

She continued to stare at him.

"Olivia, will you marry me?" he asked, getting down on one knee.

Taking a deep breath, she tried to process what was happening. He loved her and wanted to marry her, but he didn't want to risk planning a wedding and getting cold feet again. She felt the excitement build up in her at the thought of finally having the man she fell in love with back again. She quickly ignored the part of her that felt uneasy and wondered how a grown man could change so easily and so quickly just because he was uncomfortable. If they were married, things would go back to the way they were. He would have no reason to be anxious, and she would feel secure.

"Will you Olivia? Let's jump a plane to somewhere and get married this weekend," he insisted.

She could almost see them standing in front of a Justice of the Peace, saying their vows. A wave of warmth washed over her, pushing her doubts deep down inside the darkest parts of her being.

"Yes, I will marry you, Luke."

Chapter Forty-Eight

She

At work the next day, she sat in her office and stared off into space. She was finding it hard to concentrate on work or the looming deadlines. She hadn't slept much the night before. She didn't feel overly tired, but she wasn't precisely rested either. It took her a minute to realize what it was, and when she did, she nearly bolted up in her chair.

She felt at peace! For the first time in a very long time, she felt at peace. It wasn't the euphoria and giddiness she'd felt when she thought their relationship was going well, but a deep sense of assurance that no matter what happened with their relationship, she was okay. It didn't matter why he behaved the way he did. It had nothing to do with her, and she was at peace.

"What's up? her colleague asked quizzically. "You look like you just heard from publishers clearing house."

"Not quite," she laughed. "No, I just realized that I'm at peace."

"Well, that is good, isn't it?"

"Yes, it is. It is very good," she said.

"So, you had a nice time in the mountains? Did the hubby go with you?"

"Yes, I had a nice time, and no, my husband didn't go with me," she answered.

"Oh well, maybe next time."

"I don't think so," she answered. "I don't think there's going to be a next time."

"What do you mean? I thought you loved getting away to the mountains?"

"I do, and I will probably go again. No, I mean there will probably not be another opportunity for my husband to come with me," she answered. "I think I'm going to leave him."

"What?" her colleague asked, the surprise evident in her voice. "Since when?"

"Since right now," she answered with a smile. "I think I just decided this very minute."

"But, are you sure?"

"Yes, I am," she said. "Have you ever felt so sure of something that you just knew beyond a shadow of a doubt? There were no "ifs, ands, or buts" about it?"

"Yeah, I guess,"

"It's just a fact," she said. "I'm leaving my husband."

"Does he know?"

"No, I'm going to wait a bit to tell him," she mused, realizing she had decided already. "I need to make some arrangements, and I don't want to deal with the drama if he knows too soon."

"Well, if there is anything I can do, just let me know," her colleague said, standing up. "You know you have a lot of people here who are willing to give you a hand moving, or anything else you need."

"Thank you, I appreciate that," she responded, gratefully. "And I may take you up on it."

Sitting alone in her office, she was amazed at what had just come out of her mouth. She wasn't sorry she had said it, not by a long shot. But she was surprised at how sure she was and how calm she felt. Their relationship had always been so full of drama and angst, that she was shocked it was ending with such a sense of surety and peace on her part. Maybe it was just shock right now, but she didn't care. It didn't matter what her friends thought, or her family, or her colleagues. It was her life, and she deserved to be happy and to take care of herself.

She took a deep breath and sat back, threading her hands behind her head. She stared at the ceiling as memories of their relationship washed over her. Whatever had happened, no matter why it had happened, she knew beyond a doubt that she had loved him. She remembered their wedding day, but this time, she didn't analyze or try to understand the past, she just let it come to her. Their wedding day, so full of hope and promise. She had been so sure it was the beginning of the rest of their lives together.

Chapter Forty-Nine

Wedding

The plane taxied into the gate just after eleven a.m. As the seatbelt sign went off, she could hardly believe they were going to do it. It might not be a big wedding, and their friends and family might not be in attendance, but they were getting married!

They were staying at the Mandalay Bay hotel, and the shuttle was waiting just outside the airport doors. They found their overnight bags on the carousel and jumped into the van. Holding her hand, he smiled down at her as they swayed with the movement of the vehicle.

"Well, you ready to do this?" he asked her

"Yup, and you?" she answered.

"Too late if I'm not, right?" he joked.

"You better believe it," she laughed.

"So, what do I have to do?" he asked her.

"Well, we need to go to the Clark County Marriage Bureau to get our license. It shouldn't take long as I filled out most of the paperwork online," she answered.

"Why don't you do that, and I'll try my luck at the machines?" he told her.

"Ha! I don't think so," she said, jabbing him playfully in his side. "We both have to be present to get the license."

"Do we have to give blood or anything?" he asked.

"Nope, just sign, pay the fee, and we're ready," she responded.

"Then we just have to find an Elvis that will marry us?" he asked, jokingly.

"I agreed to a Vegas wedding, but that doesn't mean it's going to be that tacky!" she exclaimed with a smile. "No, I will check in with the hotel, but I was told we can just let them know what we want, pay, and get married the next day."

As they arrived at the hotel, she was in awe at the over-the-top splendor of it all. It had been many years since she had been in Las Vegas, and it seemed to have grown in both magnitude and sheer presence. Their room was plush and tastefully decorated, with a king-size bed, deep jacuzzi tub, and white robes laid out on the bed.

"I thought we could go and get the license right away, so that's out of the way," she explained. "Everything else can be done on the strip, but we need to grab a cab to go and get the license."

"Okay, then let's do this," he said.

It took an amazingly short time to get the license. When they arrived at the marriage bureau, they went straight to the express line, gave the clerk the paperwork they had filled in online, the clerk checked their identification, stamped the paperwork, and they were on their way.

"Wow, no wonder people come to Vegas for a quickie wedding," he commented. "I've spent more time getting a fishing license."

Back at the hotel, she left him plugging quarters into a slot machine while she went in search of a dress. She was a bit concerned because she wasn't sure she would be able to find what she wanted. Because it was such a quick and small wedding, she didn't want a full-blown wedding dress, but she still wanted to look and feel like a bride. She glanced through some of the shops in the hotel but quickly realized that they were way outside of her budget. Stopping by the information desk, she asked the woman behind the counter where the best place would be to find a simple wedding dress.

"Best place if you need something today is a place called Brilliant Bridal," the woman told her. "You can buy them off the rack, and it's about a ten-minute cab ride."

She sat on one of the cushy lobby benches while she waited for the taxi the woman had ordered to arrive. She couldn't believe she was going to pick out a wedding dress. She felt a twinge as she realized she was doing this by herself, and that it would have been nice to have her mother or one of her friends with her, but she quickly brushed that thought away. It was the marriage that was important, not the wedding. She had to keep herself focused on that and not let anything cloud this experience for her. She watched the people milling around her as she wondered what her family's reaction would be when they returned home married. She stirred uncomfortably at the thought, as she knew the news would hurt some people who were close to her.

She made an effort to push the negative thoughts aside as she slipped into the cab and left for the bridal shop, but a sense of uncertainty stayed with her during the drive. As the taxi pulled up to the shop, she passed the driver his fare, along with a healthy tip.

Getting out of the vehicle, she looked around at the sprawling Spanish hacienda-style strip mall. The red adobe tile roof seemed especially appropriate for the hot desert climate. Nestled in between a wedding chapel and a Mexican restaurant, Brilliant Bridal looked large and welcoming with large pictures of happy brides adorning the windows. Entering the store, she was greeted by a beautiful teal and white-colored room, complete with low upholstered benches, beautiful fabrics and dresses lining the walls. The dark hardwood floors gave it a luxurious, indulgent feel and she felt herself relax as she let herself take in the room.

"May I help you?" a saleswoman, with the tag identifying her as Joan asked.

"Yes, I'm looking for an off the rack wedding dress to buy today," she answered.

"You've come to the right place then," the woman smiled at her, apparently used to brides coming in last minute to purchase a dress that many women took months to finalize.

After determining the style and price point, she sat down and waited for Joan to return with a selection of available dresses to try on. She tried not to think about what she was going to do if she couldn't find anything that fit properly, that she liked, and wanted to wear walking down the aisle.

Joan showed her four dresses to get a sense of the type of style she preferred and then took her into a change room.

"If you want to go down to your underwear, I will help you slip into these," the saleswoman said, as she discreetly looked away.

"So, is this the busy season for you?" she asked, trying to make small talk.

"This is Las Vegas, every season is the busy season for weddings," Joan laughed. "Now, I'm taking a chance here and getting you to try on this dress. I think it will look beautiful on you."

"Why is that taking a chance?" she asked.

"Because, many brides who try on their favorite dress first don't realize it until they have tried on a handful or two more," Joan said. "Then they come back to the first one. But you strike me as a woman who knows her own mind."

"You're right about that!" she answered with a laugh.

"You said you like a more classic style with character, not too over the top sexy, but definitely womanly, yes?" Joan asked.

"Yes, I'm not a 23-year old, but I don't want to look like the mother of the bride, either," she responded.

"Perfect! This one I'm helping you into is a throw-back to the roaring twenties, and is a classic Gemy Maalouf sheath gown." Joan explained.

As she turned to look in the mirror, her breath caught. The dress had delicate beadwork and beautiful embroidery around a contoured waist. The neckline was plunging, but with intricate lace that softened the line.

The beadwork and embroidery give a vintage twist to the modern plunging neckline, and the back was bare except for a string of faux buttons that met at the top with embroidery.

"The back is called an illusion back," Joan explained.

"It is amazing," she whispered.

"You have the perfect body to carry this off too," the saleslady smiled. "I knew the minute you walked in you that this dress was made for you."

"And it's in my budget?" she asked, afraid to hear the answer.

"Absolutely," Joan said with a smile. "I wouldn't do that to you. Now mind you, it is near the top of what you wanted to pay, but I think it's worth it, don't you?"

"Yes, it is," she said, as she continued to admire the dress in the multitude of mirrors provided. Truth be told, she didn't want to get out of the dress. After all her worrying about finding the right dress, it felt anti-climactic to be done already. But she knew this was the dress. It made her feel like a princess while not being a puffy A-line with layers upon layers of material. She felt like a full-grown woman, not a girl.

After taking the gown off, choosing a pair of low-heeled shoes to go with it, and paying at the large, teal-colored counter, she jumped into the taxi Joan had called for her. Hands full of bags, she was pleased with her purchases and felt the excitement building within her at the idea of getting married tomorrow. Trying on the dress had made it seem so much more real, somehow. Now all she needed was to check on the booking for the chapel, make arrangements for an intimate dinner for two, and everything was ready.

~ ~ ~

When she returned to the hotel, she hauled her new purchases up to their hotel room, and went in search of her husband-to-be. When she found him, he was sitting at a Blackjack table, one hand holding his cards, and the other a drink.

"Hi honey," she murmured in his ear as she looked over his shoulders at the hand he was holding.

"Ssshhh! I'm concentrating."

She smiled to herself and thought about how in the past he had told her that gambling was for fools and he just didn't see the attraction. Apparently, he felt differently now. Half an hour later, her amusement at his change of mind began to seem less endearing when he was sipping on another drink, still playing Blackjack and still losing. The only time he had looked up from his game was when the waitress came by with a new drink for him.

"Look, I'm going to book a chapel for us," she finally said. "Do you have any preference or thought about where you'd like to have the ceremony?"

He still didn't raise his eyes from the game when he answered her.

"Doesn't matter," he answered.

"Doesn't matter?" she probed.

He must have heard something in her tone of voice because he finally lifted his eyes and looked in her direction.

"Look, I trust your decision," he reassured her. "I'm a guy, whatever you pick is fine with me."

"Are you sure?" she asked.

"Yes, I'm sure!" he insisted, his attention already drawn back to the card game unraveling in front of him.

She left the gaming area, a frown marring her forehead. Whatever happened to showing up and planning it together? While she understood that he wouldn't have been interested in dress shopping, surely he had some opinions on the rest of the planning? If he didn't, couldn't he at least humor her and come along to help?

Despite her annoyance, choosing the location and the details ended up being fairly straightforward. Because it was only the two of them, she chose the Gold Chapel, and a special package called the "Elope" - which seemed only appropriate. After she had chosen her flowers, and his boutonniere, and two songs from the hotel's songbook, she found herself at loose ends. Wandering back to the Blackjack tables, she noticed he had switched tables but was just as engrossed as he was when she left. She let him know she would be up in their room, resting before dinner.

As she flopped down on the king-size bed, she smiled as she looked over at her wedding dress, hanging from its hanger. While she was disappointed that she had done almost all the planning herself, yet she was consoled at the thought that she would have her fiancé's undivided attention once they were at dinner. It was already nearly five, and she felt the day catching up to her. The excitement of the day and her worry over finding the right dress had taken more out of her than she'd realized, and she was soon asleep.

She awoke with a start and the sense of a lot of time passing. At first, she wasn't sure where she was, and it took a few rubs of her eyes to orientate herself to her surroundings. Once she was aware enough to remember where she was, she reached for her phone on the bedside table. She was shocked to discover it was after eleven pm.

Where was he? Had she slept so deeply that he had returned, and she hadn't heard him? Her heart rapidly thumping in her chest, she slipped into her shoes, grabbed the room key, and headed for the hotel's casino.

She found him exactly where she had left him more than six hours ago, except this time he was slumped over his drink, his cards held loosely in his other hand.

"What are you doing?" she asked, incredulous.

He looked up at her through bleary, unfocused eyes.

"Wha?" he asked.

"What are you doing? It's after eleven, and we were supposed to go for dinner!" she exclaimed.

"I've been playin'," he said, barely able to stop from slurring his words. "Where were you, huh?"

"I fell asleep!" she stated.

"So ya didn't miss me," The tone of his voice seemed to imply there was no harm no foul.

" We're getting married tomorrow, and we were supposed to have a nice dinner tonight, and talk through things, and..." she trailed off. "It's not every day you get married."

"Okay, let's grab something," He threw down his cards and attempted to stand. Swaying slightly, he seemed uncertain of what to do next, or where to go.

"Let's get you up to our room and order you some room service," she took over, shaking her head.

"No, no we can go for dinner," he argued as he began to head off towards the elevators to their room.

"Tomorrow night," she insisted with more than a touch of resignation in her voice. "Tonight, you rest."

She half walked, half dragged him to their room, removed his shoes, and sat him down on the side of the bed. While she was looking over the room service menu, he flopped onto his side and curled up on the bed fully dressed. She stood looking at him as he began to snore. This wasn't exactly how she had imagined they would spend the night before their wedding. They hadn't said more than a handful of words to each other since they'd arrived in Las Vegas and she had a feeling it would be many hours before he was ready to hold up his end of any conversation. She put down the menu and reached for the remote control. Reality TV shows would have to do.

The next morning, she sat eating a delicious crab benedict and reading a newspaper at Della's Kitchen, one of the many restaurants in the hotel. She was just finishing her coffee when she looked up and saw him walking towards her.

"Well, well, look who decided to join the land of the living," she greeted him with a smile.

"Yeah, yeah," he responded, as he pulled out the chair opposite her and sat down.

"Did you sleep well?"

"S'okay," he answered with a yawn, his hands reaching over his head in an elaborate stretch.

"Glad to hear, are you interested in finding out what time you're getting married today?"

"Sure, what time am I getting married today?"

"Just after lunch," she informed him. "It was either that, or 9 am, and I'm glad we didn't have to take that time slot, by the look of you."

"Uh-huh," he stifled another yawn behind his hand.

"It's going to be in the Gold Chapel, and I went with the Elope package."

"What's the Elope package?"

"It gives us a place to get married, someone to marry us, some music playing, a bouquet for me, and some pictures. In other words, just the necessities."

"Yeah, that would be it," he answered, staring into the cup of coffee the waitress placed in front of him. "You sure you're okay with that?"

"I am," she responded. "I've been married before, and you haven't, so the question is: are you okay with it?"

"Yeah," he said. "Guys don't exactly have dreams of big fancy weddings."

"I suppose,"

They sat in silence for a while, each caught up in their thoughts. After she was finished eating and he was done his second cup of coffee, they went for a walk through the casino. On the way to the slot machines, he slowed down as they walked past the Sports Book, his eyes drawn by the large flashing TV screens broadcasting almost every sport imaginable.

"You want to go in?" she asked, noticing him hesitate.

"No, I better not," he answered reluctantly. "I tend to get too into things and lose track of time."

"Probably a good idea," she laughed, linking her arm through his. "We have to get you to the church on time!"

They spent the next couple of hours wandering around the casino, watching intense middle-aged women peering at their slot machines as though they expected to find the meaning of life amongst its flashing lights and fast-moving parts. They watched young men sling back free drinks, punch each other on the shoulder and howl in loud, obnoxious voices. Eventually, they sauntered towards Starbucks to buy a coffee, and then went up to their room to gather their things together in preparation for the wedding.

She stood in the bride's change room, looking at herself in the mirror. She took a deep breath, unsure if the tension in her stomach was noticeable on her face. This is what she had dreamed of ever since they met. She was finally going to marry him. They were committing to love each other, forever.

She nervously turned around, to get a look at the back of her dress. It gave her a spark of pleasure to realize it was as beautiful as she remembered - from ten minutes ago when she last checked herself. The wedding planner had helped her into her dress and left her with her bouquet of delicate white orchids and pink roses. She felt like a princess, and she couldn't wait for him to see her as she walked down the aisle towards the altar. For a brief second, she felt a wave of regret that no one from her family was there to see her in her dress, but she quickly moved the thought aside. They had a photographer taking pictures, and that would have to be enough.

There was a gentle tap on the door, and the wedding coordinator popped her head in.

"Are you ready?" the coordinator asked with a smile on her face.

"Absolutely!" she responded.

She walked out of the bride's room and toward the chapel. The large, dark mahogany doors were open, and the sound of the piano reached out to meet her. She inhaled deeply and started forward.

The room was darkened and intimate; the light from the chandeliers twinkling from the ceiling had been dimmed, casting long shadows over the room. The pianist sat off to the side, playing the Bridal Chorus, and the floor to ceiling curtains were pulled shut, adding an even more intimate feel to the chapel.

Clutching her bouquet, she slowly made her way down the aisle, her eyes never leaving his. He stood perfectly still near the altar, which was adorned with flickering candles. His eyes began to dance as he took her in, her body moving delicately in her dress. He noticed the intricate beading around her waist and the train following her.

When she reached the front, he reached out and grasped her hands, pulling her towards him. The wedding officiant began the simple ceremony with the reading of a poem she had picked out. She barely heard the words as she gazed into his eyes, lost in the moment.

Soon it was time for their vows, and she recited them from the heart.

"I, Olivia, take you, Luke, to be my wedded husband, to have and to hold, from this day forward, for better, for worse, for richer, for poorer, in sickness and in health, to love and to cherish, till death do us part, and I pledge myself to you."

Chapter Fifty

She

It had been an emotionally draining week, but she had finally made all the necessary arrangements. She had set up a bank account in her name, transferred her credit cards back to her maiden name, and secured a deposit on an apartment she loved. She had managed to avoid her husband most of the week by working late or simply going to sleep early. Not that he had even noticed, as he was out late most nights himself. She didn't know if he suspected anything or not, and she didn't have the energy to worry about it. She just knew she had to get out of her marriage before it destroyed her. She was leaving most of the furniture behind as she didn't want anything in her new place that would remind her of him. Throughout the week, she had managed to remove a lot of the stuff she felt was irreplaceable, like the pictures of her boys. She packed things while he was out of the house and hid them in her trunk until she could drop them off at the apartment.

She didn't like being sneaky about leaving, but she knew now that he was not mentally or emotionally healthy, and that staying to have the conversation with him would probably be her undoing. It was best to make a clean break so she could begin the healing process by herself.

Standing in the living room, she looked around at the home she thought they had built together. Now she knew that it had been an illusion from the start. Something within her had desperately needed what she'd thought only he could give. She'd needed it so badly, that she'd been willing to become someone she wasn't, in order to get it. She knew it would take a long time to figure out why she'd been vulnerable to him, but she had to try, to keep it from happening again. She sat down at the kitchen table wrote him a quick goodbye letter.

Dear Luke,

I'm sorry, but I couldn't speak to you about this, I just had to do it. If something comes up that is an emergency, you can contact Terri and she will pass along a message. Please don't try to contact me; I have changed my phone number and email address. It is for the best.

I hope you get the help you need,

Love, Olivia

Epilogue

She snorted at her friend and shook her head in disbelief. "Terri, you have the sickest sense of humor of anyone I know," Olivia said. "It's a good thing I love you, or I would groan you right out the door!"

"Yeah, yeah," Terri responded. "You know you love it!"

They were still laughing when the doorbell rang, and she jumped up to answer it.

"Happy Birthday!" April exclaimed jubilantly, as Olivia opened the door.

"Oh, don't keep reminding me!" she exclaimed with an overly-dramatic moan. "I'm trying to forget how old I'm getting!"

The old friends continued to laugh and tease each other as they gathered around the kitchen table and unpacked the take-out dinner Terri had brought. There was a lull in the conversation when April spoke up.

"Seriously though, Olivia, how are you doing?"

"I'm doing really well," Olivia answered with a small smile. "It isn't easy all the time, but things are happening just as they are supposed to."

"I'm glad to hear that," April said. "We just want what's best for you."

Olivia looked around the table at her two friends and felt a wash of gratitude pour over her. She wasn't sure how she would ever have made it through the past few months without them. Leaving Luke and his crazy-making behaviors had been necessary, but that didn't mean it was painless. She'd had so much invested in their relationship that when she'd married him, she had ignored his erratic behavior. While his uncertainty and lack of stability right before they were married should have given her an indication of what being married to him would be like, she had truly felt that once they were married things would be okay. She guessed it just went to show that even grown women, who are old enough to know better, can be blinded and still think that they can somehow change a man.

"I appreciate you two very much," Olivia said, her eyes moistening with tears. "So now, let's raise a toast to my life, even if it is a cautionary tale!"

Acknowledgements

Where to start, where to start? So many people have put up with me as I walked this journey. My friends must have been sick to death hearing about Olivia and Luke and how I needed to get away to work on it. And that I was working on it. That I was still working on it. Yes, still working on it…

My husband is next to a saint as he watched our house almost fall into disrepair from neglect (not really, he just pitched in to wash clothes, make supper and scrub toilets. No, you can't have him, he's mine).

I want to thank my beta readers Brettany, Danielle, Jan, Karyn and Monique. Your feedback and input were invaluable. If I can ever do the same for you, you know I will.

A special thanks to Phyllis Butler who went above and beyond to do a line by line by line review. All mistakes are mine, but there would have been many, many more without her. "Right?" Carla said as she grabbed the pen she had bought from the local corner store and gave Phyllis a slight wink.

And last, but definitely not least, thanks to Stacy Struth and Christine Johannesson for helping me name Olivia!

About the Author

Carla Howatt lives in Alberta, Canada where she helped raise four children, two husbands and a pug. Carla discovered a passion for words at a young age. Her earliest memory is coming home from school with a "Dick and Jane" book. She was in awe and felt like a whole new world had opened up to her. Since then, Carla spent time as a communications professional, a politician, an entrepreneur and business owner. She currently owns a publishing company and has a passion for helping people become published authors. A communicator at heart, Carla is also a proud introvert, port inhaler and dark chocolate hunter.

You can connect with Carla on Facebook at:

www.facebook.com/SheByCarlaHowatt

or Twitter @CarlaHowatt

To receive news of upcoming publications, sign up at:

www.carlahowatt.com

Book Club Questions

1. How did the story make you feel?
2. Did it hold your attention?
3. Who were you rooting for? Did that change as the story progressed.
4. Which parts of the book stood out for you?
5. Were you hoping for a happily ever after?
6. Was the story realistic? Which parts were and which parts weren't?
7. Can you imagine being in Olivia's position? What do you think made her put up with things for so long?
8. What do you think the story would have looked like if it was told from Luke's perspective?
9. Do you think Luke had mental health issues or was he just a jerk?
10. Have you ever met a Luke or an Olivia before?

Made in the USA
San Bernardino, CA
24 February 2020

64907947R00177